GRIEFWORK

A

NOVEL

James Hamilton-Paterson

FARRAR STRAUS GIROUX

New York

Copyright © 1993 by James Hamilton-Paterson
All rights reserved
First published in 1993 by Jonathan Cape, London
Printed in the United States of America
First American edition, 1995

LIBRARY OF CONGRESS CATALOGING-IN-PUBLICATION DATA
Hamilton-Paterson, James.
Griefwork : a novel / James Hamilton-Paterson.—1st American ed.
p.   cm.
I. Title.
PR6058.A5543G75   1995   823'.914—dc20   95-7624   CIP

'A roast field mouse – not a house mouse – is a splendid *bonne bouche* for a hungry boy. It eats like a lark.'

– Frank Buckland

ONE

'. . . simply can't get them now for love or money . . .'

'Hubie? Couldn't have been him. Survived Arnhem in one piece but then went and fell off an alp.'

'. . . *La princesse est arrivée* . . .'

A child's impression, maybe, would be clearest of such conversational fragments heard among the leaves and above the tinkle of water. Pellucid, seemingly without sense or context, they were mixed into the scrunch of pea gravel beneath polished shoes, the women's scent (almost unobtainable: diplomatic bag), the heat. All these were vivid, the heat most of all. It was surely this which attracted people by night to the great structure glowing in a dark urban landscape. Such a child, late beyond bedtime for a treat, was granted a view of what adults liked doing when left to their own devices, of this place where they met.

She first saw it from far off, one of her wool mittens clasped in an adult hand, a cathedral of warmth in a cold city. She would remember a part of the Botanical Gardens as having been cleared for an allotment of sprawling potato plants and dank rows of beans. Elsewhere there seemed to have been some hacking about, probably in a search for firewood, with a tree or two felled entirely. She knew from afternoon walks wearing an itchy wool helmet with earflaps the ornamental lake, silent and unstirring. Its golden carp, like the exotic waterfowl, had long been eaten. She knew the muddy water occluded by duckweed through which a few balding mallards had cracked their passageways. By night such familiar things were invisible. Almost everything became invisible save for the magic oasis at the gardens' centre: the crystal pavilion domed and lobed like a Byzantine Taj Mahal, delicately girdered, its panes streaked with steam and plastered with leaves. Strange times to all except a child, to whom no times are strange. She wouldn't have known to wonder why the gardens had not been completely laid waste. Why had the Palm House remained unsmashed, its plants undespoiled? Apparently some old man had worked throughout the war feeding shrubbery, dried beet pulp, railway sleepers into the furnaces which maintained a few hundred square yards of the tropics in the midst of freezing Europe.

'*La princesse est arrivée . . .*'

This immense stove house was laid out like a church, a temple to nineteenth-century horticulture which followed instinctively some cruciform model: St Paul's Cathedral in London, perhaps, or St Peter's, Rome. The central area beneath the lantern (on whose summit an elaborate weathervane spun in the fitful maritime climate) housed the palms, the tallest of which was hunched up under the glass. It was to one particular transept off this central thicket that the night people came. For here it had been the gardener's fancy to collect together only those tropical plants which bloomed at night. Recently the Society had decided to open the Palm House on Wednesday evenings between 6 and 9 pm and it had become a celebrated meeting place. People came to chat, to bury their faces in blossoms, to breathe scent. Perhaps it was the curator's private quirk or maybe there really was a scientific theory which held that bright lighting would upset the nocturnal shrubs' flowering patterns. At any rate the electricity was never turned on. Instead, and adding greatly to the ecclesiastical aspect, candles were stuck in sconces among the fronds and branches. In this way the masses of plants were from most viewpoints gently backlit. Many a chapel-like bower lay buried deep in leaves with a candle burning at its centre.

Some nights nobody at all came. On others the Palm House presented the aspect of a cocktail party, something scarcely seen nowadays in this depleted city. Well-groomed people strolled the gravel chatting quietly or else met in knots, glasses in hand (for a few brought worn silver hip-flasks), idly fingering a spray of leathery leaves, their laughter filtering up with forbidden cigarette smoke to the traceries of ironwork far overhead. Especially this winter they arrived shrunken into their coats, many of the women in pre-war furs but clenched and pinched from their walk through rattling sleet. Once past the double set of doors and into the steady 27°C they began to expand, slowly, skin colour emerging in streaks as through a breaking bud. From the world they had left outside nothing penetrated except similar quiet refugees and their accompanying puffs of frigid air. The streets beyond the high seventeenth-century wall which bounded the gardens were largely deserted after dark, as if even now people could hardly break the habit of years of curfew. An occasional tram swayed past the wrought-iron gates but its electric groan was not audible within the Palm House. Nor were the distant mourning cries of ships as they gingerly negotiated the docks' shallow approach, Polish freighters bringing coal.

'*La princesse est arrivée . . .*'

Who were these people? Grandees, mainly, or what nowadays passed for them. Diplomats, a few aristocrats (rumpled as from years in exile living out of trunks), celebrated bohemians, professionals. In short, the only people other than criminals who had the confidence to move about after dark. Leon noticed how quickly they had regained their poise even though their ranks had thinned, as if their expensive clothes were overalls and the traumas and dishonours of the past years no more than a light soot which could be brushed off with a few gestures. *Well, thank God that's over. Here we all are again.* (Not quite all, of course. Hubie and the rest had signally failed to make it back from the camps and battles and glaciers.)

On such nights Leon lurked as the genie in this enchanted forest. He was on duty, the terms of his employment required it. When it came to nine o'clock he alone could announce the time, ring a little bronze bell and lock up. Besides, he lived here and behaved like someone in his own house. His battledress trousers, stained at the knees with mould, had been stolen from a retreating army. On his bare feet were perished rubber galoshes, the unintended legacy of a German staff officer who had been suspended by his ankles from a balcony, his hair a black wick dripping blood in curlicues on the pavement below. In these galoshes Leon moved noiselessly along the winding paths toting his wand of office, a thick-barrelled brass spraygun polished bright with daily use. Carrying this had begun as a nervous habit, something to occupy his hands while he . . . well, what, exactly? The Society, in the voice of Dr Anselmus, wouldn't say. 'Remain on duty. Make sure, you know . . .' But make sure of what? It was hard to imagine a diplomat absentmindedly carving his initials on the venerable trunk of a cycad, or a magistrate's wife setting fire to an aerial fern. He was left to saunter, to circulate without giving the impression of actually policing this steamy patch of jungle. He spent much of his time fetching and steadying the several pairs of light step ladders for visitors who wanted to climb up and sniff blossoms out of reach.

There was wide acknowledgement that he was a genius. He alone could make anything grow. (It was claimed that, piqued by a challenge, he had once thrust a yellow cane walking stick into the soil and within a fortnight the whangee had sprouted a pair of tiny leaves and had since turned into a stand of bamboo. Such saintly apocrypha were just the thing for recovering from a global overdose of reality.) Only Leon could have kept all these wonderful plants alive through the terrible years. He was surely quite uneducated yet he knew the names of everything, even in Latin. It was further said and believed that he was a healer, a herbalist, a homeopath, an accomplished witch, a satanist who conducted the sorts of voodoo ritual appropriate to the jungle. What, for example, had he done in the war? How had he avoided conscription? *Exactly.*

All of this caused night society to make way for him with a complicated respect as he moved about his paths and alleys with his syringe, frowning at leaves and sniffing at soils. He listened to gossip while extravagant rumour reached him from behind screens of foliage. His aloof, Delphic aspect produced its own delightful frisson. Like a mongrel or a holy man he transcended the usual social distinctions. Night after night his big pale ears were privy to intrigue, scandal, corruptions and amours. The rationing scams, the bombed-out property deals; where nylon stockings and perfume might be had, undyed petrol or a ton or two of good coal.

Meanwhile, who was this fabled princess, constantly on the point of arriving, whose least mention excited such interest? She was beautiful, that much Leon had observed for himself. She was the wife of some Eastern ambassador – Burmese? Laotian? Bornean? – and turned up from time to time at these nocturnal gatherings accompanied not by her husband but by a dark, unsmiling equerry whose polished head was always respectfully inclined but who threw glances up and out like tarnished knives. And who was *he*? everyone wanted to know. Bodyguard? Lover? Chaperon? Perhaps an elder brother, fierce and protective? They did look alike, though of course all sorts of Easterners looked awfully similar. Interest and speculation coagulated about her, much encouraged by an enigmatic quality she diffused like scent (as to that, she seemed only ever to wear the faintest trace of Lancôme's 'Cuir'). This enigma had nothing to do with the alleged inscrutability of Easterners, for an eager observer – and there were many – would notice subtle shadows pass over her features like codicils to the conventional grimaces of pleasure and interest which diplomats learn as weanlings. Often when her attention was not engaged it slanted off to one edge, drawn upwardly with an abstracted sadness. There would, they thought, be much for her to be sad about, stuck in a cold northern clime in a crisis of food shortages, petrol rationing and power cuts, thousands of miles away from the lush shores which hid, in her admirers' fantasy, her native domain. (On paper, had they tried to draw it, her envisioned palace would have turned out part pagoda and part Aztec temple.) Nor did the enigma depend on her being uncommunicative. She spoke excellent French and, if not voluble, was capable of flashes of surprisingly malicious wit. This, unexpected in a diplomat's wife, was hugely charming. Her escort, then, was probably not an interpreter.

A good few of the Palm House's visitors, Leon knew, spoke little or no French. He himself knew only the odd word, which but made his great secret more piquant. This secret was that occasionally the princess would come all alone during the day and spend an hour among the plants with him. Then her demeanour was different, more a private face, he liked to think, unafraid of being earnest and studentlike. For she was very young and wanted to know things. She came to learn, took notes in alien scribbles, never resorted to French. She was seldom difficult to understand except when trying to pronounce certain of the plants' Latin names. So far as he could tell none of the 'night people' – as he thought of these temporarily dispossessed dining-and-nightclub denizens, these stymied opera-goers – none of them knew of their liaison. And yet to have such a secret in a glasshouse ... It was this which enabled him to saunter among them, brass spraygun loosely held, meeting their brittle pleasantries with an icebreaker's prow, acting the oracle to queries about compost.

'No smoking,' he abjured the Italian chargé-d'affaires. With a certain frozen patience this man detached his cigarette from its long ebony holder and made gestures of disposal with it at arm's length while tucking the holder away inside his jacket. This had been carved to his own design in Abyssinia, oval rather than round so as to fit Egyptian cigarettes. Leon retrieved from a ledge a disgusting jar holding half a gallon of mahogany-coloured liquid in which floated like dead cockroaches the unravelling butts of sundry cigarettes and cigars. To this he added the chargé's. It vanished with a hiss. 'Smoking damages the plants. Anyway, what's the use of coming here for the night blooms if you drown them in tobacco smoke? It makes no sense.' Clearly expecting no reply he turned away with his jar.

It was to his own circle of friends as much as to this fanatical gardener's back that the chargé said, 'Personally, I come here to get warm. It's the only warm place in this city, possibly in the entire country.' There was laughter. These little tyrannies did much for Leon's reputation. The smokers themselves quite liked public admonishment and the surrender of cigarettes which, God knew, were hard enough to get even on the black market. There was something reassuringly nannyish about his grumpy reproof, and to have suffered one of these acts of confiscation had its own cachet. Just now the episode was forgotten as there came the far-off squeal of the outer door, followed by that of the inner. Faces peered around fronds. '*Eccola* ... *!*' '*Voilà! Elle est arrivée.*'

13

What, then, was it this sealed figure brought in with her, apart from salt and gulls (the North Sea's freezing breath trapped in fur) and a dusting of snowflakes instantly turned by the heat into dewbeads supported by hairs? Not just a token of the exotic but a waft of days which recent history seemed to have declared dead. Into these shrunk and bitten times stepped the princess with her reminder that stylishness starts in the heart and may, nurtured, expand outwards into fantasy, intrigue, and powerful worldly gestures. This impression was strangely mixed with concealed disdain – concealed because quite unknown to those whose respect before this creature's beauty also crudely said: 'You've unfortunately caught us rather on the hop, my dear. At any other times than these we could have shown you what civilisation means, since we're its inventors and representatives. Unluckily it will be a few years yet before we can get the treasures of Europe back on display: the Beethovens, Bachs, Rembrandts; the scholarship, technology, social progress, good taste and the rest. For now, to mark the oddness of this temporal hiccup, we'll agree to meet by night in a greenhouse and make rather too much fuss over the golden emissaries of outer darkness.' Or something of the sort, while the golden emissaries crunched their way towards them, candle-flames bending to their passage, the princess smiling a general shy greeting while her equerry slewed his gazes from shuttered slots.

'Drink the contents of a spittoon,' came into Leon's mind as he watched them approach. 'That's what I'd make anyone do if . . .' This was the most repulsive image he could think of, no doubt prompted by the jar of deep brown reeking liquor he held. *'If anyone laid a finger on her'* was what he meant. As she passed him the princess caught his eyes and fractionally inclined her head. Her equerry's unsmiling look lasted rather longer on his face, as if the revenge of spittoons or worse were equally a part of his scheme. The gardener turned his attention to where, far away off the central aisle, a candle had gone out.

Leading from the main walkways were subsidiary paths and alleys which appeared to be sunken, so high grew the plants on either side. In fact their height was partly delusory since the original designers of the Palm House had planned for them to stand on broad brick piers at low waist level, making their care less irksome. These piers had once slanted off the main aisle with precise regularity, like the spines of a fish's backbone, with a gap between the end of each and the side walls. Over the years, though, they had been altered to accommodate growing plants, bequests and acquisitions, in some cases plinths having been added between spine and spine, making it necessary to go around by another route to reach the plants on the far side of these barriers. Meanwhile the old limewashed bricks had sprouted moss and ferns on their vertical surfaces, nourished by warmth and the moisture running down, while the level slate tops of the piers had become buried ever deeper beneath spilled mould and humus, potting shell and twigs, until the plots themselves had all but vanished and the fake tropical scene was rooted in an artificial ground level several feet above the gravelled paths. Once off the main walks, therefore, the visitor became mildly lost in a maze of sunken forest tracks, now and then brought suddenly to a halt. Only the central and outer passageways remained clear, though even here sprays of leaves had in places arched across and pressed themselves to the glass in blind obedience to light.

The candle, he found, had blown out. The area was distinctly cooler. Stooping, he wet the back of one hand at a tap and moved it across the panes until he found a gusty jet of black air. The usual place: the join between brick footing and the beginning of the glass wall, between mortar and ironwork. He returned to where he had stowed the jar of cigarette juice and came back kneading a ball of putty. He moulded a thin sausage between his palms and stuffed it into the crack. Good enough for tonight. Such literal stopgaps aggrieved him, reminders of a general state of tattiness and disrepair. He wiped the steam from the glass in front of his face. For a moment it was as revealing as a slab of jet. Not a light showed anywhere outside. The entire Palm House might have been rushing through deepest space, an empty quarter of infinitude. Then he had the impression of slight, constant movement. He turned and relit the candle. By its glow snowflakes could be seen licking the panes with softly dabbing tongues.

There was a commotion away beyond the palms. The intervening plants and leaves swallowed up sound and the steamy air further damped it, the noise of exclamations and hurrying footsteps reaching him oddly, arced up and bounced back down from the high curved roof. He remained for one moment gazing at the glass and the silent crumble of flakes beyond, then sighed and made for the disturbance. Once around the stand of palms he came upon a group gathered about a drenched and sobbing child. Her hair was stuck flat to her face in streaks, the red wool dress clamped to her small body. A dark heap at her feet was her shed coat. There was a good deal of 'I didn't . . . I wasn't . . . ' on her part and of 'You did . . .' and 'Why were you . . . ?' from the various adult faces bent over her. The Italian chargé raised bachelor eyebrows expressively and reached automatically for his cigarettes, caught Leon's eye and produced a slender gold pocket watch.

'I'm so sorry, I'm afraid she fell into your tank,' said a woman. 'Stupid child. I can't think what she was doing.'

The tank was one of several sunk in the floor, bricklined pits four feet deep which had once been used for watering and humidifying. That was before the Palm House had been plumbed for piped water as well as for a steam heating system.

16

Nowadays the tanks were seldom used and had become largely hidden behind ferns, nearly always kept full by the height of the water table hereabouts, for the Botanical Gardens unfortunately occupied one of the city's lowest sites. 'Do you like newts?' asked Leon.

'No,' said the child. She sniffed. 'What do you mean?'

'All these tanks have newts living in them. Newts and frogs and South American toads. There may be a few Florida terrapins left. Quite harmless, the lot of them. You'll have given them a nasty shock.'

The girl herself seemed uncertain whether this news might bring on fresh howls. There was a lull during which she dripped and hiccupped. Maybe the kindness of this gardener's tone reassured her that he was not telling her about newts to cause her further distress but to interest her.

'I'm most terribly sorry,' the woman was saying.

'What can it matter? She couldn't possibly have done any harm. It's only water.' What an amazingly dense creature, he was thinking; she hasn't yet seen what it means. 'So. Now what?'

'We'll take her home at once.'

'Then I hope you've a good cure for pneumonia,' Leon told her. 'There's some new American stuff on the black market, people say. It's made from mould or yeast or something.'

'Penicillin,' someone said.

'That's it. The wonder drug. But I never heard tell it could resurrect the dead, which is what you'll need if you take her home like that.' He looked towards the night which pressed about the glass. There was a suggestion of swirling. It was now eight-thirty but this minor emergency implied that nobody was free to go home until it was over, a general feeling compounded by reluctance to consider forsaking the warmth for what lay outside.

'It would be death,' said the princess unexpectedly. She

17

had come up and was regarding the child with the friendly amusement of one perfectly used to seeing children put beneath a village pump or caught in a tropical downpour on their way home from school. 'In this cold – impossible.'

'Come,' said Leon to the little girl. 'We'll soon have you dried out.' And though he was speaking to the child his eyes – having first paused at the princess – did include the mother. He led the way along the nave to the far end of the building, past the double entrance to a door set in the end wall painted with the legend No Admittance. 'Welcome to the stokehold,' he said with an odd loud formality and rattled the knob, being first through the door. By the time the others were inside the child had only the faintest impression of quick movement beyond the pool of bright light cast by a shaded bulb hanging above the table, maybe also the sense of another door silently closing. But this notion was soon lost in the rough maternal flurry of being stripped. 'Here,' said Leon, handing the woman a fleece-lined flying jacket of greasy leather. For an instant the girl stood in a puddle of her own clothing, fish-naked in the brick room, then her mother wrapped the jacket around her. He indicated a burst sofa along one wall, picking up the clothes and wringing them out in one of three large stone sinks. He vanished briefly. There definitely was another door, for a wedge of light flashed in the gloom. Returning, he said, 'I've hung them over the furnace pipes. You're not allowed to go through there. Fifteen minutes or so. I'll be back.'

He left, and the door into the Palm House closed behind him. Mother and daughter looked about them. The room was indeterminate, either a living room used by a gardener for his hobby or else a potting shed doubling as a habitation. It smelt not unpleasantly of leaf mould and bacon fat. The wall with the sinks also held a long draining-board or work-top on which stood a dozen shrubs in pots. On shelves above them was an assortment of packets and bottles including three more of the cigarette jars, all full. From a nail driven into the end of one of these shelves dangled a great hank of bass or raffia like a palomino's tail. On the wall hung a curled and dusty calendar still showing March 1938. That month's maxim had read: 'You cannot see Beauty with miserable eyes.' The table was bare except for a teapot and a newspaper.

'Are you still cold?' Leon asked the girl when he came back. She looked silently up at her mother as for permission to nod, which she did, uncertainly. He went to a dark cupboard and pulled out a bundle of twigs like the head of a small besom. Having examined its label under the light he went back for another. Then he knelt before a grate which neither of his impromptu guests had noticed in his absence, having been frozen into a kind of silent paralysis preventing either thought or sight. With a pair of bellows the gardener blew up some guttering coals into redness, thrust the twigs in until they were alight and rose to his feet with this crackling brand. He waved it vigorously to extinguish the flames, continuing to flourish it in front of the girl as she sat so a bristle of red-hot streaks crossed her face rapidly from side to side, trailing behind them wafts of thick aromatic smoke.

'What are you doing?' asked the woman, anxious but in his hands.

'Warming her.'

It was not cold in the room. Several stout, lagged pipes emerged from the boiler room and, hung with cobwebs and cloths, plunged through into the Palm House beyond. The roof overhead, though, was a great source of heat loss, being long rectangles of rippled glass of the kind which has a mesh of reinforcing wires embedded in it, pitched up in lean-to fashion against the Palm House's end wall. The light revealed the underside of a grey dusting of snow. It was obvious that if ever the furnaces next door were allowed to go out the room would become uninhabitably cold despite the grate. The girl, meanwhile, slumped drowsily, cheeks flushed.

'What is that?'

'*Palabrinus astea*,' replied Leon, inventing syllables for the woman and waving. 'It warms the innards. Don't ask me how. It just does. Doesn't it?' The child nodded sleepily, shrunk into the flying jacket with her legs drawn up in the mound of springs, kapok and ticking next to her. He laid the smouldering twigs in the fireplace and went to retrieve her clothes. Again the dim wedge of light showed momentarily, then once more as he came back, shaking out the pipes' indentations from the small garments. 'Hem of the coat's still damp.' There was a smell of scorched wool. 'Never mind. She's warm now. Dress her and take her home at once. She'll be fine if you don't loiter.'

They emerged from this rathole of a vestry into the candlelit nave, the shrubbery piled up on either hand in dark banks with here and there the waxy glint of leaves catching the sheen of a vagrant ray. There were movements and voices from the far end, around and beyond the palms. At the entrance doors the mother rammed the wool pixie helmet over her child's head with punitive zeal, the girl looking suddenly back at Leon as she did, so that a scalloped point meant for the centre of her forehead skewed across one eye. 'What's your dog's name?' she asked.

'There is no dog.'

'I heard him all right,' said the child with mittened hands clapped to the sides of her head, twisting. 'I expect he's brownish.' The doors squealed and banged behind them.

The continuing snow had turned the night people's reluctance to leave into worry about further delay. Now began a general drift into the central Palm House, noses bidding flowers a last farewell, scarves and coats which had been opened or shed rewound and rebuttoned. Within ten minutes the place was empty. Leon caught a knowing, salutatory glance from the chargé, then watched the princess's retreating back as she leaned on her dark companion's arm. In the light's feebleness they had hardly gone half a dozen steps before being swallowed up in the whirling dark. He locked the outer door, shut the inner and began dousing candles. Light withdrew gradually, stealthily, to the sound of his softly crunching passage. Now and then a branch rustled as he stretched an arm between two plants to reach a hidden sconce. On galoshed feet the darkness spread and as it did the atmosphere thickened, the plants grew denser and taller until by the end, when he was walking back and putting out the last staggered flames on either side of the central aisle, a forest closed silently in behind him. This retreat of the light worked its nightly magic, acting on him as a melancholy balm. Many of the night-flowering species he had planted became more strongly scented the darker it was, diffusing their drowsy fragrance in hopeless expectation of the great silent moths whose pollen-dusted bodies they yearned to attract. The right kinds of moth were thousands of miles away, yet still the flowers drenched the air with their languorous frustration, filling his lungs with the perfume of endless possibility.

Not far from the entrance door he laid an affectionate hand on a tamarind of which he was especially fond, having inherited it as an unhappy sapling and coaxed it into a young tree nearly ten feet tall. He had felt a certain sympathy for it because tamarinds were displaced here, being native to the semi-arid regions of India and Africa. Yet with care they could also be grown in monsoon climates and this particular plant had been raised from seed sent by the botanical gardens in Singapore. He liked its long racemes of golden flowers and its feathery leaves but his real reward was its essential acridness, the strongly acid fibrous pulp inside its dusty brown pods. Was this not his own

21

nature too, a lone and difficult creature of both sweetness and forbidding acidity?

'We're in the right place,' he told it, patting its trunk as a gust of wind sent flakes of frozen snow hissing against the panes. 'We wouldn't last five minutes out there tonight.'

For he talked to his plants, of course, even as he could often bring himself to say no more than a few gruff words to his visitors. 'I thought you couldn't speak,' the chargé had said on his third visit when Leon had lectured him fiercely and at some length on soil acidity after he had caught the Italian pouring a bottle of white wine into a pitcher-plant's tub. 'Quite undrinkable,' the diplomat had explained. 'Quite unthinkable,' retorted the gardener. 'I suppose in somebody's sitting room you'd simply tip it down behind the sofa.' This sally had made him mildly famous and proved his fearlessness as a man apart. The sitting room image was apt and revealed why Leon never considered the building he lived in as 'the Palm House'. In his mind, at least, the place was simply 'the House', neither glass- nor hot- nor palm- but his own unqualified habitation and focal point of being whose curved panes housed him as did his own skin. In chatting to his plants he was not so much addressing a collection of intimate house guests as communing with himself. It was often easier for him to put his thoughts into plant voices. He found it less inhibiting.

Nowadays the voices he gave them had become quite sophisticated. Long before the war, when Leon had just arrived in the Botanical Gardens, plants had spoken to him using the elemental speech he had always bestowed on wind and waves. During his rise to curator he had been obliged to meet more and grander people – not simply administrators like the director, Dr Anselmus, but highly informed amateurs with conservatories of their own, visiting dignitaries from other gardens all over Europe, even social butterflies who, re-emerging from the war's enforced hibernation, were beginning once more to flutter round his House as if it were a buddleia coming into bloom. From all these people he had caught new modes of expression, new voices. Recently he had noticed his plants adopting their own conversational tones. Since the coming of the night people, especially, several had taken on a brittle sarcastic quality which revealed unsuspected currents. What could only be described as bitchiness and rivalry was opening interesting fissures in what had once seemed the uniform dumb harmony of green and living things. These days he hardly even needed to walk his forest paths in order to overhear his plants. Long after he had gone to bed their discourse continued softly, whispers which he could distantly hear until the moment he fell asleep and again not long after waking. He had come to recognise distinct generic voices. The palms were overbearing, the *Annonas* by turns spiteful and tender. In their joint company he was drawn osmotically upwards and out of himself as if his very being were as fluid as sap. Sometimes these dialogues told him things he hadn't known he knew. Not the least strange aspect of this odd man was that he was thus able to be unself-aware while providing a half-amused, knowing commentary as though he were standing a long way off from himself or as if it were all happening in a distant country.

The last candle made of his bending face the ancient mask of a tyrant or a priest before it, too, winked out. Leon paused then as he always did, looking back on a world which only he ever saw. It spread away to every horizon, a tessellated land whose each plant was distinct yet thickly nested among its neighbours. Small water noises tinkled where voices had been muffled. Newt and terrapin nosed their way about invisible tanks while drops condensing inside an acre of cold glass pattered down on soil and leaves. Sometimes he could hear the tightly-wound shoots of bamboos and lilies squeak as they thrust upwards. As his eyes adjusted, dabs and dots of green light marked patches of luminous fungi whose spores had arrived with the plants in their Wardian cases (along with mites and pests and noxious insects) and had thrived in the congenial warmth. And, as he waited still longer, a directionless radiance seeped into his eyes. It was so faint as to be without colour, yet had an intensity of its own powerful enough to permeate the universe. This was starlight filtering through the thin layer of snow on the roof. Where was this place really, this sublime kiosk? Rushing through space? Sunk in the sea? It was here and everywhere and nowhere possible, and it always made him shiver with pleasure and humility, as one looking up at mountains. From his mouth issued gentle, unvoiced whispers, almost sighs: *shuuuff . . . ssiiih . . .* which, as soft as the starlight was dim, surely penetrated every corner of the cosmos. They were the repetitive gesture of someone who, quite without knowing it, lives in a state of constant sorrow.

Already thinking of the *Annona*s he was going to re-pot first thing next morning, Leon slipped in through No Admittance, turned out the light inside and crossed the darkened room unerringly to the boiler room door. Inside, the dim 40-watt bulb was on, hung with cobwebs. To his eyes it dazzled with detail. Much of the floor space of this large room was taken up with the furnaces themselves, with bunkers full of small coal and logs and with heavily lagged tanks, pumps and pipes all set with gauges at strategic points. The floor was immaculately swept. On it in one corner lay a large mattress. Leon turned the light off and went over to kneel on it. By the red glow spilling out of the open firebox doors a figure became visible drawn up on its side beneath a sheet, a plane of face amid a tangle of gypsy tresses, an eyelash trembling in mock sleep. With the tenderness of someone opening a longed-for present the kneeling man drew down the sheet, exposing a naked back which he bent forward to kiss. 'The happy land,' he murmured. 'Arabia felix.'

During the night when he awoke with practised punctuality to feed the boilers a glance through the window into the yard showed it was still snowing. In the morning when he got up and went into the Palm House the light's effect produced a tingle of remembrance, something to do with what winter means for northerners. So well did he know the smell of snow he thought he could sniff it even inside, in a temperature of 27°C, looking out at the Botanical Gardens lumpy and quilted in the grey early light. Not yet bright, the pallor nevertheless drove in through the glass from all sides, leaching out the plants' subtle greens. Their extravagant shapes suddenly looked clumsy, the palms tattered, everything ragged and sprawling as if the nature of heat was to bleed away all rigor of outline, corrupt the purposeful and self-contained. The ashy light beat upwards from the wastes outside, the roof beneath its rug of snow darker than the sky itself. Over Leon there came the feeling, beginning at the base of his spine, which he remembered from childhood: a heavy thrill brought on by clouds black with snow massing and spreading overhead, shedding that bruised radiance, avatar of dislocation and extremity.

Meanwhile his favourite tree, Tamarindus indica, had spoken of him in the dark hours as he had lain on his shared mattress. The vocabulary was that of the night visitors and the books he had read. The tone – now tart, now mournful – was entirely his *own. To his drowsy mind the plant's gentle mockery was proof of its affection, while its longing expressed something which seemed as much a part of him as the blood sighing in his ears:*

'We're all of us devoted to our gardener, of course, as he moves among us with his golden wand. However, those of us capable of thought – which is most of the species in this House with the obvious exception of the bananas, who are famously dim – object now and then to the ludicrous qualities he assigns us. We've come to the conclusion he can't help his anthropomorphism, and leave it at that. Nevertheless I do think he ought to be more scrupulous before bestowing on us characters such as "lone and difficult creature" or however he describes me. My neighbour on one side, a very handsome African orchid tree called *Monodora*, will vouch for my being easy-going and companionable; or he will if he has any sense. He himself is due for an annual bout of the dumps which always happens when his flower buds start to form in expectation of spring. It's worth it, for since he's completely leafless when he does flower the blooms hang most spectacularly from his bare branches, at which point he becomes loquacious in a triumphalist vein which is quite insufferable. The rest of the year he's an excellent listener and a good friend, giving off sympathy and a faint smell of nutmeg.

'As for my "forbidding acidity", this is a human palate speaking. What to our gardener is twelve per cent tartaric acid is to me an expression of the best in me, what honey is to a bee. Sadly, no-one will ever really appreciate it since the birds and animals who would happily feast on it and scatter my seeds never visit this House. It's one of the minor moans I burden poor *Monodora* with. My chief complaint is far more serious and difficult to express and concerns – I may as well come clean – my neighbour on the other side. It is of course hopeless, and I accept it. She's far younger and smaller than I.

As if that weren't enough she really has no business to be in here at all. If our gardener considers that I'm displaced I can't imagine what he'd think of her; but by some wilful – and for me merciful – blindness he hasn't yet noticed her. How she survives is equally mysterious since it ought to be far too hot for her in here. Yet she does, bravely and miraculously. Very well, as I'm going to have to say it sooner or later: she's a hemlock. Yes, yes, I know. Ridiculous and unseemly. Grotesque, even. A mere baby. A biennial. Don't imagine I couldn't say your lines for you, and more eloquently at that.

'So it's something I keep to myself. Sooner or later I'll probably confide in *Monodora*. One more of love's curses is that it will out: it makes one as reckless as if it were an achievement one yearned to brag about instead of an incubus beneath which one crouches, even though it did descend like manna. I can never tell her, of course, it's unthinkable. Worse than the shame of hearing one's own trite and stumbling words would be her expression of naive puzzlement. After that there would be nothing for me but the axe and the flame. No, there is such a thing as dignity and besides I love her far too much to wish to cause her the least upset. I can't believe I'm the only case of frustrated affection in this House, anyway. In fact I know I'm not. Now and then one hears things said in sleep, confessions, laments and suchlike. It's probably the common lot, again with notable exceptions. The palms, of course, are above all that sort of thing, being too busy fancying themselves as the philosopher kings of the plant world. Don't raise your expectations too high, is my advice. I've never heard any of them express a single worthwhile thought. The lotuses are a quite different case. I'd wager there's not a plant in the House who hasn't at some point or another been kept awake by their carryings-on. You never heard such screaming and bitching. That being said, one has to admit their outrageous remarks are often very funny.

27

There's something inherently comic about their situation, too. Talk about a divided community. Half of them are trying to be religious and the other half sordid, and we can all hear which half has the more success.

'Oh! It's so beautiful when the gardener blows the candles out. When the last light is extinguished a sigh goes through as a billion cells relax at once. I talk too much. I know it; and I only do so because I lack the freedom and courage to whisper to my little hemlock those few words I want to say, and then for all I care the roof can fall in and we perish in the snow which tonight is stealthily patting the panes.'

TWO

Picture a boy beside a grey northern sea, a distant figure whose neutral tones blend easily into the landscape. His faded dungarees, stuck with dried and curling fish scales, are the silvery blue-green of the sea holly scattered in clumps among the dunes. His hair is the melancholy yellow of rock samphire shaken by wind in cups and hollows. The landscape in which he moves is pared down to three elements: land, sea, sky. Each of these has a superficial scurrying quality beneath which it is as static as a grim metal poured long ago and set. To one horizon stretches rumpled water raising an infinity of failed castles. To the other, a terrain of low tufted dunes and saltings trembling stiffly in a flat wind and reaching inland past the invisible estuary. No trees, no vertical objects break the tyranny of the horizontal save only three wind pumps, vastly distant from each other and appearing bigger and closer than they really are, like oil drums in a desert. Although these are the late 1920s the sky remains as innocent of the aeroplane as it was when it frowned upon Europe's last retreating ice sheets.

The boy smells strongly of fish oil, and is quite unaware of it. From before dawn he was helping his uncle empty the smokers and pack the boxes: bloaters sweating amber droplets, the twisted batons of eels. They were still nailing the lids when the lorry called, though in this land its arrival could hardly be said to have caught them by surprise. Its insect crawl had been visible for ten minutes, its rattle over sluices and the bridges made of loose railway sleepers audible even above the sea's beating pulse. He had helped with the loading, drunk a pint of milky coffee, walked off along the shore to a point where the house he had left, with its line of huts, looked no more than the cluttered superstructure of a wrecked ship stranded far away on tidal flats. Now in the distance beyond it are Flinn's palish gleams: roofs greasy beneath stray sunlight, the steely flare of greenhouses. Most prominent of all is the menacing white stump of a lighthouse which dominates the town and at night intermittently blanches his bedroom curtains with its beam.

Ten years earlier the lighthouse had set the course of his life, and so cardinally that it was only of late he had managed to make a story from what had been an inarticulate wound. A space had at last opened up in that ever-receding landscape to accommodate a remembered figure and the images which clustered around her like birds about a distant statue, immobile in sunlight. Immobile, for there is no movement in memory; there are only instants which paint the fluent living with the rigidity of death, even when they are most in motion. Yet this boy would have said how vividly as a five-year-old he remembered his mother's bicycle spokes, *sprrixx*, as she pedalled away up the track across the polder to Flinn, the sun sparkling off the twirling wires, merry as mills. So he had stood as he always did when she went shopping in the village, watching her out of sight. It took a long, long time. The pedalling figure shrank to a gliding blob, now disappearing behind a stretch of stiff bushes, now sinking into invisible declivities, reappearing heraldically proud, crossing a bridge over one of the cuts. *That creeping dot was his mother.* At the same time he thought of anybody else in

30

the distant village who might happen to be gazing inland rather than seaward: how they would notice movement out there among the kale fields, a creeping dot with a speck of colour to it which slowly grew and resolved itself into Christina in her orange headscarf escaping from that foul-tempered brother of hers and her poor little boy for a quick round of cards, some purchases and a good few glasses of schnapps (which Leon could smell when she returned). And so he watched everyone and everything out of sight: boats putting out, a heron flying, the lorries coming to fetch smoked fish, a white steamer crossing the horizon and leaving its long thinning smudge. They all trailed behind them a hollow never quite filled by their return, carrying away part of him with them so he could look back and watch himself watching, just as he was sure his mother never once glanced over her shoulder to glimpse her melancholy child dwindle behind her. *Sprrixx.*

One day in Flinn marketplace there had been a stir of interest as a lorry arrived bearing a huge lump tethered beneath green canvas. The driver asked the way to the lighthouse, possibly out of self-importance since it was clearly visible from all points in Flinn and, indeed, from many a mile outside. It stood on a low sandy cliff not a quarter of a mile away and had been blind in its eye for nearly a year since the heavy steel trolley on which the half-ton lens revolved seized up one night. The year was 1918, and even at the end of the world's first mechanised war the arrival of a lorry in Flinn was an occasion and a large group followed it along the sandy track. It would be a three-day task to instal a jib on top of the building, haul the new mechanism up, swing it in and seat it in its bed. A crew of trained engineers was sitting in the cab with the driver, and the keeper of the only inn for some miles began cheerfully throwing open windows and airing beds. The weather was propitious: a high blue summer sky with a few mare's tails languidly unravelling their tresses across

Europe. Scattered lark song ascended flutteringly on weak thermals from among the dunes. The sea rocked and glittered to the horizon. The work began.

On the second morning Christina pedalled into town with her string bag, took a couple of glasses of refreshment and asked where everyone had got to. Told, she hopped back on her bicycle and soon joined the crowd of onlookers. It was at one of the more interesting moments. The men were getting ready to haul up the revolving mechanism, a task almost as delicate as remounting the lenses in it since it was as finely engineered as a watch. It lay in a cradle of mattresses on the back of the lorry, steel and brass glistening beneath a film of light oil. Before the order to haul was given the keeper waved everyone back and the spectators drew off to one side, just far enough so that if the rope broke (as many of the adults and all of the children were hoping it would) they were sure of a ringside seat without being in danger. The men hauled, the rope creaked, the pulley high up on the lighthouse squealed, the mechanism rose slowly into the air. As it did so the upturned heads tilted ever further back until they looked to the foreman up by the jib like a patch of daisies in a meadow. When the load neared the top there occurred one of those brisk claps of wind which come from nowhere and pass into nowhere, a stray lump of summer air perhaps detached from a stiff breeze a week previously and loitering lazily in its wake. It did no harm whatever to the precious mechanism now at the lamp room's sill. All it did was catch and throw back one of the curved lattice windows. Being heavy, it moved quite slowly and jarred to rest with a thud against a wooden stop bolted to the stonework. The foreman, intent on his job, scarcely glanced up but called out 'Latch that, Jon,' his gloved hand on the quivering rope. As the window struck the stop a single diamond pane flew from its mounting and twirled languidly down in a bending trajectory. Hardly any of the onlookers even saw it. This fluttering glass blade took Christina at the base of the neck and killed her where she stood.

Her child being five as well as living in isolation made it easier for the unplanned conspiracy to emerge and bear him the news that his mother had been taken seriously ill all of a sudden and wouldn't be coming back for a while. He accepted this as any child must an adult account of disaster, at face value. At the same time his speechless part must have wondered at the incongruity, at the perfectly everyday fashion in which, only a few hours before, she had pedalled away expressing at the last moment a fake exasperation at his demand to be brought the peppermints he knew she would bring anyway. These delicious mother-and-boy games were snapped off short, at once and for ever, at midday when a motor car drove inexpertly into the yard, temporised by reversing too close to the smoke house door and cuffing it off its hinges, and reluctantly disgorged some pale village women who at once closeted his uncle. After only a few minutes they came out again and got back into the car. One of them reached out of a window with a wild smile and dropped half a bag of liquorice (which he didn't like) towards Leon's chest. His hands came up an instant too late, the bag fell and bounced off the running-board and there was a fossil moment. For ever afterwards the image would recur of a crumpled white bag lying on sandy ground in the sunlight, hazed about by an engine's sound and the sweet pungency of a black tailpipe. Then the exhaust receded, the motor car departed, and everything was over.

His uncle, bereaved brother turned cantankerous guardian, remained an unknown quantity. 'He's got his own problems,' as the teenaged Leon was later to learn in the village, though he never found out what they were and by that time cared less. It was no good trying to impute to the man either a particular cruelty or emotional incompetence, especially not in a time and place which did its best to deny subtleties of feeling unless they were put into the shorthand of convention. It was easy for his uncle to offend no code but also to give no clue to his own motives when with malign scruples, as weeks lengthened to months, he met his little nephew's tearful demands to know when his mother was coming home with vague news of her progress from one special sanatorium to another. It soon became impossible for the child to ask while looking directly at his uncle. The stoniness was unbearable. Anguish masked as stoicism? Rage at being badgered to come up with fresh fictions? He gave up asking. One sunny morning she had gone away, *sprrixx*, twinkling off as she always did twice a week, but she had never come twinkling back again and now she never would. That much her bereft child knew. His conviction remained that somewhere beyond the limitless polder, somewhere out in the wide world his mother lay in bed or tottered about in a dressing gown smelling frowsty and looking grey as she did when she had one of her colds. And since he could see her thus, he thought she could surely see him too. How, then, could she bear not to come home and take him in her arms?

In those days Leon howled a lot for his mother. But neither the culture nor the landscape encouraged self-indulgence, and bit by bit the impulse was translated into more appropriate forms. In this way the habit began which marked the rest of his childhood and adolescence of endlessly wandering that desolate littoral in search of driftwood, birds' eggs, coloured stones, the sounds of water and wind, bobbles of black tar – for any, in fact, but the one thing. And after a time these treasures and their long searches engendered a life, as an oak gall's tiny grub becomes surrounded by accretions ever denser, larger, more rugose, in final shape and substance utterly unlike their begetter and yet faithfully its home. When he was ten he was allowed to go to the village school if there were no fish to be cleaned and spitted, and sooner or later the insouciant brutality of childhood dragged him to the churchyard and confronted him with a small plain stone bearing his mother's name.

'There,' they panted in a circle around him. 'Now will you believe us? Anyway' (said their leader), 'it's spooky here. I vote we go down to the lighthouse. Or no,' he added with unexpected kindness, 'not there. Wim's trapped some sparrows in his greenhouse. Let's make his cats get them. Come on, Leon.'

The balder a fact, the more equivocal. This one had immediately split into unrelated parts. Thereafter his mother existed in two tenses simultaneously, past and present; or, like an element, in two allotropes, the one dark and supine in a grave and the other still whitely refusing to come home. Either way it added up to abandonment. At about this time he had begun to avoid looking at the lighthouse and to hate its beam: the long empty finger sweeping over land and sea as if levelling them, ordaining or demarcating an area of blight. As he lay in bed its insistent pulse on the flimsy curtains seemed like surveillance. There were two flashes every twenty seconds. As dusk fell these blips hardened into spokes of light whose inexorable quality added severeness to evening's melancholy. As if that were not enough the foghorn mounted on a low concrete hut at the lighthouse's foot sent forth its bellow into the frequent sea mists. These hootings into nowhere sounded, muffled by fog and the remoteness of his house from the village, less strident and more like the regular groans of mortal illness. A territory was defined with Flinn lighthouse at its centre, the circumference of its horizon constantly retraced by the ends of light beams and sound waves. To Leon, glancing up suddenly from where he might be crouched over a drowned gull or the filmy mantle on a peat pool, everything seemed to rush soundlessly outwards into illimitable distance.

The child became the boy, ignorant of all that lay outside

Flinn except as fragments of schoolroom learning. Tucked into shrubs against the wind, himself to himself in small unknown places, he watched the sea and thought of it stretching back from its nearby line of constant collapse to behind the horizon, on and on until it returned somehow, wrapping the world in a wrinkled sleeve. His mind fled away over its surface to far-off nowheres and diluted his grief by smearing it ever thinner across dreamed deserts or forests whose canopies sagged beneath carpets of celestial butterflies. By such lonely acts the faintest heartening echo sometimes came back to him as from temple gongs struck by his thoughts or as scents jarred from distant blossoms.

The boy became the yellow-haired dungareed youth who at every opportunity walked off alone until his uncle's house was a distant wreck. As he walked he talked in a lively conversational tone to the one who accompanied him. Maybe once, when he was small, he had had the invisible companion whom so many children befriend until one day he or she vanishes, unmissed. This boy talked to his self as it grew, and it spoke back in his own voice or in the speech of waves and wind. Of what did this language consist? Of absolute purity, for one thing, unmuddied by any notions other than his own. His stark and orphaned life contained no music. No impassioned dominie had ever read him poetry with a traitorous glint of tears. Had he had a musical upbringing the sea's voice might have come to him in the accents of dead composers: the compulsive sequencing which floods the lonely and impressionable child by the shore who constantly hums and whistles his self. Instead the water, the breeze, the birds, shingle and plants were for him an endless syllabary. In correctly hearing and learning to pronounce each sound he talked back to the world which surrounded him, and in talking back intensified the one who spoke.

The principal sounds of his life included these, made without the larynx and in a fervent whisper: *Shuuuff* was the voice of the onshore wind which comes in summer puffs and beats against the first dune-crest, curling up its face and striking the exposed roots of eroded tussocks on its lip. *Ssiiih* was the steady breeze of grey April or October days through samphire and grasses. *Grockle* was medium-sized abraded stones tumbled by a retreating wave, a sound peculiar to winter and which had always pleased him because at a time when the sea appeared uniformly thick with cold this unexpected hollowness at its roots suggested aeration down below, a valiant lightness permeating upwards. There was a whole vocabulary to describe the noises made by different waves depending on mood, the direction of the wind, the colour of the sky. The sounds he attributed to birds were legion. None of them, had he known it, much resembled any of the standard transliterations used to identify them in books. At some point, after an age of lonely repetition, the words he had assigned these noises had hived off and now stood on their own, names for things which had become the things, had become his companionable whole. Long after he reached the city as a young man he would repeat them when alone, quite consciously, or maybe no more unconsciously than a prayer: something affirmatory and consoling; something heaved, iterated, meant.

For, central to this boy, to his companionship of himself, was a solemnity which could not be put into words but which had the status of a vow. He had promised that no matter what happened he would always remain true to the person he now was, to his unseen companion who alone knew what he endured. What he knew he could not describe except by the feelings it brought, as a merganser brings with it its marvellous plumage out of a grey sky. When a herring smack from Great Yarmouth went aground on the Shaleybanks the clouds cracked apart that afternoon and let out a ray so narrow it illuminated a single spar which burst into gold, the rest of the craft remaining as dun as its sails. It produced in the boy a fretful ecstasy which recurred whenever

37

the weather looked the same. What were such episodes if not cement, building up dab by dab an identity which would last and in which he could be free?

Very occasionally something stranger and more momentous happened whose plumage was iridescent fire and which could descend while he was putting on a shoe or threading the fluker wire through the eels or watching a Dutch skipper haul up his glistening lee board like a swan tucking up its black web. Suddenly everything broke open. All the syllables and voices spoke at once, together but each intensely clear, and for an endless flash there was equally *shuuuff* in a wave and in the flare of a gull alighting, *grockle* in the sheen of marram grass bending before the breeze. Afterwards, when everything had settled back, he could never recapture this as knowledge. He could only remember the suffusion of calm, as one most intensely remembers a great wind by the silence which falls when it is spent and rings on in the mind. He yearned for these things but could never make them happen. Nor did he tell anyone, for there was nobody to tell other than his constant companion who already knew.

He had once tried to confide in Wim, whose father had four long greenhouses behind the town. These were crammed with row upon row of tomatoes and it was Wim's task to help with watering, pinching out, tying up trusses, spraying washes. Wim was bigger than Leon, a year older, with sticking-out ears and farinaceous skin. Despite constant eczema which cracked painfully and wept he preserved a cheerful spirit and vagrant passions, pushing potatoes up exhaust pipes and dyeing cats green. When Leon timidly broached the subject of his 'funny feelings' Wim's great ears had lit up bright red and he did things which made little sense but caused Leon to think of gutting and roes. It seemed after all that Wim had not understood, and Leon never tried again. Much later he could vividly recall that scene of cross-purposes: the bright October sun shining hot through the glass on the back of his head, the smell of crushed tomato leaves, the translucent ears and milt.

One other constant companion was a chronically weak chest. Sometimes on winter mornings when it was still dark he hardly had the strength to light the candle, get into his clothes and totter downstairs gripping the rickety banister. The first breaths of searing sea air or the close tarry fume of the smoke house would bring on a fit of coughing which forced him to sit for minutes, wiping tears from his eyes. On three occasions he had been taken in a cart to the cottage hospital nine miles away, the first at the age of eight, the last when he was fourteen. Each time the treatment was the same. He was put to bed in a warm room and well fed, while every so often a tent of curtains would be drawn around a frame overhanging the head of the bed. A nurse would bring a steam kettle heated by a spirit lamp and set it on a chair with its long tin spout poking through a hole in the curtains. From this spout came steam with an assortment of aromatic flavourings added. The doctor was a great believer in variety, on the grounds that a physiological system as complex as the lungs needed more than a single specific. One morning it might be menthol crystals implanted in a blob of sponge through which the steam passed; later that afternoon it could be benzoin or Friar's Balsam. The steam helped and Leon would lie back in his semi-delirium while the hot resins opened up crackling passageways in his chest. The first time the doctor doubted he would survive, had believed the infection would spread. He looked thoughtfully at the gasping child, thin to the point of gauntness, called for constant nursing and hot camphorated poultices applied to the chest every two hours and wrapped in yellow oiled silk. He spoke of invasion, capillary bronchitis, pleurisy. With his old wooden stethoscope (to which he loyally clung, maintaining that flexible rubber tubing distorted sound) he listened to the *râles* in the boy's lungs. His head was turned towards Leon as he did so, face balanced on the wood tube so that to his drifting patient it looked like some kind of blancmange on a cake stand. The doctor listened as the crepitations roared up, his eyes fixed nowhere, expression rapt as a child's with a seashell pressed to its ear. Since chest complaints were so common hereabouts he had a fine ear and could distinguish shades of sound which told him much. Above the loud undertow of crackling noises, for instance, that thin squeak was not a good sign. It was the remaining air from the alveoli squeezing back through the clogged atrium into the bronchiole and slowly shutting down another group of air sacs. Areas of the left lung were already producing a dead, meaty sound to auscultation. 'Time for an expectorant, Sister,' he would murmur, straightening up at length. 'Squill, I think. Tincture – no, *vinegar* of squill, together with syrup of Tolú. Tomorrow morning tar-water, preferably birch tar. Is he drinking?'

'When I wake him.'

'Plenty of hot milk. Sweet, with a lump of butter. Look at him. How can he fight like that? Poor little scrap. Bowels?'

'Not so far, Doctor.'

'Hickery-pickery, then. Nothing stronger. We can always increase the dose. Carry on, Sister. I'll be back tomorrow morning.' He looked again at his patient, picked up his silk hat from where it lay over the boy's feet and shook his head.

But that time Leon had pulled through, and the next, and the next. By his early teens he was left with permanently weakened lungs. He coughed a lot, became easily short of breath. Down in Flinn he excited pity. In his delicacy and unparented isolation he stood out, even on that harsh coast where conditions differed little for most people. Indeed, many were fond of him. He was gentle and polite; and if he seemed remote and always to be talking to himself it was construed as proof that 'part of him was already on the other side'. In this view people were touched by sickness as by sainthood. He was really only waiting for a fatal complication to set in – pneumonia, consumption – and he would finally go all the way to the churchyard where sickly children ended, his coffin leaned on by a sexton with a pole to stop it floating up as the soaking clods were shovelled hastily back.

None of this happened. He survived and he left. One day in 1929 when he was about sixteen he walked to the town, hitched a lift on a cart full of Wim's father's tomatoes and vanished citywards. He forsook the cold, salt-laden yawn of sea, sky and polder and with him took a private landscape and an unseen friend. Not physically strong but entirely self-possessed he wandered for some weeks before finding a job as a gardener's boy in the distant capital. A month after he had left, his uncle and two companions were drowned while fishing, caught in a squall which became a great storm. Had he survived, the uncle would have returned to find his dwelling roofless and sagging, the smoke house blown flat. In this manner he was saved from ruin by disaster.

So carefully had he watched sails, waves, grasses, skies, that maybe Leon allowed himself to be guided by the wind. A quartering breeze on his thin shoulder-blades veered him diagonally to the railway instead of the bus station. An icy clout to the side of his neck knocked him into the first train rather than the second. At any rate, some explanation should be advanced for the uncanny accuracy with which he fetched up at the Botanical Gardens of all places on the very day there was a vacancy for a low-ranking employee, and this at a time when half the streets of Europe were restless with low-ranking employees looking for work. His companion about him, he moved among these listless folk in a purposeful way, one eye on the clouds. He had already been down to the docks crowded with shipping and admired the forest of masts and rigging, the funnels' stained livery. But the wind was steadily onshore and he was blown back towards City Hall.

Not far from the centre was a park. With one of his remaining coins he bought a bun, unconsciously divided it into two and ate as slowly as he could, sitting on the grass. Children kicked a football, the pages of an abandoned newspaper lolloped before the breeze. A hundred yards off was a row of plane trees beyond which he could see the flicker of traffic on the boulevard. He watched a brace of sheldrake cross the sky, quite high, then lose height rapidly to slant steeply behind the tree tops, wings downcurved. '*Hutt*,' he said. '*Hutt.*' This was the air passing through a duck's tight wings as it braked for landing. He got up, brushing off crumbs and leaves, and made for the trees.

On the far side of the boulevard was a fine high wall bending with the road so as to suggest a large enclosure. He crossed, wincing at traffic din, and came to a pair of iron gates, one of which was open. He wandered in past a little lodge, the wind now squarely at his back. Some way off beyond a screen of willows a small tarn glittered. On it were several dozen waterfowl. Leon approached. Many of the larger ones were odd indeed. There were emerald shanks and weird crests and crimson excrescences like tumours around the base of the beak. He looked about him with amazement. Although the grounds had been landscaped they were laid out not as a park but as an elaborate garden. There were a few expanses of plain grass lawn which together might have constituted a pleasance, but the general effect was more serious and even scientific in a way he found reassuring. On all sides was a profusion of unfamiliar plants and trees, all well maintained and labelled. Used as he was to the North Sea coast he was overwhelmed by the richness of the garden, by the colours and scents, the nooks of shade, the rockeries and summer houses.

Butterflies staggered above banks of honeyed trumpets whose name was painted on the wooden marker planted beside them. He seemed to have fallen into a paradise. He wandered about, slightly stupefied.

'We can't leave this, can we?' he kept remarking. 'Oh no, we can't leave,' came the reply. The wind had dropped, the sun beat hotly back from the brick walls of potting sheds and outhouses. Along the paths moved nannies drowning in light, the silver spokes of their perambulators glittering like pinwheels, *sprrixx*, while around them trotted their older charges, some of whom wore velvet leggings, for the day had started cool and dull. His chest paining him with excitement, Leon sat on a bench in the shade of a camellia gazing across at the Orangery (which of course he did not recognise as such). At once he fell victim to a strange fugue. In an instant he watched the seasons changing, the trees stripped and black with mist, the cold blaze of snowlight, the nursemaids and sauntering couples bundled up and brisk. All this he saw taking place in a withdrawn silence as if out of earshot. '*Ssiiih*,' he whispered when it was over, already rooted to the garden by virtue of this perspective. And then he noticed between trees the tall glitter of the Palm House. Approaching it he saw there were a couple of lesser conservatories not much different from Wim's father's greenhouses. He paid them little attention. It was the Palm House which drew him, with its crystal dome and flashing weathervane shaped like a golden ship, full-rigged and holding its course into the eye of the wind. The panes of this immense glasshouse were misty with condensation but he had the impression of green bulks of foliage and, beneath the dome itself, of actual trees.

Seeing a couple leaving he let himself in through the double set of doors and stood in wonder, breathing the hot damp reek. This incense went straight down in his lungs, clearing airways, easing tightness. He walked the spongy paths, admired plants

43

whose shapes he had never imagined. If the walled garden outside were itself a fragment of the seventeenth century, this indoor land was a patch of primordial terrain. It was as if once, unknown ages ago, a tropical forest had covered this part of the Earth until one day people had noticed it retreating and had clapped a greenhouse over a remaining tentacle like a tumbler over a butterfly, preserving it intact as the rest shrank away and vanished for good. Altogether he spent an hour in there, alone but for three visitors who came and went. There seemed nobody in charge. He left and after a search found a fellow in a leather jerkin and gaiters who directed him back to the lodge.

'Little sod,' a vaguely official-looking man was saying to a red-haired woman sitting at a typewriter in the office. 'We're missing two hundredweight.'

'You mean he's nicked them?' asked the woman incuriously.

'Clean as a whistle. Imagine, two hundredweight of trellis straps.'

'What on earth are they?'

'Those nail things for driving into walls to hold plants up. They've got a lead tag on them which you bend over the stem to grip it. It's the lead he was after. Any scrap merchant'd give him a good price for . . . Yes?'

'I want to do your glazing,' said Leon.

'We've got a glazier.'

'We *had* a glazier,' the woman reminded him tartly.

'There's a lot of panes missing or broken,' Leon insisted, adding truthfully, 'I'm good,' thinking of all the glass he had helped Wim replace. There was hardly a winter storm which hadn't taken its toll.

Whatever wind had blown him here was evidently still blowing his way. Within half an hour he was engaged as a gardener's boy for a pittance and with permission to sleep in a potting shed where there were some bales of peat and a horse blanket. 'Can't think why I'm doing it,' the man kept saying. 'No references, nothing. And especially after all this. I suppose you've not got your eye on anything? There aren't any trellis straps left but maybe you're planning to start a black market in putty?'

'I'm not a thief.'

'No,' said the man with a slight stare. 'I don't believe you are. I wonder what it is you are, though? Apart from being mysteriously punctual?'

'A good glazier.'

Not only that but a willing and reliable worker. By the year's end Leon had made a niche for himself in the Gardens' hierarchy of labourers. True, it was near the bottom; but in some way he had made himself indispensable, or at least was off the list of those who might be dispensed with if the worsening economy made layoffs necessary. Wearing his leather jerkin and gaiters (obligatory for all staff members, a remnant of eighteenth-century uniform) he mastered various kinds of maintenance while learning all he could about horticulture. For the first year he was not allowed to have anything to do with the plants, many of which were rarities from all over the world. He asked questions and remembered answers, watched and watched. He lived in the potting shed, ate at workers' cafés, bathed once a week in the Palm House boiler room, had his own key to the wicket in the main gates. This by itself was a measure of the peculiar trust he inspired.

'Very odd boy,' as the head gardener remarked to the Palm House curator. 'Talks to plants.'

'Not just to plants. Sits there in that tin tub in front of the furnaces carrying on to himself. I can hear him from the next room. Sort of nonsense full of squeaks and groans and things. You wouldn't say he was potty, though, would you?'

They thought for a moment, warming their hands on the

mugs of tea they were holding. The dried mud on their palms husked over the glaze. 'Not to talk to, no,' said the gardener. 'That's what's odd. Remember that painter they brought in? The one who'd been gassed in the trenches? Now there was a fellow off his onion. He didn't just talk to himself. Went about shouting at people who weren't there. Gave me the willies. But young Leon's not like that. When he's on his own he talks to himself, right, but when he's with you he talks perfectly normal, doesn't he? No, he's not potty. And I'll tell you what, that boy's got the greenest fingers I've ever seen. You know when you're losing a plant? You've tried everything short of sitting up with it at night? Point comes when you think sod it, that's it, heave it up and put it on the bonfire. Old Leon'll come by and say "Don't pull him up, Mr Smy, don't pull him up." And he'll mess about with it and make sort of hissing noises at it as if it was a horse and blow me, a week later there'll be this little green shoot. Soon as winter's over I'm having him off maintenance. It's a waste. You could go out in the street right now and in five minutes find thirty men to put a washer on a tap or patch a water butt or dredge dead leaves out of the lake.'

'And glad of the work.'

'Exactly. No, I'm having him off that. The lad's got something. Wants watching, though. A lot to learn. He will keep talking to visitors. Caught him at it only this morning. Willesz had put him to cleaning out that runoff tank at the back of the Orangery and he'd got this barrowload of sludge and muck, looked like a blackamoor, pushing it along a walk if you please, not even going round by the wall. When I came on him there he was, bold as brass, stopped out there in the middle talking to this young lady. "Since when," I asked him soon as I could get him away, "does the Society encourage filthy dirty gardener's boys to talk to ladies and gentlemen of the public? One, it's against regulations and two, it's a question of manners." He knew better than to give me any sauce but it's not the first time he's done it.'

'Nor the last, probably. Not if it's young ladies he likes chatting up,' said the curator wisely. 'I sometimes wonder if he's not having quite a bit of fun on the side after hours in that potting shed of his.'

'Blimey,' said the head gardener. 'Never thought of that.'

'Well, he doesn't seem to want to leave it. My wife tried to get him to lodge with us. You know how soft she is and she's sort of taken a shine to the lad now that our two have left the nest. Doesn't like the sound of his cough and he's too thin – you know how they go on. Fine by me. Shove a bed up in the attic, it'd be better than kipping between peat and straw, but he wasn't having any. Respectful-like but no, he was happy where he was. Perhaps that's why. Ask me, he's on to a good thing. Not many kids his age have a little private roof over their heads with their own key and nobody asking questions.'

'Can't have that,' the head gardener said dubiously. 'Not on the premises. Bring the Society into disrepute. Think of the headlines. Orgies in the Orangery. They'd have my head.'

'You leave him be,' said the curator, draining his mug and standing up. 'He isn't that sort. He's not one of your tearaways. Been here what, a year? and nobody's ever caught him doing anything worse than talking to ladies without washing his face. Don't stir until you have to, my advice. We need kids like that. Boys nowadays, they come and go. Don't want to learn a trade. Not like it used to be. Our generation, it was for life, man and boy. These days you need to encourage the good ones.'

'Maybe,' was all the head gardener would say.

If a dark figure ever was glimpsed accompanying the Gardens' most junior employee as he stole at night between boulevard and potting shed, nothing further was said. And if in after-years Leon looked back at these times – which he seldom did, being no common nostalgic – he could clearly recall only details about particular plants and an immense disseminated happiness. With its bowed, peg-tiled roof, its tiny grate and small-paned windows locked solid with generations of paint and cobwebs the potting shed was his first home, tucked into an Eden behind high walls which had a comforting hierarchy, customs and dress. The shed's very smell was a source of contentment and was made up of creosote, hay, mice, winter wash, tarred twine and the linings of nests. Already the preceding years had blurred and run, infancy and boyhood, into a long self-loyalty beside an aching sea. The gilded galleon atop the Palm House, sails crammed and stays humming, tacked auspiciously into steady breezes, heading for foreign lands to bring back strange pods, seedlings, cuttings, tubers and corms for nurture and cultivation. It was the order that was so satisfactory, the artifice. The natural world's abundance was too dissipated, too squandered. It was diluted and thinned by distance, by vagaries of climate, by accidents of geology and the wrecking hand of man. A botanical garden, though, could be a living museum, richly concentrating varieties which in nature might not even share the same continent. It was something to set against limitless polders sucked at by a limitless sea until all the flavour was gone. True, those tough maritime plants were subtle and beautiful in their hardiness. Yet the shivering spaces in which they clung and thrived, the marsh grasses rooted in the seep and glitter of draining water, all told of something hollow and unquiet which he wished not to think about. Only now and then in winter or in stormy weather when the gulls drifted inland with their pained, angular cries did they bring with them a breath of the past, for a moment producing in him a sense of unravelling. It was marvellous the grief a mere bird could bring, crying and bent against a drab sky. Quickly he would turn back to hoeing around the *Crinodendron hookerianum* or swaddling a clematis against frost, rendering the gulls powerless and keeping at bay the sad chill they brought. With him at all times was his companion. Like a lone mountaineer who is so certain of a presence that he automatically halves each bar of chocolate, Leon knew he lived with an angel perched on his shoulder, his own familiar, guide and friend.

Sometimes at night, nested on peat or straw, he would stare up through the potting shed roof as if it were transparent. His being was sucked up by the stars like moisture in sunlight until there was nothing left and he was dispersed throughout the universe. Even in this grand revolve the Gardens remained in view, a patch of earth whose hallowed quality was emphasised by its being an island within a city. He could get no further than this simple perception. More often than not his vision would lose altitude and sideslip into nothing more than a banal aerial view, no doubt inspired by newspaper pictures taken from airships and aeroplanes. At night, at least, his home was a mysterious stain surrounded by the streetlamps and illuminations of a capital city stretching from harbour to zoo. His own dark island gave off only secret gleams as muted as brushed silver: from the lake which held the moon spellbound in its pane and the Palm House itself whose myriad facets glinted with suppressed power. A fox barked. All these images mingled and swirled while, sitting on the ridge tiles not six feet overhead, the barn owl which lived in the hexagonal turret of a summerhouse revolved its head soundlessly and coughed up a pellet of mouse fur and skull plates less thick than fragments of a ping-pong ball.

Not even the wind bore the faintest whisper as, many hundreds of miles away to the east, maniacal speeches were cheered by vast crowds in floodlit stadiums.

Overheard:

Acalypha hispida: He was very interested in survival in those days, wasn't he?

Brownea grandiceps: Very. His own, primarily, but also ours. Quite a leap. Humans have a different perspective on these things. They've got various grand phrases like "The will to live" and "The life force" which have religious or moral significance for them. We're a good deal less pretentious. I mean, why invent difficulties? Do you remember him lecturing us about something called "Occam's razor"?

A: Vaguely. Didn't that tamarind he thinks so highly of, the one by the door, make a joke about "Bunkum's pruner"? Just a bit of mickey-taking. Our gardener's so *earnest*, isn't he?

B: He's making up for lost time. In any case it's obvious just looking around that our own life force must be pretty simple and uniform. Whether we live or die depends on conditions being right. If you ask me, survival's a straight-forward matter. Look at that moss he has such problems with on the outside of the House up beyond the palms. He's always going on about it rotting the bricks and making the glass green at the edges. It's because that end faces north. It doesn't happen on the southward-facing parts because conditions are wrong there. Not enough damp or shade or nourishment. Any plant can understand that.

A: True. With the right conditions there's no stopping us. But give the man his due, he also understands it. There's something in his character which responds to the principle of "all or nothing". When it comes down to it there's very little flexibility built into most living things, not even humans. For the majority of creatures everything has to be just so, and within quite narrow limits. What else are all these thermometers for?

B: Survival.

A: Exactly. We happen to be particularly sensitive to cold. Our lives hang on a few degrees, which isn't true of humans. But they have their own problems, our gardener especially. It's to do with their hearts, I think. The conditions for life may be fine, but they can still lose this "will to live" of theirs. I've always thought the gardener's will was really more a matter of stoicism. He's very absolute, I've noticed. If he can't have what he wants he'd rather have nothing. I approve of that, don't you? It's how we all feel. Anyone here would prefer to grow and blossom and die in due time than merely survive in a sort of straggly half-life. Who wants to live on those terms? One has to be a bit brisk about these things. Our gardener is, and that's why I admire him.

B: Me too. Better nothing than the wrong thing.

THREE

Several days' snow had left the Palm House practically deserted, with few visitors by day and none at night. Leon presumed they had little faith in the buses and trams which ran the sketchiest of services past the Botanical Gardens' main gate, and equally little coal to dry their shoes and thaw their feet once they did arrive home. On an auspicious morning when it wasn't actually snowing he allowed himself to hope for one of the princess's surprise visits.

He had spent an hour or two potting up *Annona muricata* seedlings, a task which had been delayed. This was a small tree whose fruit the English knew as soursop and the Spanish as *guayabano*, hinting at a non-existent connection with guavas. He had never seen this fruit but knew it from illustrations to be dark green, vaguely pear-shaped and covered with soft spikes, sometimes growing to the size of an irregular cantaloup melon. There were thirty seedlings, and he touched their first glossy leaves with affection. It never staled, the pleasure of watching seeds which had formed inside fruit warmed by a tropic sun in a forest eight thousand miles away sprouting into an alien world, duped by heat and light and moisture. Such a light, too, as no *Annona* would ever normally see. The snow outside riddled the Palm House with its glare, blotting up colour and replacing it with brilliant blacks and whites and greys. So strong were its effects that it had the qualities less of light than of a chemical which, when people were dipped in it, etched brutal discriminations. Anyone below the age of twenty it turned into children; anyone above it aged. The cold which accompanied this light afforded its own litmus test, too, the young going pink and the old blue.

Leon had been outside to see if there were any fox tracks. In his apprentice days before the war there had been a population of foxes in the gardens but it was some time since he had heard, seen or smelt one. They, too, might have been eaten. He found no tracks and the cold air had brought on a spasm of coughing so violent he had staggered back indoors bent over, his face suffused, legs weakening at each step. Once inside he had sat heavily down on the gravel – the sensation was more of having been pushed to the ground – while the steamy vapours slowly eased his lungs. There was, he vaguely knew, something else, something connected with the heart. 'Lungs and heart,' as the doctor had said years ago, tapping the varnished tube of his stethoscope on the palm of his hand, 'lungs and heart. No use thinking of them as separate. They're both bedfellows in a sick chest.' For a moment on the gravel Leon had felt the weakness spread upwards throughout his body like hemlock so that even his vision grew momentarily dim though with red streaks like sunset. 'But of course we're none of us up to snuff,' he told himself when he was back on his feet. 'Short commons for everyone. What can you expect on half rations?'

Even as he returned to his seedlings he felt optimistic about the future. Things could only improve. Here were thirty little plants where a month or two ago had been none. Probably half of them would wind up in other gardens, at Kew outside London, at the Hortus Botanicus in Amsterdam, the Orto Botanico in Florence, in Paris, Brussels, Edinburgh, The Bronx. Obviously

Berlin and Frankfurt would have to wait. Who knew what was left of those once-magnificent gardens? Strangely, many of the learned societies which administered such places had managed to remain in touch throughout the war. It had been amazing how amid bombing and shelling and with an entire continent in convulsions of militarised chaos, a network of private links and public services like veins beneath the skin had pulsed on in some sort of fashion. Late in the war Leon had been caught in an American daylight raid when the whole city centre had been cleared of people, tin-helmeted wardens herding everyone off the streets and into shelters. His last sight before being pushed underground had been of a postman, open leather satchel in a steel basket on the handlebars of his bicycle, pedalling among the last raid's uprooted cobblestones while troops and gunners dashed for their positions. The postman was holding a letter as he rode, reading the address. It had flashed upon him how layered reality was, not at all a single thing. The postman belonged to another, concurrent version, like a ghost of prewar days passing through in a dream. By such means had the Royal Botanic Society kept in touch with brother bodies, exchanging professorial greetings, learned papers, even seeds and cuttings, the hideousness of human behaviour made to vanish in the contemplation of a new rose or a batch of tenderly coaxed seedlings.

It made him happy, then, to imagine these little plants leaving him to join another collection elsewhere, new life being passed from hand to hand, propagating itself together with knowledge. Was he not a midwife in his mould-stained apron, bringing into the world difficult infants in this great incubator, rearing, training and strengthening them until they could flourish on their own and be ready to leave if need be? His children. Up and down the nave, in aisles and transepts, beneath the dome, his children, rampaging with vigour. Only when placed in the context of the snowscapes outside could they be seen as delicate.

On their own terms they burgeoned fit to cover the Earth.

Towards noon the sun broke weakly through to light up the south-facing angles of the Palm House roof. There the snow melted from the panes' topmost edges and sagged to form wet crescents of palish sky. At ground level the temperature remained below freezing, the snow pristine but for the twiglike tracks of birds and the scars of his own flounderings. This layer also transfigured the gardens, hiding signs of damage and neglect. The head under-gardener had been pensioned off, having lost a leg in a tram accident during the blackout. Two other gardeners had been killed in air raids and several boys and men had never returned from conscription into the army. Evidently the Society did not yet feel financially secure enough to fill their vacant posts. The beautiful seventeenth-century mansion attached to the gardens and forming the Society's headquarters had been requisitioned by occupying forces and left partially ruined. The current priority seemed to be to restore the house before the gardens. Nothing was quite certain. Meanwhile, snow covered all evidence of indecision.

Leon was suddenly prompted to drop what he was doing and go and look at his lotuses. He had scrounged some immense aluminium roasting pans of military origin which now were laid out in a double row where the winter sun fell through the glass. The pans were filled with water up to the rims of the flowerpots they held, each with its sacred lotus. The pots themselves were no longer visible, being hidden beneath the plants' circular pads and many-petalled flowers which placidly basked in the faintly blue snowlight. He had acquired the seeds from Burma just before the war but had only recently turned them out and grown them and discovered to his relief that they were a nearly pure white variety instead of the usual effeminate pink. The profound silence of these two complementary whitenesses separated only by a membrane of glass now brought a moisture of satisfaction to his eyes. He relished the intense juxtaposition of two worlds whose huge disparity in miles had simply been compressed into a temperature differential of thirty degrees centigrade. Suddenly taken with the idea of stuffing the entire Palm House with lotuses he found a box containing a last couple of dozen seeds, filled a jam jar with water and took six of the hard, greyish-purple nuts which looked like small olives, pierced the rounded end of each with the point of a nail and dropped them in. Within a few days they ought to have germinated and could then be potted out to join the others in the roasting pans.

In early afternoon the sun was a reddening ball balanced on the roof of the Temperate House when Leon heard the squeal of the entrance doors. He was far away, adjusting the padded zinc halter which, by means of a long cable strung from a bracket, supported the venerable head of a cycad, *Encephalartos altensteinii*. Grown from a seedling by a founder member of the Society, this ancient palm fern now had a stem nearly a foot thick whose rind, marked by the print of every stalk it had ever produced, was reminiscent in its spiral dotted pattern of something briefly glimpsed as a lump of coal cleaves in a grate. He paid no attention to whoever had entered until aware of a motionless presence at the edge of vision.

'Good afternoon,' said the princess.

Evidently her own skin contained a substance impervious to the corrosive reagent in snowlight, for she looked neither younger nor older but only slightly paler, wrapped in furs with ice melting from the welts of her boots. A cylindrical muff hung from her neck.

'Why is nobody here?' she asked, glancing about in surprise. 'Outside it's – the whole world is – *derelict*. Only here is life and warmth. You're like a heart, I think, beating and beating in this frozen body of Europe.'

How small she is by day, he thought. He found this saddened

him. Outside the mysterious persona created for her by the night people she appeared defenceless. The snow only exposed her further. He mounted a step-ladder to tauten the stay.

'Why are you putting wire around its neck?'

'It's been wired for years. Probably since last century. Too heavy to support itself.'

'Surely it can't be? In the wild there are no kind gardeners.'

'No. It would have collapsed and decayed long since. Except in freak circumstances it wouldn't have lived as long as this. Guess how old it is?'

'You said they put the wire on last century, so I'll say a hundred years. But a hundred years for a plant in a pot must be impossible.'

'I believe the Japanese grow miniature trees in pots to a far greater age. This cycad's a hundred and seventy-three years old. We're almost certain it's the Western world's oldest potted plant. Beautiful, isn't it?'

'Not very,' said the princess. 'It's all bent and quite undistinguished. If I saw it like that in my garden at home I should tell my gardeners to pull it up.'

'Exactly. That's why it's beautiful. It's a survivor, and all survivors have beauty. It has everything against it. By present standards the cycads are primitive, some say the most primitive plants still alive. See its stem and the shape of the leaves? They say "palm", don't they? But look at this – a cone. It's so ancient that botanists claim it hasn't yet reached the evolutionary crossroads of deciding whether to be a palm tree or a conifer. Propagation's slow and difficult. Already you can see it shouldn't be here at all. It ought to be a hundred and sixty million years in the past. But here it is. Add to that its rarity, and people like you and your gardeners, to say nothing of the cold only a few feet away which would shrivel it within minutes, and you'll understand why I think it's beautiful. For as long as we can keep it happy and protected this *Encephalartos* will remain one of Europe's most celebrated plants.' He caressed the thick, woody trunk.

For a moment she watched his hands, then said 'I think you're a strong man.'

'What?' he glanced up absently.

'A strong man. Someone who doesn't care what people think of him. Who's free inside himself. Who dares tell diplomats and aristocrats to stop smoking.' She wiped mist away from a pane with a fur cuff. 'I like that kind of power. The other kind is – what was that expression? – two-a-penny.'

Leon only murmured 'power', musingly, an aside which might have been no more than a conventional politeness while his attention wandered.

'We've all had a surfeit of tyranny,' she continued. 'You here in Europe, we in Asia. Swaggering generals, swaggering armies, police chiefs, politicians, mayors, landowners, petty officials, criminal bosses. In only the last five years my country has been liberated by the Japanese – according to them – and now by the Allies – according to them. Nobody bothered to ask us, but we were perfectly content six years ago without all these liberations and massacres.' She moved to another pane and drew a neat line of curlicues in the condensation. From each letter, if indeed it was writing, a drop of water gathered and ploughed its way downward, increasing in size and momentum. 'A river of dead children, this I have seen. From one side to the other. Like little logs floating. Now they tell us things are back to normal again, it was a hiccup of history. So what are we to think of all that power? Those swaggering generals?'

She turned from the window and Leon, who was still caressing the cycad, gave a start and said, 'Me? I'm just a gardener.'

'One who would tell a swaggering general to stop smoking in your Palm House, I've no doubt.'

'Maybe I have hidden motives. I'll show you something.'

She followed him obediently as he walked back and took from its shelf the half-full jar of fermenting cigarette juice. He shook it and she watched the brown liquid tumble and froth, the fragments of paper and shreds of tobacco whirling. 'Not power,' he said. 'Self interest. As always.'

'I don't understand. Oh, maybe you don't like the smell of cigarettes. But that's a private dislike, not self interest.'

'No. This juice is valuable to me. I need it. So I collect cigarettes from people who smoke here. Before the war I didn't bother because I had a tobacco supply. Now there's a market even for the stubs. So if I can take nearly whole cigarettes away from people like that Italian diplomat who comes here, I'm in luck and it makes me vigilant. As soon as they light up, there I am with my jar and what you call my power. It's no more than a need for nicotine.'

'A need?' she asked uncertainly. 'You mean, you . . . ?'

'Drink it? Inject it? No, just spray it on the plants. Nicotine's a wonderful pesticide.'

'I'll pay you a compliment,' she said, 'but it's the truth. You're a better gardener than any in my country. You understand our own plants better than we do ourselves. How can this be, since you told me once you've never been further than this city and that place by the sea where you were born?'

'I've studied,' he said with a certain haughty modesty. 'I don't think it matters where a plant comes from. They're all the same, really. Of course, some prefer heat and others cold, some need more water or a different soil, a lot of light or plenty of shade. It's just a matter of knowing these things and then paying attention to each plant to get the balance. Start with the idea that things *want* to grow, that they have to be actively dissuaded from growing. You've seen that patch of concrete by the main entrance? You can't at the moment, of course, but when the snow clears have a look as you come in and out. They put that down only three years ago for the commandant's car' (an immense Mercedes with little silver flagpoles on each wing sporting swastika pennants) 'and already there's grass coming up through the cracks. The other sort of power. There's no mystery, you know. A gardener like me doesn't really have to do anything much except watch and listen. The plants do the rest.'

'Then why do the plants in our gardens at home not look as good as the same varieties you have here, thousands of miles away in the wrong climate?'

'I couldn't say.' Leon put the nicotine jar back on the shelf. 'Perhaps your own gardeners aren't really gardeners but just men you employ to keep order. Also, I suppose your plants are in their natural surroundings, at the mercy of storms and pests and wild animals. And children throwing sticks and catapulting stones to get the tamarinds and mangoes down.'

'How do you know that?' she asked in astonishment.

'I assume. All children everywhere must be the same. Here it's plums and pears. Why should your village children be any different from ours? You're leaving out something else.' He indicated the great indoor jungle. 'Beautiful, yes. But also largely sterile. Some of the plants reproduce themselves but many don't. No birds come to drop seeds. No bees or bats exchange pollen. There are a lot of singletons, shrubs which are the only representatives of their species here. In order to keep the strain going I need to import more seeds or seedlings, grow them up and pollinate them by hand. It's the main part of our project here, to make all our species more secure. That's the drawback to an artificial environment. Back home you don't need to worry. Nature takes care of everything. A more reliable hand but rougher and readier than mine, and that's the only reason why these plants may seem to be in better condition, just as I may seem to be a better gardener than yours.'

When two strangers hold each other in slight awe, even if their awes are of a quite different variety, it can produce its own stilted intimacy. Of course he was flattered by this rarefied creature descending from her charmed circle of diplomats and emissaries, magic people who lived in a world above that of common hardship and rationing, trotting through the snow to watch and question him at work. And flattery of manner, combined with veiled homilies about power, could scarcely avoid bordering on the erotic's secret territory. The furs with their beads of moisture like sweat or secretion; the slender brown finger writing on the window a message recording atrocity or desire – he would never know which. A point was reached (as he shut off a stopcock and began unscrewing a leaking tap) when a proposition was in the air, though utterly shapeless and undefined. Something about the waning afternoon light bouncing off the snow outside cut the Palm House adrift on its own island, starting an intangible process whereby two strangers become survivors, who in turn become inhabitants, who perforce change from allies into intimates skipping only, maybe, a stage of friendship. The process was set in motion, rendered the more titillating since neither knew which stage had been reached. It was the moment of unbearable delicacy which can lead to unbearable delight, or else to an abrupt and unaccountable loss of interest.

'I've no right to ask this,' she said without the least impertinence, 'but are you happy here?'

'Happy?' It was the sort of job which could be done without a vice, merely needing a small adjustable spanner which he took from the shelf next to the nicotine jar. Nobody had ever asked him a direct personal question in his life. He unscrewed the handle from the body of the tap and examined its rust-orange washer. 'I'm content enough, of course. To have survived the war. Those things.'

'Everybody must have some longing, some dissatisfaction. This is a major Western belief, I thought.'

'Ah.' He found a pair of pliers, gripped the plunger and unscrewed the little brass plate which held the washer.

She retreated fractionally. 'Many people, for example, may be quite content in the ordinary way but still have a hankering to travel, for example. The trip of a lifetime to see – oh, I don't know – the Pyramids or the Taj Mahal, the Amazon or Tahiti. In your case it would be hardly surprising if you wanted to see the places where all these plants grow naturally as part of the landscape.'

'Your own country, for instance.'

'For instance.' A small shoulder rose and fell beneath the fur, releasing a fragrant breath of 'Cuir'.

It occurred to him that even allowing for her tropical origins she must be feeling the heat but he lacked the courage to suggest she remove her coat. 'Of course I've thought about it. Naturally I'd be curious. But I know I never shall. It's not the point. My job here as curator carries full-time responsibilities and besides, travel that far must be very expensive. I never could have that sort of money. So I never consider it.'

'Oh,' said the princess, 'all things are possible, you know.' This was said without archness and he took it at prosaic face value.

'Football pools? A lottery? I never waste money on things like that so I'm never likely to make any, either.'

'But you surely take holidays now and then? This Botanical Association, whatever it's called: presumably they're normal employers and not slave drivers. An expert like yourself is unique. Every so often he needs a sabbatical for research. You're not some ordinary gardener.'

'The Royal Botanic Society gives its employees holidays, of course,' he said a little stiffly. 'Excuse me a moment.' He left the princess standing there and went away down the nave. The No Admittance door banged softly behind him through the muggy atmosphere. Almost at once he reappeared. She sighed and poked a finger at the pieces of dismantled tap. He returned with a new washer which he began to fit. 'I'm sorry. What were you saying?'

She was more than equal to this small rudeness. 'If it has slipped your memory in two minutes one would certainly think your brain could do with a holiday even if your body doesn't need one.' Quite unexpectedly this made him smile. 'Say you didn't go abroad, say you couldn't bring yourself to leave this damned freezing dilapidated *derelict* city, you could at least stay at home and let someone else look after your greenhouse for a fortnight. They surely couldn't ruin it. You must have assistants.'

'Not proper assistants,' Leon told her. 'There isn't the money. Just some labourers. And yes, they could ruin it quite easily. Only I and . . . and only *I* know how the boilers work. When you say stay at home, this is my home. I live here.'

She repeated this in amazement, adding, 'On these premises?', and looked about her as if expecting to glimpse a camp-bed half concealed by shrubbery.

'Yes,' he said, now almost shyly. 'Have for years.'

'Oh, but – '. She had been on the point of saying, 'Then perhaps you, too, are a *singleton*' but was stopped by the squeak of the entrance doors. The light was going steadily now but the neat figure was easily recognisable as he approached. The dark overcoat and suit, even the muffler at the throat marked a visitor from an exterior world. The man's eyes sliced Leon's face in passing, then he spoke to her in a mellifluous babble.

'He's worried I should return unescorted in the dark,' she told Leon. 'He points out quite correctly that this is still a dangerous city full of poor and desperate people who might take advantage of an obvious foreigner like myself, especially a woman. Well, I'll go now, but with more than customary thanks for a fascinating and enlightening afternoon. Your magic place is a partial cure for homesickness, Mr Gardener.'

'Leon.'

'Mr Leon. I have a feeling your life is going to change soon.'

The effect of these words was immediate. 'Oh, don't say that,' he cried.

'I didn't mean for the worse,' she said reassuringly. 'Quite the contrary.'

'But I don't want change. No, no change. I'm content, as I said. Thoroughly content.' As if in placation he added, 'I have something for you, princess,' in a formal tone. The equerry's face had dimmed to a dark blur but still housed the glitter of eyes. Leon went over to the roasting pans and picked out a perfect lotus in its pot, dripping, while supporting its leaves with the other hand. 'We'll wrap this in sacking and you shall take it home. Keep it in the warm, in water up to the edge here. Near a window so it can see the sun. Only please don't tell anyone because the Society wouldn't be at all happy that its curator is giving plants away. Though in fact these are mine, acquired at my own expense.'

'Oh,' she said in delight. 'Look,' she showed her companion, 'basimbun.' She laid a moth-light hand on Leon's arm. Not for the first time he noticed the erotic pleasure involved in giving, as if the gift and its acceptance were earnests of greater intimacy. When they left the equerry carried a shapeless ball of hessian in front of him like a tyro-anarchist a bomb. The outer door closed behind her, severing a tentacle of 'Cuir' which curled upon itself on the threshold.

'A delicious person, don't you think?' he asked himself as he lit a candle or two in the empty Palm House. Today was a Thursday; the gardens closed at four and there were no night visitors. As he locked the entrance he noticed it was starting to snow again. He hoped the water wouldn't freeze as it had in 1942, nearly leading to disaster. A raid had uncovered, but miraculously left undamaged, the mains supply in the boulevard half a mile away. After a day or two's exposure to the intense cold the pipe froze and no water came through to feed the heating system. By sheer good fortune he happened to glance at the thermometer on the boiler and had damped the furnaces down in time. Such reflections scurried through his head as he moved restlessly about. 'What does she mean?' he asked a carob whose curious bean had been a vague substitute for confectionery in the war. Not that sweets were once again available, but now the emergency was over one seemed to miss certain things less, others more. Likewise a thick stand of sugar cane nearly dominated one of the areas off the rotunda beneath the dome. It had gone unrecognised by all the occupying forces throughout the war and Leon had used a washing mangle to squeeze out the juice, boiling the smashed fibres to extract what remained. By careful rendering down he had produced a clear syrup which had been a great luxury during the sugarless years.

The afternoon had left him in a state of undefined excitement with a dark current running beneath. 'What does she mean?' he asked again. 'Ssiiih.' He lit a candle and then blew it out. 'Change? No, no. We remain true to what we know, don't we? For ever. What else? Travel. Unravel. Strange winds. And for what? What sought? What found? After all these years? Drop it all? Abandon ... ? But how beautiful she is. Fit to plant.' For this was the image which came to him, an instinct that precious things should be rooted in good soil and tended so as to preserve them, to coax them into further blossoming, to keep them in place. It was only the image of a horticulturist, not that of a madman or a murderer, and was accompanied by feelings of wistful tenderness.

How hungry he was, he thought as he walked back towards No Admittance. The door was slightly open and the electric light outlined a figure in the gap. Backlit in this manner it was featureless, but there was in its attitude (one hidden hand evidently on the handle inside) something which suggested a creature poised for sudden flight.

'Arabia felix,' said Leon gently with a smile. 'We're here.'

For a long time Leon was sure he could hear the lotus's receding voice:

'One moment we were floating in such beautiful pale light, our leaves gently interlapping, and the next I was wrenched up and bundled away into total darkness. Before I could see no more I was held up for inspection by a lady of startling beauty. Oh, that I shall one day see her again! I should like to gaze and gaze at her. She reminds me of the past, as if we had met before in some other place. Yet it's impossible. There was only ever the House. Yet I seemed to have – not a memory, exactly, but an instinct of *rightness* when I saw her features from close up. Most of the faces bent into mine have been pale and pudgy with gigantic noses. But hers . . . Delicate nose, delicate eyes. I'm sure I know them from somewhere far, far away. Or long,

long ago? Something about the skin colour. It has to do with love, perhaps, or just a dream, one of those dreams that infect a whole life.

'A strange sensation now; I believe they're unwrapping me. Yes, they are. It's getting lighter and oh! Light! There's a world outside, after all, and I must take stock of it. Very well: I find myself back on my feet, as one might say, floating in a pot next to a window. The view is extraordinary, I'm so high up. Or it will be tomorrow, for now it's quite dark outside though I can still see a canal with boats frozen into it and a little bridge with people going over, some of them on bicycles. Lights are coming on. There'll be all sorts of activity to watch. And clearer, since this window isn't misty like the ones in the House. Here it's just like looking through air instead of glass so it seems almost a miracle being perfectly warm while out there it's obviously very cold indeed. The people are all wrapped up as I was for my journey here, and leave footprints in the snow. Being higher, the light is different. It's not so blanched but bluer, a bit the colour of the smoke from cigarettes when they're first lit and before there's any ash on the tip. (A sudden homesick pang there, remembering how our gardener would suddenly appear and the cigarette disappear.) The air's much drier in here which I suppose explains the lack of mist on the glass. That doesn't matter since I'm floating again and so can't dry out for the moment at least, but it's a curious sensation. It gives everything a harder edge.

'The room itself is full of soft things: carpets, cushions, rugs, sofas, curtains, in gold and stripes. Mirrors, too, and pictures. A great fireplace with logs burning in it. (I wonder where she got those!) All very grand, and I can imagine parties in here with noblemen and people like that. Hardly my sort of society. If I feel at all awkward or out of place it isn't that which makes me feel humble, though, but the princess herself. A girl who looks quite like her – the same dark skin and hair and eyes though a lot younger, almost a child – has come in wearing a sort of red robe and carrying a tray with silver things on it.

'And all the time I can't clear my mind at all. Thoughts rush at me, the strangest new feelings and impressions. Yet underneath them is a single theme, I think, something bruise-coloured and heavy. It has to do with her, now drinking her tea alone by the fire. She, too, is thinking. Why do I imagine she's thinking about the House? Even about Leon, our gardener? It's as if she's looking back at him and wondering if he's looking back at her. Distance, that's it. It's about separation and distance. Sadly, I can't judge because not only do lotuses have almost no sense of time but I was blind throughout my journey here. For a moment then I thought I glimpsed a huge expanse of sea – an entire ocean, perhaps – but surely we couldn't have travelled that far? More like the other side of town than the other side of the world. Where do these stray images come from? I believe it's still connected with the gardener. Maybe I'm not just his simple gift to her but more his emissary: a doleful homesick creature half proxy and half spy cunningly planted so as to be nearer her than he himself can be?

'In any case how very beautiful she is as she sits by the fire with the dancing flamelight on the side of her head! Why doesn't she turn on the chandelier? But she doesn't and the room gets darker and the flames leap about the bulbous shoulders of the teapot and her face stares over and over the rim of her cup as she thinks of him. She's sublime and belongs elsewhere. Being a lotus I feel close to her since I do, too.'

FOUR

When the sun melted the snow on the Palm House roof the
moon refroze its edges into a crenellated coastline which ebbed
away down the glass until snow fell again. There was a moment
in early afternoon when the rays lacked sufficient heat to gnaw
any further and the day's new boundaries were complete. On one
particular afternoon sunlight blazed the fringes of its map into
gold filigree and fell through as topaz rain into the princess's
hair as she walked the length of the aisle. Leon was wandering
about looking at vistas, at juxtapositions, discontented with a
chance massing of too many dark greens at the jade vine's foot.
Harmony, balance; the plants' disposition was critical to their
overall effect, and their overall effect might elevate an interesting
collection into a work of art. Passing the young tamarind he laid
an encouraging hand on a branch and was at once distracted by
the approach of the princess's aureoled figure. At the sight of
her youthful Asian face in its golden nimbus his heart staggered
momentarily beneath the weight of memory. When she said 'I
may be going away, but first . . .' it seemed to fly apart and,
riding on a fragment, he was carried back to 1928 and found
himself on the beach with Cou Min staring helplessly at where
a splash of dried seawater had left, like the evidence of tears, a
floury patch of crystals on the delicate skin between her earlobe

and cheek. The whole story could be contained in one short summer of nine weeks, in which time the thin boy with the fishy dungarees had suffered the other pole of his life to be fixed. By the end he was the complete human being, a little celestial body wobbling bravely on its twin axes of loss and longing.

The arrival in Flinn of a Dutch fisheries expert had greatly excited the townlet. Extravagance of any sort entered neither the lives nor thoughts of its inhabitants, with their dour muling and muted dolour. The spectacle presented by Dr Koog was of royalty. They were not to perceive that the prodigious limousine in which he drew up outside the inn was a battered maroon shooting-brake, a vast jalopy disgorging an exotic retinue, chests and coffers of treasure and fine raiment and finally Dr Koog himself, a gentleman of aristocratic mien with muttonchop whiskers, a high white collar with rounded points and a crimson tie which lit up the square. It was some time before the townsfolk could see the car for what it was and the treasure chests as a collection of scuffed cabin trunks and leather boxes full of oilskins and scientific equipment – epibenthic nets, nests of circular sieves, microscopes and Nansen bottles. By then the boys were referring to Dr Koog's whiskers (strictly among themselves) as 'bugger's grips' and his exotic retinue had resolved itself into Mrs Koog – a dumpy lady with a gay laugh – and two foreigners who acted as servants. These were from one of the Dutch colonies, Bali or Java or somewhere like that, a mother and daughter presumably acquired as one acquired a tan, in the course of government service or private enterprise. The inn door finally closed behind them, the car's engine ticked as it cooled, and three or four urchins too young to be intimidated squatted by the chromium hubcaps and fell into hysterical giggling pleasure at the sight of their own distorted faces and bulbous tongues.

Leon, on his way home from an errand, had been as diverted

by this magnificent arrival as everyone else until he saw the servant's daughter. In that moment he became possessed, wholly taken over by an inflooding of such amazement he could scarcely breathe. His very blood forgot to circulate. He even stopped coughing. Blessed the young to whose diary pages – scribbled in tears and pry-proof code – come doomed and wistful words like 'unattainable' which their hearts refuse to take seriously. In their imaginings the attainment is ever-present and any day now will be happening. To fall in love on the instant so that it has the effect of everything collapsing at once drenches the rest of time, or at least the rest of that summer, with a vibrating unreality. Certain migraine sufferers have advance warning of an attack when a shimmer appears above objects or haloes them entirely. Others are also filled with a strange exaltation despite knowing that it always leads to a darkened room and a shattering ache. The rest of that afternoon shuddered about Leon in just such a way as he went home along the track across the polder. Without warning his life had fallen into pre-today and post-today. A singleminded canniness of devotion was born which began at once to plan tomorrow. Unreality supervened again the moment he went to bed that night. As he lay in the darkness he scarcely noticed the lighthouse flipping its spurts of light across his curtains. He was in thrall for the first time to the addictive incense which rises from a pillow receiving confession. Her face was as close as the inside of his own eyelids yet beyond his reach. Try as he might he couldn't get her beloved physiognomy into focus. It had been more than a glimpse he had had of her, too. He had gorged his eyes as she carried boxes and bags and rugs between shooting-brake and inn while he stood not five feet away. He clearly retained the impression of black eyes, of skin the colour of the honey Wim's mother made, of a cheek flat or infinitesimally hollowed so it contained the merest wisp of diagonal shading such that the backs of his fingers might have

smoothed it away. But he couldn't fix her features. The harder he tried the more they skidded off and congealed into those of the tobacconist's daughter whom he loathed, even (God help him) of the tobacconist himself. Exasperated by his own disloyalty and by the perverse waywardness of his memory he fell eventually out of unreal waking into real sleep. When he awoke with a yielding tingle of instant recall at the change which had come into his life the lighthouse's beams were already invisible on the paling curtains and his mind was made up.

Putting on his cleanest clothes he ran downstairs, wrenched his bicycle from its shed and pedalled into Flinn. There he presented himself at the inn to learn what he could and, before timidity and resignation could get the better of him, to offer himself. As what? As anything: drudge, messenger, lover, car cleaner, boat rental expert, lifetime companion, slave. The first thing he learned from the innkeeper, quite forcefully, was that it was barely six o'clock and a gentleman like Dr Koog was hardly likely to be afoot after the previous day's long journey. Afoot, afoot, afoot; Leon morosely hopped down the inn's three steps and sat with presumption and temerity on the great car's running-board, leaning his head against the cover of the spare wheel half recessed into the wing and gazing up at the shuttered and curtained windows. The innkeeper came out and told him to take his reeking bum off guests' property. So he went down to the little harbour and sat on the jetty instead and watched fishermen unloading withy creels of flatfish and herring, haddock and gurnard while a summer morning crystallised around him. The early sun did its best to squeeze from the glittering grey North Sea a suggestion of tropic tints so that flashes of green and violet leapt from the lit edges of taupe sills, lapsed and collapsed in time with his heart.

To telescope judiciously, to haste things on: at ten to nine that morning Dr Koog engaged him as an 'experimental

assistant', the august lineaments of which title concealed the outlines of a dogsbody. He would be responsible for carrying equipment down to the boat and back up again, for cleaning it, repairing torn nets and performing such other tasks as might crop up. Dr Koog was friendly and had renounced his imperial collar and tie for an open-necked soft shirt. As he talked Leon's eyes wandered, trying to see around the man of science so as to catch a glimpse of the girl descending the stairs. He was unlucky in this but went home with a lifting sense of enterprise and success. By a legitimate ruse he had brought himself into the orbit of his beloved object (whom he couldn't yet name) and so fully had he embraced his new persona an oddness never struck him: that roughly eighteen hours ago he had never heard of Dr Koog nor tried to find buried in his pillow the face of a Javanese servant girl. But the next morning when he started work he saw her outside the inn, coming down the steps behind Mrs Koog. At the time he was talking to someone and his mouth continued to speak as he fixed for ever her red dress, her fledgling breasts mere hints beneath a white organdie bertha. *That* was how her face looked, framed by raven hair gathered in a thick glossy plait tied with a blue ribbon. *That* was how her fractionally plumper lower lip protruded as her heels elastically bumped each step to show she was fourteen and not twenty-four, just enough left of the child to make coming slowly down three steps less than a prosaic affair.

'. . . about hiring a suitable boat?'

'What? Sorry, sir, I didn't . . .', for it was apparently Dr Koog himself to whom he was talking.

The scientist raised a hand cheerily towards the retreating backs. 'My wife's off to do her shopping and we've no time to waste. She's on holiday. I'm not. Find a boat, get started, that's the thing. Know anything about fish?'

'My uncle's a fisherman, sir. I help him smoke the catches, mend the nets, stuff like that.'

'Know how to tell a fish's age?'

'No, sir.'

'Sex?'

'You mean like cock fish and hen fish, milt and roes?'

'That's it. Perhaps I'd better explain what I'm up to. The governments of all the countries which have North Sea coastlines want to find out more about the way fish breed, where they lay their eggs, what they eat, what makes a good breeding season, where they go when they migrate. That sort of thing. Once we know, we may be able to improve our fishing practices. At the moment we're taking far too many young fish and certain varieties are becoming scarce, as I'm sure you'll have noticed. Some areas are badly over-fished. There are limits to what we can go on taking and taking, year after year. If it was on land we'd say the animals were being hunted out. Not the least of our problems is that we know next to nothing about fish. Now, a boat. With an engine. There's one we might use lying away in Holland and I can always get that but I thought maybe we'd try for something local first.' Dr Koog had already steered Leon down to the jetty. His breezy energy was contagious and the boy felt there was nothing he couldn't arrange, no obstacle he mightn't overcome. With a man like Dr Koog behind him he was sure that getting to know the daughter of his wife's maid would be a pretty straightforward affair.

After some enquiries and haggling a suitable boat was engaged, a steam smack which had seen better days, and Leon's *aestas mirabile* was launched and under way. In some respects the doctor was scarcely less marvellous than the girl. He clearly believed that since Leon had volunteered for the job he might as well learn from it. He took the trouble to explain whatever he was doing and encouraged the boy to ask his own questions.

They spent roughly half each week at sea, generally day excursions but now and then going out at night. The rest of the time Leon was his lab assistant. Koog turned one of the inn's attics into a makeshift laboratory suitable for sorting and classifying specimens, preparing slides, writing up notes. It opened up a world the boy could never have imagined. He was proud of his dexterity with a knife and could split and gut a herring in a neat double movement, but Koog was less impressed by this skill than by a casual aside of Leon's that he sometimes put his head in the sea and listened to the fish. In the first instance the doctor showed him how to perform a simple dissection and explained a fish's basic anatomy, since like many fisher-folk the boy was utterly familiar with the creatures and almost entirely ignorant of them. In the second he questioned Leon closely about what he thought the sounds were that he heard, and whatever had made him listen in the first place? Leon blushed and begged him not to mention it to anybody since the villagers already thought him peculiar enough. Unfortunately he couldn't identify specific creatures by their sounds but only knew the sounds were there. What was more, although at one time or another he had seen most of the species around these coasts his ability to name all but the commonest was slight, and even those he often knew only by their local names. All varieties of squid, cuttlefish and octopus were referred to as 'stickers', for example. They were winged stickers, bony stickers and round stickers. Dr Koog listened attentively and then with the aid of the specimens they caught and the illustrations in textbooks (such books! such pictures!) showed him how very different each was, with different abilities and habitats. He soon saw that the creatures of the sea were as subtly diverse as the plants he so minutely discriminated, that the crude commercial relations he had with them disguised everything which made them interesting. The revelation lay in his grasping the idea of an unsubjective taxonomy. The private method he had devised for classifying natural things evidently had a parallel. All unbeknownst to him science had been assorting them according to criteria he would never have hit on in a million years, fitting them neatly into trees or setting them on the rungs of ladders so it became possible to trace an orderly relationship between everything.

While all this was going on he had made other discoveries. The girl's name was Cou Min – at least, that was how it sounded. She was half Chinese, half East Indian. On his recent travels to those parts of Asia Dr Koog had been accompanied by his wife who, owing to an attack of malaria, had been too ill to return to Holland in time to give birth. The infant was stillborn and Cou Min's mother had devotedly nursed Mrs Koog and, both husband and wife were convinced, had saved her life where the local Dutch doctor was evidently failing. In recognition they had offered the woman a permanent position as Mrs Koog's private maid, a post she had been only too glad to accept since her own husband now lay in a cemetery in Batavia. There was another thing Leon learned which made him gloomy indeed, which was that Cou Min spoke only Chinese and a Malay dialect. Her mother communicated with the Koogs in kitchen Dutch as opaque to Leon as Chinese itself; her shopping expeditions must have been a fine linguistic gallimaufry. Of the entire household only multilingual Dr Koog could converse with his new assistant with complete ease.

This frustration was made worse since, to give the girl pleasure, Koog would sometimes invite her on his field trips. To judge from her evident enjoyment and lack of fear she was perfectly familiar with the sea, though not with one as cold. She would sit on a coil of rope bundled up in thick clothing while her eyes took in everything. Whenever Leon's met hers he experienced an eviscerating pang. He would contrive to sit beside her and judiciously exaggerate the sea's motion so his body bumped against hers, at which he flashed her an easy smile of apology behind which a raving yell of hopeless love was bitten back. Once when they were delayed by a lost net it was past ten at night when they turned for home and as light left the sky and dark welled up from the sea his hand, after some minutes' stealthy manoeuvring, fell against hers and with a soft involuntary exhalation he kept it there, or it stayed and held hers of its own accord, being clearer in its intentions than its owner was. This breathless moment prolonged itself while she didn't stiffen or object or draw hers away. And then gradually her not drawing it away became sheer passivity and he could no longer pretend this was the demureness of a young goddess but some paralysing inertia or indifference with, maybe, deep cultural roots. He didn't let go, of course, since any contact on any terms feeds lonely hours and days of a lover's life, sustains dreams, quickens the air. At first he had kept his face averted but later looked into hers, puzzled, and found the dim oval likewise turned to him. But the eyes remained invisible, their expression unreadable until they neared land enough for the lighthouse to sweep its double flash across, in whose brief exposures he believed he saw a smile.

But the weeks passed and by broad daylight he read the same ghastly benevolence about the mouth whose contours his own had sought in the plump creases of his pillow, and in her eyes his own beseechingly caught the mere evidence of uncommitted liveliness. Her glances were everywhere, frank and inquisitive, young girl in a foreign land; and wearily it seemed to him she cast the same expression on a bag of cherries, the innkeeper's dog, the contents of one of her master's newly hauled-up dredges, as she did on him. Leon tried using Koog as an innocent interpreter, having him ask her if she were cold, if there were fish like this in her country, whether she went to school. Although some of the questions got through, Koog had a habit of answering them for her, absently, and such replies as he did extract were probably modified by their passage through the same indifferent filter. Leon thought the doctor wasn't especially protecting her; it obviously never entered his head that she was anything but a child, and a native one at that, towards whom nobody could feel anything other than the vague and undifferentiating kindness due all children. Certainly he seemed not to notice the wandering of his assistant's attention whenever Cou Min was present, nor see his trembling fingers as evidence of strain rather than debility.

'That's a nasty cough,' he would say as Leon was bent double by formalin fumes and could feel the scientist's eyes counting the line of vertebrae knobs beneath his shirt. 'We must get some weight on you.' But this, too, was vaguely said and the zooplankton in the water column soon rose up again and regained his attention.

Yet with each sun Leon's heart lightened in expectation as he cycled into Flinn after the usual acrid exchange with his uncle (who was little mollified by the small sums he brought home in place of his previously free labour). Some days he never even glimpsed Cou Min. On others, circumstances would conjure her arm beside his own and he would marvel at their different colours and ache to pass his fingertips over the tiny hairs trapped at her elbow's crease. Or else his eyes would be offered her leg, casually raised as she tied her shoe, the hem of her dress falling momentarily back or catching a stray favonian huff of breeze so as to permit his gaze access to unbearable depths of tender, apricot thigh. Those evenings he cycled home exhausted, worn out by the effort of maintaining his balance, riding the lurches, acting the uncomplicated, eager apprentice. It was impossible. Language, culture, constant supervision and sheer adult incredulity placed Cou Min on the far side of an insurmountable barricade.

Who at fifteen could ever imagine that everyone in his

town, throughout Europe, in the entire world, might be constantly filled with similar hopeless longings? That this sweet ailment which had descended on him sooner or later afflicted everybody? And who would conclude that at the centre of this universal longing there resided a tenderness so intense, so yielding, that it constituted a form of racial frailty? How out of sheer thwart and desperation protective guises were donned so that each morning from bedrooms the world over men and women stepped wearing armour – suits and overalls and uniforms which mediated the permissible and damped private anguish. But fifteen-year-old Leon was naked before his longing, even as he longed for nakedness. When he repeated her name into his pillow his scalding breath came back to him smelling of damp feathers. Behind squeezed lids he tried again and again to assemble her, to will her to stand before him, smile, reach out to place her hands behind his neck and draw him to her. Yet with faithless malignity his memory supplied only morsels in soft focus. In fantasy he was able to adore at leisure the sweet jut of an ankle bone beneath its short white sock; an ear transluced by pelting summer sun; the backs of her calves (modestly kissing as she stood waiting while adults talked) tensing and relaxing to her rocking on and off her toes; the tender nape so artfully hidden and revealed by the shining pigtail. Yet these wonderful details refused to coalesce into Cou Min complete. Instead they drifted about like motes in strong sunlight. Behind them floated her presence, by now as much part of him as his own beating heart and equally beyond sight, like the familiar figure glimpsed in a dream, so well known that its real identity is never disclosed.

And thus, sadly, passionately, he sang the Fragmented Beloved, dissolved in her own beauty.

Since everything about this summer was revelatory he also discovered how much being in love sharpens the senses even as it paralyses the intelligence. Had he been the diary-keeping sort he might well have headed one entry 'The Day I Smelt Her Knee', an event which took place without any contrivance of his. Once again they were at sea. Dr Koog and a crewman were hauling up a dredge of bottom samples, using a sheave. Leon had just turned away as it came aboard. The boat lurched, the heavy dripping net swung into his back, the end of its steel header catching him behind one ear. Half stunned, he was thrown to the deck where he slid on all fours like a dog on ice, thudding into Cou Min's legs where she sat on the edge of the engine-hatch coaming. He never quite lost consciousness but experienced a dreamy, prolonged sublimity where his vision was narrowed to an area of russet knee and he breathed the scent of salt wind on sunbaked skin. Even as it seemed he could stay there for ever the singing in his ears grew fainter, hands grasped at his shoulders and he was helped back on to his feet, unwillingly restored to the world. Had he been writing this up later while nursing the ragged remains of a headache, he might have gone on to list several other of Cou Min's intoxicating scents including those of her hair and her upper arms. Her clothes, too, had an innocent fragrance like the warm ghosts of coconut oil and the waxy smell of children's bedding. And had he been writing reflectively years afterwards he might have been tempted to enlarge generally on the smells and sounds of the young as opposed to those of adults, for his adolescent self had engraved Cou Min pungently and for ever in more than merely the visual dimension. The very young might not be aware of noticing such things, but it is by subtle as well as by obvious means that they choose their loves from among their peers and coevals, from appropriate calves and puppies. Is this not true? (he might have written, with monumental vexation at the years which made it impossible to complete that summer – now destined to remain for ever unconsummated and lost to proper expression.) Is it not so, that young skin and hair smell different? That the young sound different not only when they speak or sing but when they eat and even when they digest? It is adults whose teeth clack and whose jawbones crepitate so irritatingly when they munch; who leave lavatories stenching of the fermented ichors of coffee and tobacco sputum; whose breaths are accompanied by the shrill whistlings of nasal hair. How visually led people are, then, to imagine that this vast spread of difference could be squeezed down into matters of looks alone! Women in particular went to great and costly lengths in order to appear young, with their creams and diets and rinses, as if age were only wrinkles, fading and middle-age spread. Yet a blind person could tell in an instant they were fakes. No matter what art and artifice she employed no woman could ever go back to smelling and sounding as she had at Cou Min's age. Her very breathing would betray her. The body's clock is not read in the face or hands but in its sonorities and the leak of glands. The interwoven sensualities of youth are fully understood only by other adolescents, for whom they are new (if sometimes a little on the rank side) and free from the corruption of nostalgia.

One thing Leon certainly would not have noted in a putative diary was his theft of Cou Min's handkerchief, carried out with the unthinking response of the hardened criminal who stoops hawklike on a dropped wallet. This had fallen out of her sleeve when she brought tea up to her master and his assistant in the laboratory. Dr Koog had just explained how for the purpose of rough identification it was convenient to divide the flatfishes into three kinds: the turbot family, which included brill and megrim and had their eyes on the left side of their heads; the plaice family to which lemon sole, dab, halibut, witch and flounder belonged, whose eyes were on the right; and the proper sole family – also right-eyed – essentially represented by the Dover and sand soles. With a magnifying-glass Leon was examining the rosette around the nostril on the underside of a sand sole they had caught that morning when Cou Min knocked and entered with a tray. He broke off to watch her softly chiming progress and imagined running the lens over her entire body. As her hand dropped to the door handle on her way out a white wedge of handkerchief fell unnoticed from her sleeve and lay on the threshold like an abandoned sandwich. Quickly he went over and scooped it up, eliding this swift gesture into the act of picking up a teacup and bringing it over to the doctor who was still intently probing the sole's apertures with a pair of forceps.

He never really got closer to Cou Min than this. He had thought to recognize in her a fellow outsider, adrift in a strange place and an alien culture, surely isolated by her youth in the enforced company of adults. In vain his own feelings of dissociation, in vain his certainty of this bond between them. They had everything in common but a language. The summer went on passing; passed. He learned a good deal about fish, about marine organisms, how to use a microscope and at last see for himself what he had always intuited through the *grockle* sound of the sea threshing its roots around pebbles: that it was alive throughout with unsuspected creatures now shimmering in their prismatic colours and intricate shapes in the sunlight which bounced up from the swivelled mirror. What he saw was a glimpse, just as what he learned was a glimpse; but it would be impossible for him to return to the crudeness of smoking bloaters. Once this summer's turmoil had abated an intellectual disquiet would be found heaped like clouds out of which blew a wind fit to drive him away from Flinn and carry him as far as the capital.

And one day he was near the jetty, just far enough along the beach so that the water was not agleam with the restless rainbows of spilled engine oil, rinsing out plankton sieves in the shallows. When he straightened, dungaree legs rolled to his knees, he saw her standing a few paces off. He waded back and laid the sieves on the sand, heart beating with the certainty that she could only have come on a private errand. For the first time she smiled directly and unequivocally while holding his eyes. Then she said, in passable dialect, 'I may be going away.' And directly she spoke he realised it was true; she had purposely troubled to learn a parting line to convey that she had known all along what she meant to him, an act of politesse, even of sad mercy, which ran him through. 'I thought you couldn't speak . . . Going? But when?' he blabbered. 'You can't go, Cou Min. Not now . . .' Not now they could speak to each other, he meant, but they couldn't. She only shook her head helplessly, her one phrase of his language exhausted, her message delivered. When he said, 'But I love you, Cou Min. I honestly, truly do,' he reached out involuntarily and grasped her hands, whereupon her tiny wrists – surprisingly strong – swivelled so that she also could exert a fond pressure. She spoke a soft sentence or two which conveyed less to him than a sandpiper's cry. It was then that he saw the smear of dried salt dusting the cheek by her ear, the floury bloom minutely textured by the silky fuzz growing beneath, and was so immediately overcome with longing and despair that the remains of the strength which had sustained him week after week left him at once and he fell weeping to the sand. Involuntarily he reached forward and, drawing himself to her ankles, kissed her feet.

Oh, the payment exacted for love which has no return! The humiliation, the later self reproach; the inevitability of the malicious onlooker (in this case Wim's older brother) who hurries off to spread the riotous news. A thespian act upon the beach! A ham melodrama in which weirdo Leon falls at the feet of his Chink goddess, a slant-eyed servant's brat! In public! Not ten minutes ago! Probably if we're quick they'll still be at it!

But we're not quick enough, for that was the end we witnessed, five seconds after which Cou Min squatted briefly and laid her hand on the boy's trembling head. At this touch he sprang to his feet like one brought to his senses and turned back to the sieves and the sea, brusquely blotting his cheeks with shirted biceps while she walked away down the beach, at the jetty giving a small shake to her head as if to free the lustrous pigtail. The next day she left in a taxi together with her mother and Mrs Koog while the doctor stayed on for another week to finish his research. It was only then that the Dutchman appeared to notice his assistant was heartbroken rather than sickening for flu. After a little he explained, no doubt kindly, that Cou Min was engaged to a wealthy Chinese in Batavia – had in fact been affianced since she was nine, such was the way they did things there. He was under oath to this merchant grandee to return the girl on his next trip to the East Indies, which was to be before Christmas (it was now the first week in September) when they were to be married. A few days later the doctor himself left. Leon mutely helped him repack the maroon car with boxes and containers heavy with specimens. At last Koog held out his hand.

'Best assistant I ever worked with,' he said. 'I'll miss you badly, young man. Take this book – no, go on. From time to time you may want to refresh your memory about some of the fish we've seen. They're all there. The herrings, especially, would merit your earliest attention. And here's my card. If ever you're passing through The Hague be sure to look me up. I should be back there by next summer. Well,' he paused and glanced at the sky over the harbour as if for inspiration. 'Don't waste it. I mean your gift. You notice details. You appreciate difference. You like discriminating. It's a rare thing at your age. Perhaps you can make it pay. Something scientific, I'd suggest. Go off to the capital and get yourself an education.'

With this breezy farewell the doctor sped away. Leon never saw him again, nor any of his entourage. Later that day, flicking listlessly through the book he had been left, he discovered wedged between the pages describing the *Clupeidae* four rosy banknotes whose value together was more than his uncle earned in six months, enough (before his uncle found and stole three of them) to get him to the capital and enrol in some sort of course, had he chosen. And so that fateful summer ended. His own traitorous memory added an ironic postscript, for he found that no sooner had the Koogs left than he could visualise Cou Min entire, standing, sitting, squatting, running, looking at him and smiling from the other side of nowhere with that smile reserved for the dead in photographs.

Eighteen years later he watched the princess walk the length of the Palm House with her hair burnished as the sun's rays fell through the golden ice-frieze high above her, and heard her speak Cou Min's own words: 'I may be going away.' They produced a distant pang, an echo revived, precursor of loss, inevitable bad news, endings. 'But,' she went on, 'first I have a most serious offer to make to you. You don't believe me? *Je vous assure.*' Yet once again they were interrupted by the timely appearance of her lance-eyed shadow.

That night Leon blew out the last candle and instead of going to bed lingered for a while by the lovelorn tamarind. On hearing it speak he sat sympathetically on the brick pier beside it, knowing that eavesdroppers seldom hear good of themselves but also knowing it was his duty to listen. Tamarindus indica spoke softly, however, almost so as not to be overheard in its self-communing:

'Did I once accuse our gardener of anthropomorphism, of tainting us with human ills? I think I'm tainted anyway, with that fatal unrest which takes over when mindlessness has run its limiting course and one is free to suffer. At any rate he touched me this morning and I understood at once. Oh, not because it was me: it was quite absentminded. It wasn't a caress but something more wistful. Hardly a week goes by without somebody touching me but it isn't the same. The visitors like to touch – despite the notices – because we're rare to them, tokens of the exotic. The assistants have to touch, we're part of their work. They vary from brutal to considerate. But our gardener's like none of these. His is the gently musing touch of an unhappy man. If suddenly we could all burst into flower for him I believe we would, in blithe disregard of seasons and genes. The dark truth of this place is – *wasted love*. Scents and fruitfulness and all manner of budding and burgeoning: wasted. None of it goes any further, no matter what he says about sending seedlings hither and yon through the world. I sense it in his touch. The fruit drops and no seed germinates. The flower opens in futile splendour, the leaf falls. We writhe inside our glass.

'What I learned today is that he's little different from us. In a sense, are we not his flowering? Do we not speak for him? (And what comes of it? Dumb growth.) Nor is there hope for him outside. The sea wind blows across the dunes and marshes of Flinn, the world unlocks itself from war and finds nothing tender surviving. So much has been lost, and too much loss leads to this: to a gardener's gestures or a priest's, acts of succour and generosity which began long ago and with something quite else in mind. Though what should we care? The skills work none the less. His motivations are no-one's business but his own. It may be that nobody else even notices; quite possibly I wouldn't myself had I not felt his touch and seen his face. Such love! but of another time and still animating him, like the light now reaching us from a long-extinguished star. However, I mustn't get sentimental on his behalf: I'm no doubt wrong in reading all this into him and, in turn, committing my own vulgar error of botanomorphism.

'Nevertheless, I do have to go a bit further. I'm an intellectual – through no choice of my own – and there's no stopping thought. A saving grace if ever there was one for there's not much to do but think in a place like this. What else do you suppose happens when you're rooted in earth? I used to gaze down despondently at the antics of those in my vicinity but nowadays I daren't let my fond and betraying glance slide over my little neighbour for fear I'm unable to tear it away and she – in all her touching hemlockian innocence – becomes baffled and dismayed. So I admire the architecture instead, which never stales, although in these last eight years the paintwork certainly has. I've a childhood memory of when they did it inside and out in gleaming white and the House seemed twice as spacious, the roof floating off among clouds on the far side of a bright gulf. Of course everything does look larger when you're small but some new paint would definitely help. Even so, there's plenty to admire right down to details such as the cast-iron pineapple finials everywhere which I love. It's also impressive that such a slender ironwork skeleton should be so strong, as it obviously is. Especially now, in this overstayed wintertime, one can hear the wind at night clouting the glass and flinging hundredweights of snow at it so the whole building seems to stagger, yet the warmth goes serenely on. All that happens is a momentary change in pressure as the structure flexes, iron and glass bending in order not to break, which I can feel in my stomata since they're acutely sensitive.

'An eccentric thought has just struck me – a new way of looking at this caged world of ours. Mightn't it be seen as a memorial? Our gardener may *think* it's some sort of living museum devoted to observing and preserving, but really it's a memorial to a previous world. Maybe that's what all museums are? Memorials to previous states? No; the thought's gone. It was just a fleeting idea set off by his touch this morning and the contemplation of all this ironwork . . . Come to that, mightn't grief quite efficiently frame the structure of a life? At once unbending and flexible, sombre yet airy, truthful in its inability to conceal itself? Its support would remain when all else had clouded or fallen away.

'Too fanciful, no doubt. Just because for a weak moment I allow myself to be overtaken by melancholy there's really no call to reinterpret everything in its purplish light. I've no doubt our gardener's no gloomier than anybody else and this House is exactly what it purports to be – no more and no less. But how easy it is with time on one's hands to slip into that parallel world of longing and sad fancies. Keeping my voice scrupulously low so not a whisper of sound can leak from a single stoma I need only say "Little hemlock. Oh, little hemlock", and understand what moves him also. Feeble creatures, we are.'

FIVE

Just as an overtired child may not be able to sleep when finally allowed to go to bed but grumpily kicks hot blankets as night wears thin and a new day shows through, so (one might fancifully think) there is a time for marriage which, bided over, slips past and turns into a differently dawning future. Within very little time the night denied, the pairing instinct cooled, are as one, unmissed. This was what happened to Leon, who was evidently not intended by nature to toss fretfully on a marriage bed. Once he had stopped being a gardener's boy, a wheeler of dung, a mere stercorifer, he blossomed into a horticulturist accomplished enough by 1938 to step into the mildewed shoes of the Palm House's old curator. That had been his ambition from the moment of first setting foot inside the Gardens, and the intervening years had been those of purposeful apprenticeship. They were also those of his potential hymeneal prime – if ever he had one, which in retrospect looks doubtful. In any case it remained unfulfilled. Instead he studied with singleminded zeal as though at the college he could not afford, and by night the cobwebby panes of his potting shed glowed to the lambent apricot of midnight oil.

Not that he was erotically anaesthetised, though it remains a good question what might have caused him unqualified arousal.

From time to time plenty of the strollers and saunterers in the Botanical Gardens glanced, were intercepted glancing, and left wondering what it was had been shot from the eyes of the tall, samphire-haired young man as he squatted with secateurs stilled in mid-snip. Nothing unquiet in itself though disquieting all the same, withdrawn yet longing, gentle but avid. A mad monk? they wondered, for Rasputin was still a recent enough figure to supply yellow press imagery. Not only had Rasputin been hypnotic and hard to kill but a demon lover as well. Or so they said. It might be worth finding out. Nothing serious, of course; just a dangerous little dalliance. To trifle with a strong young gardener would be a welcome respite from the Biedermeier gallantries of yet another dentist. Such thoughts passed through several brains of both sexes.

What, though, passed through Leon's? Plants, for one thing. Plants in their kingdoms, divisions, classes, subdivisions, subclasses, orders, families, genera and species. By dint of much study he was making himself at home in the beautiful Linnaean edifice, the vast echoing palace down whose succession of halls, corridors, rooms, chambers and antechambers one could track a particular cupboard wherein, on a particular shelf, would be the very specimen one sought. Far from cramping the natural world into labelled boxes the system allowed it to proliferate endlessly as fresh cupboards were built, new shelves installed. He was surrounded suddenly by a universe of knowledge with himself at the centre, a universe whose tendency was centrifugal and seemed to flee him as fast as he tried to master its details. It filled him more with wonder than despair.

This fascination did not in any way eclipse or thrust into abeyance his emotional life. It *was* his emotional life. Into it, and into the crystalline goal of the Palm House whose swinging weathercock glittered ever in his upturned pupils, he poured all his unhappiness and longing and private language. Deep within, like the embryonic plumule clenched in the heart of a seed, lay the folded outlines of his boyhood resolution to be true only to the one who walked a beach and talked to the sea. It would always be there. If ever it were allowed to shoot and grow fully one might imagine a lofty and gracile tree of unknown species burst through into upper air and unwreathe its gleams against an azure sky. Heraldic, unique, it would stand alone and quiver to a celestial wind, shedding the soft husking of eternal voices. Or something of the sort. The god which slept within was not to be expressed in any human syllable. *Ssiiih*, it whispered to him late at night when his eyes watered with yawns and set afloat the oil lamp's teary flame. *Shuuuff*, it eased itself through chinks in the shed roof to comfort him. *You are not alone. I shall never leave you.*

Not alone in the potting shed? Draughts apart, no, not on a few occasions in his eligible years. There was, for example, Greta, the wife of the owner of Geller's, the city's largest and oldest department store. The day? The wind? The gleety seep of gland? Maybe the look on her face as he finally snapped shut the secateurs and rose from his crouch. He didn't know who she was then, of course. Bourgeoise, a good ten years older than he and with the faint down on her cheeks which by the time she was sixty would be a uniform fluff. She had with her two facially pretty but bodily plain little boys with plump corduroy bottoms and expensive model motor cars on strings which banged and crashed among boulders of gravel on the path. Incredulously, Leon found himself letting her through the wicket gate into the nightbound gardens at nine o'clock. It was clear that the first glimpse of the potting shed's interior by lamplight acted on her like sunshine on morning-glory. A bloom of hidden fantasy opened its unnatural petals before his eyes as she visibly checked out the props and assembled them into a tableau. Excited by the detailed nature of her requirements he obeyed each of her nearly articulated demands that she be stripped and spread ungently over a bale of peat, her face buried in it, pegged beneath fruit-cage netting. He had found himself standing naked but for gardening gloves, in manly state and tearing an access in the net, for the mesh was fine enough to keep out little birds. Her cries were soon muffled by peat. They went on a long time and only acquired a despairing edge when he paused for breath. Much later she was sprawled on the cold brick floor, limp, her mouth and face smeared with peat crumbs like an infant's with chocolate. Within minutes she was back in her tweed armour, shaking scraps of three-thousand-years-dead vegetation out of her hair.

'My God,' she said hoarsely. 'You're a sheikh, you know that? I demand a return match and I shan't accept a no.'

She came back a few nights later, but although the anticipation initially kept Leon aloft he never managed to soar as he had. This second time round the identical playlet appeared too contrived, on a third night too silly. That part of him ineluctably surfaced which didn't want to grind people's faces into bales of mould and grapple through netting *a tergo*, O Greta. When she had left he raked and patted his dishevelled bed in whose lignin and fibres he could smell her scent. He lay in the dark listening to the owls and was swept with an old sadness, unable finally to see any connection between what he had just done and what he had longed for that lost summer at Flinn. A semi-resolution evolved that he wouldn't do it again, though he broke it on a handful of occasions for lust of an experimental nature. Excitement came mainly from the hope that he might find whatever it was which would satisfy him; like many people he never did. The nearest he came to liking a participant in these investigations was in the case of a young male student at the University studying botany who was destined to die seven years later in the park a couple of hundred metres away, strapped to a plane tree in front of a firing squad, protesting in vain that he be allowed to keep his spectacles on. (Whom, then, did the obligatory blindfold protect?) But over and above all these diversions, or behind and beyond them, stood the Palm House and Leon's dormant internal tree ready at any moment to sprout, untouched by casual nocturnal goings-on. The owls hooted and a fox barked in the frosty air, each sending up a tiny cloud which unravelled in the same breeze that swung the galleon, with a scrawny sound, under full canvas towards fabulous lands.

It was a cold blustery March day when the old curator failed to report for work, victim of an overnight stroke. He died the following morning at almost the exact moment when, hundreds of miles to the southeast, the new Austrian chancellor Artur Seyss-Inquart announced the *Anschluss*. Leon, who had been the curator's assistant for two years and for most of that time had largely run the Palm House, was sent for by Dr Anselmus and told the job was his if he wanted it. He responded with a decorous show of reluctance, for he had been fond of the old boy, but within the week had outlined to Anselmus various plans which were obviously not the fruit of a few days' hasty thought. They included reorganising the House the better to display its treasures; the installation of a new heating system; closer links with similar establishments abroad for the exchange of specimens; the creation of a seed bank for tropical species; and more consideration given to the general public, who might even make contributions in exchange for being allowed to take home cuttings of some of the hardier plants and grow them themselves. This was, he said, calculated to excite interest and participation. Dr Anselmus, who had never heard anything like it, said such a proposal would need careful evaluation.

'This is primarily a learned society,' observed one of his fellow board members, a man whose waking hours were largely devoted to the task of trying to breed a black hyacinth. 'We have centuries-old connections with the University here as well as with the larger scientific community. The public are welcome to see the Gardens – our founders expressly desired that they should. But they are no place for showmanship and flim-flam. One of our own salaried experts rearing cuttings for ignorant people to let die in overheated sitting rooms, indeed. Never heard such a thing.'

Neither had the others. That aside, they were generally in favour of Leon's energetic approach. It was still too soon to say it but his predecessor had let the place sag a bit over the last few years. It was widely agreed that Leon alone had kept it in some sort of order, noticing cracked and broken panes which the old man's rheumy vision had missed and showing an instinctive grasp of the boilers' vagaries. Above all he had the gift. Things sprang into life beneath his hands. At his behest stands of bamboo whisked upwards, trembling with vigour.

As soon as his appointment was confirmed he moved his quarters into the Palm House. For the first time in eight years the potting shed window ceased to kindle to the nectarine glow of learning. Within a month one of the panes was mysteriously broken and a thrush built its nest inside. And now it becomes a little clearer, that matter of not marrying, not pairing. He thought in a gardener's timescales. Where he planted a nut he saw a tree, saw also how it would chime with surrounding plants in ten years' time, how high the leaves would hang and what coloured shade they would cast. This peculiar fatidic talent overleapt clumps of years in a nimble act of aesthetic and botanic imagination. It was the extension of a habit of seeing the past similarly demarcated by episodes which threw long shadows across elisions of time. This was a life divided by important staging-posts, not one geared for diurnal domesticity. In the absence of a person the unifying thread was work, the vision, the thing glimpsed dimly or in flashes as though picked out by a lighthouse on a darkling sea. Even so, he sometimes lost sight of any future and a sentient malignity rose up between himself and his work. Then it became easy to understand a lighthouse as projecting fat wedges of darkness in between its blazing apertures, for the lens still revolved behind its shutter and the light was constant. Yet light withheld had a different quality to ordinary darkness. It would fill the room behind the No Admittance door, seeping down at night from the slanted panes overhead, distilled from the cosmos pressing against the glass.

Maybe these occasional moments of nocturnal dolour were such as come to all those who of a sudden hear their own hearts in the dark and cannot forestall the chill arithmetic which leaps ahead, only to be brought up short like a guard dog on a chain. It sickens, this jerk of knowing trees planted now will never be seen fully grown; that a garden planned and sown will remain only a sketch, a landscape destined to be filled in by other hands and no doubt in the wrong colours. (The phantom of continuity hoots from a corner of the canvas.) The unwived man lies kithless in the dark and imagines his children, pretty and affectionate and talented, bearing away his seed for ever . . . No; it's meaningless. A faint injunction in the blood, that's all. Prettiness fades, affection becomes contaminated, ex-talents wear blue collars. The arithmetic is no longer simple, the melancholy multiplies. Leon moved his mattress into the boiler room so he should not have to face the stars. The glow of the furnaces, their chinkings and siftings and muffled internal collapses was comforting and reminded him that at his back, on the other side of a thin brick wall, lay a tropical forest. The black spots then, were no more than a sense of anticlimax breaking in. He was here at last, master of the very heart of the Gardens in whose crystal pavilion he now lived and reigned. Beside him in the semi-darkness he once more found his lifetime companion, true unto death even if given to temporary desertion in the cold starlight of the small hours. *Here*, said the furnaces, their calm slow pulse sending warmth to every part of the Palm House. *Here*, said the shrubs whose upturned hands supported their transparent bubble of unnatural, triumphant life lost among the galaxies and constellations. A sanctuary for the delicate and the fugitive, a bright glass bulwark against the brutish and the drear . . . These exalted ideas came and went fleetingly and were generally replaced by rather prosaic thoughts. He had the sudden fancy to go down to the fish market, buy a peck of herrings, rig up a smoke box and make bloaters. This notion was so satisfactory he never needed to carry it out.

He began putting into effect some of his less controversial plans. He moved the showy *Caesalpinia pulcherrima* to a more prominent position. He also planted certain shrubs and trees – including the Balsam of Tolú, *Myroxylon balsamum* – whose resins had helped him breathe as a child. At the same time he put in a formal request to the Society for a new heating system which was shelved rather than turned down flat. We'll see next year. Meanwhile I'm sure you'll agree the place would look the better for a lick of paint. Leon thought this a strange decision. While not unwelcome it implied that the alternative to an expensive new heating plant was an economical cosmetic gesture, whereas in reality the painting of a structure like the Palm House was a complex and costly affair. Since the roof surfaces were curved they required an elaborate framework of scaffolding whose configuration needed constant altering as painting progressed. However, as the framework retreated downwards it revealed a spreading area of glass scraped of industrial grime and freshly polished, supported by an airy cobweb of white glazing bars and topped by a regilded weathercock. The effect was of such lightness and sparkle that he stopped worrying about furnaces and boilers. By the time it was finished three months later his palace appeared to float slightly off the ground, and when glimpsed from the other end of the gardens between trees in full leaf could have been an enormous dirigible of fantastic design beginning its ascent, bearing aloft a cargo of sweating greenery.

He hatched another of his plans strictly in secret. It was not that he was as radical as the Society's trustees feared, simply enthusiastic. To him the Palm House was no mere laboratory or extension of the University. It represented a mysterious world apart, full of wonders which otherwise would never be seen in a cold northern country. He wanted more people to appreciate it. He got in touch with the reptile house at the nearby Zoo and they sent over six pairs of little jade terrapins which settled down on the marshy margins of the tanks. But at the back of his mind was the desire for a project which would be individual enough to draw people into this world, and one day he had the solution. He would assemble a collection of night-flowering varieties so that if visitors wanted to see them in bloom they would have to come after dark. The idea excited him and he mulled it over constantly. It seemed like an inspiration. On a lower level was the thought that he might also set aside a small area for plants which yielded spices, believing it would surely interest people to see a pepper plant with its berries, a nutmeg tree, some members of the ginger family such as cardamom and turmeric, a clove tree. He thought he could prevail on the keeper of the dilapidated Temperate House to provide space for an extension of these culinary plants to include such things as a tea tree and also one or two of the umbellifers from closer to home like coriander, fennel and cumin. There already was a cacao tree hidden away in the Palm House so he moved it to a better position and painted a new label for it, beneath *Theobroma cacao* adding the words 'chocolate tree'. All these plans would take time to realise, obviously. He submitted a list of plants to the red-haired secretary (now showing ash among the flames) and in due course seeds and cuttings began arriving from other botanical collections, from private and public sources around the world. One of the first things to come was a box of rhizomes from a Malabari importer in London, and it was not long before the first red and yellow cardamom flowers were opening in the steamy heat.

Good days, these were, full of energy. Within the freshly painted Palm House Leon reigned like a monarch or officiated like a bronchitic high priest, while all around his texts opened in the balmy dampness and spoke messages brought from afar. He understood their spiced and scented words and spoke back to them as he came and went fondly anointing, tying, pinching out, re-potting. The incense of regeneration, the calm satisfaction of growing things rose into the air and glittered. The spectral dust of a rainbow-spray caught by a shaft of sunlight through a pane could not have beguiled a visitor more than this authentic tropical reek. It had always been there, of course, but under Leon's regime it had intensified and was now shot through with other things, subtleties of a melancholy which was now of listless afternoons, now of a nameless longing. A garden always speaks of its gardener in ways other than the obvious, and a stove house is no exception. Something of Leon's character diffused throughout the building. In any case it enticed people in. They wandered and stayed longer than formerly, reading the labels or just sitting on the benches now provided in the central aisle. They noticed the quality of the silence, accentuated by the hollow pock of drops falling on to broad, tough leaves and by the sparrows which hopped in through the ventilation louvres up under the dome and fluttered and twirled in this indoor summer. Far from acting as a crystal drum to magnify the noises of the outside world, it seemed the glass skin was enough to exclude most sounds entirely. Just occasionally the faintest clanging of a tram's bell or the hooting of a motor-car horn penetrated as from a long way off, so that elderly ex-colonials who had sticked themselves over from clubs smelling of leather and gout to spend a quiet afternoon could dream they were once again overhearing Benares or Kuala Lumpur or Macassar, that the streets beyond the garden wall were thronged with rickshaw men and water carriers. Until Leon took it over the Palm House had always been closed on Sundays. Now at his insistence it was open the week round and it became something of a ritual to visit it, especially on grey Sunday afternoons when a cold drizzle fell from a low sky. Then it was a perverse pleasure to saunter through the tropical warmth, *endimanché*, exchanging glances among the leaves, some furtive, some frankly challenging. It was as if, sensing this as a place apart from the ordinary world, people were emboldened in ways otherwise reserved for intercontinental expresses, ocean liners and the beach at Biarritz. That time off could be snatched from between the sullen claws of northern Sunday piety was all the more piquant.

The gardener observed these undercurrents eddying in and out of the little blind alleys ending in swags of leaves and branches. What better place for hormonal tweakings and discreet rutting than a palace enclosing that sensual languor which everybody said was the chief ingredient of the tropics? Some nights, restless himself, he would drag his mattress out of the boiler room and lay it on the gravel path, now in this place, now that. Then the stars were no longer the stony eyeballs of eternity but the prickly decor of a languid sky draped behind plumes and fronds. He was adrift in an unmapped world, on an equatorial islet. He would lie and envisage the trysts and assignations whose whisking hems he had caught in photographic glimpses. The curl of a garment, an eyebrow, a mouth's corner; the whiteness of fingertips touching amid ruffled dark green. But there was nothing for him to con-centrate on. No sooner had he called up one image than another fell in front of it like a superimposed lantern slide. The vignettes of urban mating slithered and ran, congealing only into a general impression of other lives being lived but flirtatiously only, not intensely, not in the grip of passion. Unsleeping, he would get up and slowly walk his garden, pace out his domain, trailing whispers and syllables, the half-words of half-thought. Lonely? he wondered. Was that it, then? An ache for . . . But whenever he tried to put a shape or face to this lack it was never enough to make it solid or plausible. A rich woman in tweeds, a coquette with a parasol, a serious lad with rimless spectacles. Not enough, finally. Too much flesh, not enough of the intangible electric which shocked at the sight of a breaking bud's first gleam of colour, the soft trudge of a heron across the sky at dusk, the noise of sea wind through rimy grasses in a winter's dawn. What, then? Like the pink of a scalp declaring itself through sparsening hair, the subtext of a life rose inexorably to the surface. It was of lack; so be it. But lack fabulously dressed in sound and sight and colour and smell. It was a lack which never would have to contend with slow domestic clotting, which would stand in tears over no grave nor be wept over in its turn. Solitude's dark beam might sweep round, over and over again proclaiming the land deserted, the sea empty, the earth flat. Yet what richness managed to thrive in the brilliant interstices, the revolving splinter that lit and ever rekindled sublime pleasures! He returned with a sigh to his mattress. The soft plop of terrapins lulled him to sleep.

Meanwhile, his secret project for assembling night-flowering species was taking shape. Since many of the monsoonal varieties were trees rather than shrubs this was evidently going to take time even though several were quick growing. The attraction of the plants themselves would be inseparable from the novelty of having visitors in the Palm House after dark. That the same Sunday afternoon strollers might return and become night people was intriguing and provocative. Everything changed after dark. Something else began to show through, subtly, and people were no exception. From his first day as a glazing boy just after his arrival in the capital Leon had been fascinated by those who came to see the plants. How different they were from the fisher-folk of Flinn! They were positively exotic, these townees, with their peculiar refined accents, their witty remarks and sophisti-cation. They might have belonged to a different planet the way they chattered and drifted and trailed scent and pomade. These were the people who had money and influence, who read books and could use the knowledge. They went to theatres, cinemas, operas, ballets and art galleries. It was not long before he knew he would always be excluded from their society. No matter how eminent he became, a gardener remained a gardener. On the other hand he might well be able to woo them on his terms. His plans therefore contained an element of seduction, just as he himself was considerably seduced. He had long supplemented his book learning with eavesdropping and his appointment as curator made this even easier. As an assistant he had scurried, always at the beck and call of his irascible and whimsical old predecessor. Nowadays, though, he could employ assistants of his own by day while at night he lingered and absorbed, from behind clumps of greenery, the talk of those he secretly courted. Nobody in his childhood had ever had conversations, he now realised. They had had exchanges: more or less terse, jovial, brutal, but never these relaxed and worldly discourses full of jokes and innuendo. Bit by bit in recalling the things they said his own inner conversations acquired something of the same urbane quality, the same slight detachment which accompanied ideas. They also had an autodidact's mixture of learning and magpie knowledge. On his own subject he knew far more than he could express, so he expressed remarkably little; but when alone with his plants he would hear them voice outlandish, barely-formed opinions culled randomly from visitors on politics, banking, gynaecology, the arms trade, perfumery and the role of Antonio in *The Marriage of Figaro*.

It was one of those spring days when a balmy southeasterly breeze drifted up from Damascus and Constantinople still with enough strength after its long, scented journey to evaporate the last tatters of North Sea cloud and inflate over Europe a filmy marquee of blue silk. On such days it hardly mattered that everything was temporary, that gardeners were as evanescent as the blooms they tended. This morning the Botanical Gardens was a walled oasis of fertility full of the inaudible roar of buds splitting. The poignant rapture of the moment seized Leon as he went outside into the sunshine. There was contentment in the air. The few early strollers were well dressed and leisured. From beyond the wall came the dulled sounds of city traffic pricked now and then by a bell or a horn. All was calm and industrious. From the bare glazing bar of the broken potting shed window the fledgling thrushes were making their first flights. For an instant the Palm House sat with delicate immobility at the earth's hub. Following the gaze of some children he looked into the sky and there, high above the golden galleon, a tiny monoplane was performing aerobatics over the city. As if its canting wings were shedding a happiness caught from the very air through which they winked and flashed he felt an inward soaring so that he, too, could watch the planet's surface tilt like a plate, the sea's grey wrinkled slab slither towards the edge like scree. He even thought he could just make out Flinn, a fleck of mould far away up the coastal map caught between sea and estuary on its long spit of polder. The aircraft's mayfly gyrations went exuberantly on, accompanied, if one strained one's ears to exclude local birdsong and voices, by a drone shaped like a distant line of mountains, sagging and climbing, dipping and peaking with short patches of bluish silence in between. Gradually, as befitted its insect character, the machine drifted away on the breeze, engine popping, leaving across the marquee's roof the lone aviator's dark signature of exhaust.

Leon, no less exalted and no less alone, dragged himself back down to the Gardens and re-entered his Linnaean temple filled with lightness and energy. They would come to him, he vowed. Oh yes, they would come in their stoles of silver fox or their shapeless corduroys, with parasols and umbrellas, dainty gold watches and sturdy half-hunters. Housewives would come, and students, and old men with dandruff and cracked spats who loved butterflies. Famous actresses – why not? – and society ladies, moguls and diplomats, even – why not again? – the occasional dotty king. They would none of them be able to resist what he could offer: the ordered tropics in their midst, the spectacle of the dreamy and the exotic burgeoning in their hard-edged city. Once the right plants had been collected and had matured the heavy scent of night blooms would lure them ... He took it for granted the Society would approve his scheme once they knew about it. It would bring regeneration not just to the Palm House but to the Gardens as a whole, in perpetual danger of becoming fossilised. Everyone was so old, that was the trouble, from the head gardener to most of the Society's board. Anselmus was quite progressive but what on earth could be done with dim plodders like that cretin who spent his time trying to breed green roses or black hyacinths or something? As if almost anything in the Palm House wasn't more interesting, more subtly beautiful than some monstrous hybrid. After all, why stop at black hyacinths? Why not spend your life trying to cross a snowdrop with a lupin? A snowpin? he wondered sarcastically (for he was soaring). Or maybe trees would be more of a challenge because of the time they took to grow? *Cocos* with *Hevea*, then, bouncing its rubber coconuts? No. In his view Anselmus ought to start purging the Society of people like that and encouraging younger blood, enthusiasts who could share the vision of a true garden as something both scientific and aesthetic, vibrant with its own inventiveness and needing no trickery to succeed.

Thus he saw his own intoxicating future on a brilliant morning in spring. If there was something opaque, not fully declared, in this vision it was no doubt because few people ever managed to be wholly truthful about their own ambitiousness, least of all to themselves. And perhaps, quite without knowing it, he still entertained some fairytale fancy of attracting the one mate who could not resist him, the princess who could discern the princeling beneath the toad's warts and pulsing dewlap. In any event his motives were more muddled than were others on that sunny day. From newspaper offices and broadcasting stations violent press and wireless campaigns were even then being launched against Czechoslovakia in general as Nazi troops began sidling towards the Sudetenland in particular.

One Wednesday night some eight years later Leon was wandering, brass syringe in hand, well beyond his guests' outer perimeter. Here and there he rubbed the steamy glass and pressed his nose to it to see if the snow had begun again. Like a shy child at a party who instinctively moves towards the darker regions of the house, he watched from afar his night visitors clustered by candlelight beyond the palms. A low hum of chatter came back

to him, together with the occasional clink of glasses. When he passed the Balsam of Tolú, now a sturdy young tree sixteen feet tall, it addressed him clearly:

'I'm glad for your sake, now you've got your way, and it was a nice idea in any case. It's high time the visitors here learned to use their noses. It's a pity some of them don't wander down this end, break a rule and pluck one of my leaves. I'd happily spare the odd leaf in order to be more widely appreciated, though I fear I already know what they'd say. "Ooh yes, it's like – " they'd crush and sniff a bit more "but very faint. It's like – you know, sort of medicinal. You have a go," and the other would say the dread words: "Friar's Balsam, that's it," and they'd move off, reminiscing about childhood inhalations. Depressing that I could be confused with anything as crude as Friar's Balsam which, though indeed it contains my resin, is mixed with all sorts of other things such as bitter aloes and extracts from various *Styracaceae*. Just as well they'd only be smelling my leaves. If ever they were to cut my bark they'd find that my sap hardened into a golden brown exudate, crystalline and redolent of an aromatic form of vanilla with a rich dark bitterness underneath. It would no doubt remind them of clot-mouthed black bottles in gruesome surgeries, of all sorts of punitive gargles and liniments. In point of fact my gum has many happy uses, including as a fixative in perfumery, but you wouldn't expect them to know that. I, on the other hand, am sure I detect a definite trace of myself in the princess's scent, "Cuir", as Lancôme thoughtfully re-named "Révolte" in 1939. But as I stand here watching and sniffing and listening to those visitors who do pass me I have to conclude that modern people are progressively abandoning all but one of their senses, abject before vision's crushing hegemony. They damage their hearing with raucous jazz, clog their palates with tobacco, wear gloves so they needn't touch anything and finally cut off their noses to spite the stone masks they've turned themselves into and from which they peer fretfully with greedy, insatiable eyes. But that's their affair.

'I'm touched you should have chosen to raise me. I've always taken it as an act of homage, a recognition of your own childhood indebtedness which overcame any silly idea of unhappy associations. (People and their unhappy memories! They shun them with such fastidious horror one can only conclude that's where they chiefly reside, and would do far better to throw open a few windows than keep up this wearisome pretence of having moved house.) Perhaps on reflection it was less a matter of homage to me than of loyalty to your former self? Although the idea of a former self also strikes me as inaccurate. We are who we were always going to have been. What was my own former self? A seed gathered in Colombia? (I'm told Santiago de Tolú's rather a pretty place on the coast not far from Panama.) A plumule? A radicle? As I was, so I am now but bigger. As I am now, so will I be, but unfortunately not much more so since as a fully grown adult I ought to reach a height of a hundred feet with a trunk four feet thick and I can't see that happening here. But the point is we none of us change, we only somewhat transform ourselves. I didn't personally help towards your survival as a child, of course, so I never saw you in those far-off days. Yet I'm sure you can't have changed so fundamentally. I imagine all one need do is look around at this House and see your old obsessions respectably disguised as a vocation. I presume this goes for a good few people.

' "I ought to reach a hundred feet," I catch myself saying. Is this, then, one of my own obsessions? But no, I don't think so. Really, I'm perfectly content and not a bit anxious about the future. How could I be – you ask – seeing that balsams have a reputation for self-satisfaction to the point of smugness?

Something to do with having been esteemed (over-esteemed?) for so long and associated with all those myrrhs and spikenards and frankincenses and other costly gums of mythic resonance. All I know is, I can supply something for the human nose and palate to get to work on. Now this probably *is* a mild obsession of mine. It's heartening for us to see our gardener beguiling his visitors' olfactory, if not sapid, sense before it atrophies entirely. You're even making their eyes work harder by insisting on candlelight. I wonder if you don't have a satirical streak in you as you confront these townees with the vestigial whispers of their ancestral past? As they once were, so may they discover themselves still to be! Already some of them are wearing pelts, I notice.'

SIX

In the early days of the occupation Leon had commissioned a notice which said 'Beware of Tropical Snakes' in five languages. He screwed this to the Palm House door where it remained throughout the war. He never discovered if this simple ruse had saved his private capitol from ransack and destruction, but in one way or another the Botanical Gardens were largely spared the invaders' attentions which, like the blast of bombs, took unpredictable and freakish forms. A grey scout car had nosed in through the gates one morning and stopped, blocking them. Soldiers had deployed with rifles at the ready, expecting ambush. When nothing happened besides the temporary capture of a couple of terrified orchid-fanciers the troops had relaxed and wandered around, poking into potting sheds and summer houses. Leon, standing protectively at the door of the Palm House, overheard them say, 'Just a lot of boring old plants. This is no fun. I know – let's go to the Zoo.' The scout car had backed out in a cloud of blue smoke and roared away. The Society's director, Dr Anselmus, had shortly afterwards shown a high-ranking German officer around the Gardens but this gentleman, while keenly interested in plants, saw Leon's notice and declined to enter the Palm House despite his escort's assurance that the snakes were 'not much in evidence these days'.

It was the luckless Zoo a mile away which had attracted all the attention. It had even been bombed. American or British pilots discovered that a line drawn between two prominent features, the penguin pool and the bear pits, pointed directly at the Ministry of Telecommunications in the centre of town. This building was well defended by anti-aircraft emplacements and though some way off, the younger and more nervous aircrews, lined up on their target and finding themselves flying directly into a lethal barrage, sometimes jettisoned their bombs early and peeled hurriedly away to safety. During one of these raids a bomb fell within thirty yards of the lion house, causing severe damage. An elderly lion, bewildered by pain and noise and bleeding from a concussed eardrum, loped its way slightly crabwise out of the Zoo grounds and along boulevards of shattered lindens. It caught sight of and attacked its own reflection in a music shop, scattering bright golden saxophones and severing an artery. A detachment of soldiers found it exsanguinated, gallons of dark lion blood running across the pavement and into the gutter. For good measure they riddled its lifeless body with 9mm rounds before whacking out its teeth and cutting off its paws for souvenirs. Then they hitched it behind their scout car and dragged it away, polishing tram lines and the metal studs of pedestrian crossings with its dusty pelt. Back in barracks its remains were roasted for the officers' mess. The roaring, redfaced excitement that night, the uniformed men swaying outside trying to urinate on the Milky Way, suggested the catharsis of tribespeople after a long and dangerous hunt.

Strangely, it was not until the last few months of the war that the city folk, wearied and gaunt after nearly five years' occupation and food rationing, had begun to think of the Zoo as an untapped larder. It was touching how long their inhibitions had lasted, how sacrifice had been piled on hardship yet precious food was still diverted to keep the animals alive. That final winter, however, when the occupying forces could see their doom and began to be less interested in maintaining civil order than in saving their own skins, bands of famished people finally ransacked the Zoo. They found very little. Exotic menus had long since passed through the ovens of the officers' mess and indeed the officers themselves: cassowary Kiev, giraffe steaks, panda pie, llama sausage. Three elephants, two hippos and a white rhino had provided hundreds of troops with tough but nourishing meals, while to the highest-ranking officers had gone one *bonne bouche* after another: koala tongue pâté, lion tamarin in raisin and kümmel sauce, buttered marmoset. By the time the populace arrived there was not much left alive in the tanks and cages. Most of the reptiles had long since died of cold, though such was their hunger a few people would undoubtedly have overcome taboo and phobia for a plate of constrictor stew or fried monitor. The last two sealions were eaten, together with a brace of Tasmanian devils and a scrawny dingo. The Zoo was now a desolate and overgrown wilderness full of cages containing nothing more than an end of chain, a drinking bowl of green water, a drift of dead leaves. Before long some of the refugees roaming in directionless tides across Europe had taken up residence in the cages, lit fires of brushwood and had a roof over their heads.

Behind the Botanical Gardens' high walls, within the steamy glass palisades of his private land, Leon's beleaguerment had increased with each new threat. There are ways of retreating from the world which nevertheless involve an awareness of its doings. The gardener remained in touch with how things were beyond his precinct; its survival depended on knowing the nature of possible menace. Going out only to collect his rations, he was taciturn but listened well. In this he resembled an extension of his own House, the sheen of war-grime on whose glass looked steely from outside but admitted more light than one would have thought. Once he was back inside his taciturnity vanished. The trickle of visitors had now dried up altogether and days went by without his seeing anyone other than the blurred shapes of the few old gardeners moving slowly about outside. His own conversations grew steadily. The assiduous study, the self-tuition went on and spilled out in long harangues with plants whose sophistication and articulateness now equalled his own. They were fit company, and the enabling pact he shared with them in private made it a pleasure to limit himself in the out-side world to few and dark words. When occasion demanded, though, he could come up with a schoolmasterly outburst right there on the street. When in 1943 two identically-hatted men in civilian clothes stopped him in Palace Square and asked to see his papers, the folded rag which Leon had produced after much searching through pockets filled with tarred twine, dried seed pods, corks, washers and copper glazing pins had not at first satisfied the inspectors. They had, indeed, collared a frightened passer-by in order to show Leon what an identity card ought to look like.

'It got damp,' said the gardener truculently when the other card had been handed back with sinister courtesy and the man scuttled off, sick with relief.

'It looks as if you'd buried it. Maybe the same thing ought to happen to its owner. Look at it – you can't even read it. "Place of work . . ." Something about a garden, is it?'

'The Botanical Gardens. I am the Curator of the Palm House.' Leon said this with a certain quiet dignity, slightly stressing the definite articles. He knew one didn't trifle with these little rodents from the Gestapo but neither was he going to grovel.

'Tell us some botany, then.'

'Vascular bundles, gentlemen? The drawbacks to Paris Green as a pesticide? Or maybe – ' and he launched into a lecture on

August Borsig, a German industrialist of the last century who diverted steam from his own ironworks at Moabit in Berlin to heat glasshouses in which he reared one of the world's great private palm collections, including the so-called 'thief palm' named *borsigianum* in his honour. Long before it was over the men had handed back the mould-stained document and walked off. Turning oneself into a classic bore had distinct advantages, Leon considered, and carried on his daily rehearsals.

It was not all book learning which echoed among the roof's dripping traceries as the silver midges of warplanes twirled and smoked in the skies above. In night hours fitfully lit by hectic bursts of light and shaken by concussions, as he walked his aisles in danger of death by falling glass, his plants spoke eloquently to him of loss and anguish. Sometimes he thought he heard a girl's voice. 'I may be going away,' it said and he would turn involuntarily in the blackout, straining to glimpse the beloved face, a few strands of hair crossing a cheek. But it was only a plant. 'I thought you couldn't speak,' he told it bitterly, yet even then was sure his nose caught in its vicinity an aching wisp of the fragrance – marine sunlight on young skin – of his lifetime's one act of utter homage, of the feet he had once kissed.

Just as a desire to preserve the illusion of normality had for so long kept people feeding a shrinking population of zoo animals, so by a mixture of inertia and oversight fuel was still delivered to the Palm House until the last winter of the war. True, it had degenerated from top quality coke through brown coal and peat to nearly anything burnable including dried beet pulp which should have gone for animal feed, railway sleepers damaged by Allied air attacks and tarred oak blocks blown by bombs out of tramway beds; but still it arrived. With the onset of winter, though, supplies stopped. Both the winter and the war were predicted to end at much the same time, but that was still months away. It was a matter of surviving until then. With

Dr Anselmus's permission Leon took to raiding the gardens. What with the able-bodied younger gardeners having vanished into war, most regular maintenance work like the pruning and lopping of trees had not been done and there was five years' worth of dead and surplus timber to be thinned out of the mature planes, elms and beeches.

The wood for supplementing his dwindling fuel stocks was there, but Leon was scarcely in a fit state to bring it in. The exertion of sawing and dragging combined with the colder weather went straight to his lungs. After hardly any time he was forced back inside the Palm House's sanctuary, weak and wheezing, while minatory shades of purple and cinnabar flashed across the retinas of his closed eyes. Nevertheless he and a small band of mainly elderly men did move steadily from tree to tree, heaving ladders and labouring with saws, while the piles of firewood at the foot of the trees grew.

One evening as dusk was falling he was bringing in a final barrowload when there came the familiar sounds of a disturbance in the street on the other side of the high wall. In the war's early months there had been spontaneous protests against the occupation, against conscription, against the curfew, against rationing. These had usually been put down with such overwhelming displays of *force majeure* that often there were not many fatalities. The centre of the demonstration was suddenly surrounded with tanks and troop carriers, a few ringleaders were pulled out of the crowd and either driven away to SS Headquarters and never seen again or tied to a tree in the park and summarily shot. The rest of the demonstrators were allowed to melt away and within ten minutes there was little to show for it except some brass cartridge cases and a body or two. Even the rounding-up of the Jews had been conducted with hardly any fuss or resistance. They had been driven away in army trucks to a goods yard out in the eastern suburbs and had vanished. Not a single trainload had left from the platforms of Main Station. After this initial period things had quietened down and gone back to being as nearly normal as was possible in an occupied city in wartime. Recently, however, with some sense of an ending in sight, little fermentations of the anarchy brewing beneath had begun bubbling up with increasing frequency. As the hardships grew and repression had less effect terrible revenges were taken, scores settled and reprisals exacted.

On this particular evening Leon was just the other side of the wall when he heard the sounds of an old-fashioned hue and cry coming down the boulevard. Running feet and harsh shouts passed and stopped in a knot fifty yards beyond. Out of this stalled baying there rose a despairing, piercing cry. Nearly a word, it soared up into the cold twilight like a rocket and shed tingling sparks of anguish over the entire sky. For some reason it made him snatch up his pruning hook and run for the wicket gate. By the time he had reached the street the cry had become pulsing screams. Ten or so dark shapes were grouped at the foot of the wall, some of them squatting and busy with their hands, others watching.

What was it that possessed him to intervene, suddenly to break every unwritten rule learned over the previous five years to stay out of trouble, never to interfere? He didn't even think what to shout, simply advanced with his pruning hook rigidly at his side, bellowing:

'How dare you? How dare you? This is the *Botanical Gardens*! You've no right to do your filth here! Get back to your holes, you vermin!'

Such was his tone of voice, a quality in his advancing presence, that the lynchers suspended their work and turned to face this newcomer with belligerent incredulity. They saw a gaunt man wearing ragged overalls, muddy, scratched-faced and with dead leaves in his yellow hair who shouted 'Back! Back! Back!' and wheezed audibly between shouts.

'Stay out of this, Dad,' said one who appeared no younger than Leon and might even have been older. It was still light enough to see his features, which were all muzzle. The gardener was reminded of a crazed greyhound. (A year later almost to the day, on a visit to the pensions department in the Town Hall, he came face to face with this same man, now two stone heavier and wearing a bureaucrat's cheap suit, and recognised him instantly. Then, the man appeared not to notice him and the snout he was bending over a secretary's head as he walked had fattened into that of a bear, but Leon had known him at once, might almost have predicted the ribbon of an honour threaded through the buttonhole of his lapel.) 'Stay out of this,' his wartime persona was yapping. 'You keep out. Nothing to do with you. Just some thieving little turd of a gypsy we're dealing with. I thought the Germans had cleaned out all these scum years ago.' A high moan escaped the wall of legs.

'Not here you don't.' The gardener was still advancing. 'Not *ever* here! You keep your dirty battles in your own quarter!' He was beside himself, bellowing directly into the muzzle, which opened, weakly underslung.

'What's it to you?' came through the side of the teeth. 'In any case we've finished.' And the moment passed when the ten or twelve panting men and youths might casually have diverted some of their overflowing ferocity and killed this irritating spoilsport. For a moment they stood, silently roaring plumes of grey breath. A hand came out dark with blood, offering backwards a knife. The vulpine leader took and folded it without wiping it, saying 'Why waste energy? This gyppo won't steal again in a hurry, not now we've nicked his jewels.'

With parting kicks and spits the group slouched away up the boulevard. Bursts of laughter ricocheted back along the wall to where Leon was standing, gasping and trembling, less rescuer than survivor of a moral disaster. At his feet, half lost in the shadow of overhanging branches, hunched a form whose torn garments lay around in a tattered puddle. Once on his knees Leon could see that the puddle was actual, no trick of the light. With immense effort he gathered the dripping body in his arms and rose unsteadily, leaned briefly against the wall and set off for the wicket gate into the Gardens. By the time he was inside he recognised he would never have the strength to pick it up again once he had put it down. He kicked the wheelbarrow over, spilling the logs, and managed to right it with one foot while balancing on the other. Finally he was able to ease his burden into the barrow which he trundled, a hank of black hair flopping over its lip, towards the Palm House. He opened both doors, backed the barrow inside, closed and locked them behind him. Having made hasty arrangements in his quarters he summoned his last strength, picked the lightly moaning deadweight out of the barrow, carried it through into the boiler room and laid it gently on the mattress he had dragged over to the furnaces.

In the yellow light of forty watts he inspected the victim. A young man, a youth, folded into a bloody ball with arms between thighs, quivering with the strain of hunching himself ever smaller until he might mercifully wink out of this world. His eyes were scrunched shut, his mouth and chin juddered with each indrawn breath like those of a chilled and exhausted swimmer.

'Safe now,' Leon told him. 'Hush.' He fetched a bowl of hot water and a towel while planning what he would need. In his dispassionate way he had already assessed the likely damage and knew there was no help except what he could give. The city's main teaching hospital had been commandeered for wounded German troops; the only other hospital was out in the suburbs and partly bombed. He also knew there was no transport to be had after dark and that if he were to go wheeling his patient about the streets during curfew in search of a doctor neither of them would survive ten minutes. With the end of the war in sight the occupiers' morale was low. Drunk and panicky soldiers careered through the streets in military vehicles taking pot-shots at anything that moved, cheering and roaring on. Nor would his luck hold for a second time were he to meet up again with muzzle-face and his gang. From a shelf he brought down a box of dried moss and two bottles of decoction, one of *Arnica montana* flowers and the other of marigolds. He found a clean dish, put the moss to soak in the marigold lotion and returned to his patient. With the deliberation of self-reliance he set to work. As he did so he talked unceasingly, quietly, as to two visitors whose identities merged, separated briefly, merged once more. '*Ssiiih,*' he whispered as he held the boy's head and coaxed him to drink warm Arnica mixture laced with cane syrup. 'We have to dress your wounds or they'll take chill.' Gradually he unfolded the body, opened clothing, took stock of the constant bleeding, applied a compress of moss and held it firmly in place. The patient gave no sign of additional pain but seemed to have retreated behind a grey barricade of shock.

All night long Leon sat with him while a winter wind sprang up outside. Its cloutings and rushing over the Palm House's acre of glass came through to the boiler room like the sound of a railway station's distant cavern filling with softly escaping steam as a train prepared to leave. At intervals he pressed the boy's own hands over the pad and got up to stoke the furnaces, fetch a blanket or more of the hot Arnica and syrup which he insisted be drunk. His patient lapsed in and out of consciousness and as he bathed the side of the bruised, puffy face he wondered whether one of the assailants' kicks might not have caused concussion or worse, but the pupils in the dark eyes were of equal size and responded promptly to the light bulb's yellow glow.

117

Sometimes he caught the eyes open and fixed on him without expression; at others they were closed and he could stare back wonderingly at this piece of human wreckage washed up at his domain's door. Beneath the asymmetry of bruising was a thin dark face framed by lank hair. Seventeen? Nineteen? Twenty-one? Impossible to tell. Years of hunger and fear had made everybody's age hard to guess. Europe was full of old men of twenty and children in uniform. Death might briefly restore a person's youth as the protective mask relaxed or it could make even the young look ageless, as if their features had resolved into the stock lineaments of an antique species.

Towards dawn the bleeding largely ceased and the pulse grew stronger. The pad became suddenly soaked with hot urine. The patient's eyes opened, then clouded with realisation. Speechlessly he rolled his head. Leon reassured him, fetched a clean handful of moss moistened with lavender oil. Tears of loss and humiliation leaked from closed eyelids and ran back into the dirty hair. As daylight blanched the small dusty windowpanes Leon gazed at the sleeping face and saw himself as he had been, lying in a cottage hospital not expected to live while nurses spooned hot milk and calves' foot jelly into him or else drew the tent and tried to fill his clotted lungs with aromatic steam. How vulnerable, how frail, he marvelled. Why should any of us survive? Whereas plants, unchecked, would take over the Earth in a few years and smother it with simple fecundity. From the corner of the mattress on which he sat he could see the leafless twigs of a beech scratching uneasily at the sky. It was going to be a scuddy, blusterous day which might with any luck bring down some dead wood. He was immeasurably tired.

All that day the wind blew, and the next. Having put the 'Closed to Visitors' sign in the window of the outer door he dragged himself from chore to chore, catnapping between. At noon the first day the patient's temperature rose alarmingly

and he thought he could see the first signs of infection in the still-seeping wound. To the Arnica syrup he added some powdered sulphur and a few drops of Aconitum. For hours he sat and talked, drowsed into silence, awoke with a start and carried on. Maybe he told the youth the story of his life, about the sea and the coast and the smoking of fish. Maybe he discoursed on plants and their properties, on the changing ideals of botanical collections, on the finer points of constructing stove houses. Probably he didn't talk about war and air raids and rationing and queues and the black market. They were the common incubus, too widely experienced to be worth mentioning. And besides, what could one tell a casualty of war which he was not already confronting? That twenty-four hours ago he'd been like any one of millions of semi-fugitive men, women and children concentrating only on staying alive, but that shortly afterwards he was singled out for ragged knifework which, if he survived, would change his life?

But he did survive; and by the time the wind had dropped began greedily eating the boiled potatoes Leon gave him. Only, whenever the gardener returned to the boiler room after fetching something or performing some task in the Palm House he would find the boy weeping as though he had dared a glance behind the handful of moss and seen too clearly what he had come to. No acceptable future might be devised which had mutilation as its starting point and sprang from a mattress black with dried blood beside a whispering, creaking furnace through whose mica spyholes could be seen the flap of flames. Where could safety lie? Where might the gangs of dusk not burst in with their boots and blades? Come to that, where was he? Where this bare room with no-one for company but a monologuing stranger and the steady sift of ash into cinderboxes nearby?

Leon brought the boy foul and bitter infusions of twigs or bark, held his hand and talked. But never a word could he get

in reply, not even a name. At first he thought the barrier might be that of language. He had heard the foxy gang leader call him a gypsy and certainly he looked swarthy in a foreign way. Were gypsies Egyptians? He didn't know. Was this speechless creature a Hindoostani or an Arab or else one of those strange Asiatics from far beyond Hungary? But the problem was not linguistic; the boy nodded when Leon pointed to himself and spoke his own name. Maybe he was dumb from birth, then. Or else shock had temporarily paralysed his faculty of speech. When he did indicate himself his lower lip folded behind the white upper teeth as if to make the letter 'F'. 'For now,' Leon told him, 'I shall call you Felix,' since he had heard that the correct name for Arabia was Arabia Felix.

But what to do with him? As always, the gardener walked by night in the Palm House, moving among his plants while the starlight slid off the rounded panes far overhead. Occasionally the white beams of searchlights swung hopelessly across the sky, arousing in him a distant disquiet, echoes of loss, of a steely order breaking up in disarray. He was thin, his coughs rattled up among the leaves and flattened against the streaming glass, but he believed he had never been so happy. Outside the glass, beyond the wall, unspeakable events were dragging to their conclusions. Inside, though it might echo to the hollow boom of anti-aircraft guns, was a frail temple to all that might survive. His private, long-term project for a special collection of night blooming varieties was coming along well. He was ready to concede that the scent of one or two of them was slightly sinister or uncanny: they had, after all, evolved to attract bats and moths rather than human noses. If he closed his eyes while standing in front of them he sometimes became confused about what he was experiencing, so strange were the smells and so apt to provoke disorienting sensations as of a spoken painting, music tasted, sculpture overheard. He longed to see how visitors would

react but of course the curfew and blackout made it impossible and in any case he had yet to spring such a radical idea on Dr Anselmus and the rest of the Board.

He wandered about in indecision, easily sidetracked by a grotto studded with dim green hazes. He fell on his knees, interested to see if the phosphorescence was strong enough for him to be able to see the outline of his own fingers against it. It was. The boy must stay, at least for now. He was obviously petrified, traumatised. Well then, he must be hidden. If his presence were known neither would be safe. Whatever the lad had done he looked exactly the sort of person the Germans would finish off in their final paroxysm. And as for himself, he would be no better off. Harbouring Jews was practically as bad as being Jewish. Harbouring gypsies amounted to the same thing. Racial degenerates, the criminal element . . . The epithets were well worn but still carried force in the shape of death sentences. To turn Felix free, even if he wished to go, would be to send him out to die.

'Of course he shall stay,' he told *Passiflora edulis* var. *flavicarpa*, the passion fruit vine, who only urged Leon to play safe.

'Why don't we betray him to the Germans?' came the vine's seductive voice in the dark. 'They'll reward you for sure. Some fuel, with any luck, or maybe some new glass. We're down to our last spare panes. And what about us? All right for you to commit suicide nobly, but you'll be murdering us. Believe me, once you've vanished into some camp nobody will look after this place. Not a chance. The boilers'll go out and your House will become derelict. The end. And all for a complete stranger. It makes no sense.'

'He stays,' repeated Leon with a groan.

So Felix remained, just as his name remained Felix, and just as if locked into the moment of his salvation. Physically

he healed and strengthened even as Leon's own health declined, for the gardener gave him most of his rations. Had it not been for the vegetables he grew hidden among the tropical plants he would surely have starved. Felix was back on his feet after three or four weeks, the mattress turned cleaner side up. He was much improved in appearance and seemingly unimpaired apart from being obliged to squat when he urinated, as many desert menfolk customarily do to this day. But his timidity was intense and he was reluctant to leave the boiler room. This was just as well, for keeping him hidden remained their sole chance of survival. The problem was exacerbated by the floating population of assistants who came and went about the Palm House. Until 1942 Leon had retained his prewar staff of five men permanently assigned him. After Germany's calamitous defeat at Stalingrad in the winter of that year the conscription of ever older men to make up for the losses meant he was often lucky to have two men in late middle age to help him. (Even Leon himself had been ordered to report for a medical examination to confirm his ineligible status. It had been conducted on a raw December morning and it was evident to the army doctor that all was up with Germany if she needed combatants as ill as this man. Having established that a hothouse was the only environment in which Leon could survive, he astutely said 'I should think you must be fighting for your own life as much as for that of your plants. Be off with you.') Leon might have been able to bar his own staff from No Admittance on the grounds that he lived there, but he could hardly forbid the outside gardeners their ancient right of access to the boiler room through the yard door to thaw their hands and brew tea. It was therefore necessary to devise a way of hiding Felix, and for this the boiler room's layout was helpful.

As has been hinted, the city's Botanical Gardens was not ideally situated. To its pre-industrial founders it had not much mattered that the site was low since they hadn't foreseen

the Palm House and its heating requirements. The designers of the original heating system had planned to copy that at Kew, where the problem of constant coal deliveries to the middle of a horticultural idyll had been solved by digging an underground tunnel with a track along which fuel could be unobtrusively hauled. In the case of Leon's Palm House this had proved impossible because the water table was too high. Perhaps seventy yards of tunnel had been cut from above and lined with brick until the idea was abandoned in favour of an access road behind high walls which became part of extensive kitchen gardens, covered with all kinds of espaliered nectarines, vines and loganberry canes. This little road, up which horses pulled a succession of rubber-tyred coal carts, led into the yard behind the boiler room. In order that the public's illusion of being in deep countryside should not be ruined by the sight of offices and messuages at the back of the Palm House this yard was enclosed by similar high walls, thickly grown with ivies and creepers and broken only by a single wooden door to which few of the outside staff had keys. The space thus enclosed was lined with brick bunkers. Those against the boiler room wall were for coal. Others around the yard contained mounds of pea gravel, compost, peat and crushed shell, while still other sheds housed the glass stores as well as collections of tools, whiting and huge rolls of disused blinds like the sails of an obsolete schooner.

The boiler room therefore had two aspects. To Leon and Felix it was an annexe of the Palm House itself which, because the public were excluded, seemed yet more private, as befitted its status as their bedroom. To other gardeners and the men who brought the coal it was more an extension of outdoors, though complete ease of access was denied them by the curator's eccentric rules and often forbidding presence. Leon now imposed a strict rota for when the gardeners could come in and warm themselves. At all other times the boiler room door was bolted from within, occasioning much puzzled speculation. This routine enabled Felix to slip away before the men came in. He needed merely to have a safe hiding place in case of a proper search, and this was afforded by the aborted tunnel. Having given up on their original scheme, the Palm House's designers had ingeniously turned it to advantage by devising a way of ducting the smoke from the furnaces along it, running the flue underground for a considerable distance until it could emerge behind a spinney, disguised as the remaining tower of a ruined mediaeval keep, a triumph of nineteenth-century taste. This kept the smuts away but the sight of smoking battlements cast over that part of the Gardens something of the sinister fraudulence of a crematorium. The advantage to Felix was that the first part of the tunnel was a perfect hiding place. In the boiler room itself the huge lagged flue gathered smoke from the three furnaces, further impelled by steam as in a railway engine, before plunging through the floor next to a coal bunker. This bunker was now largely filled by an electrically driven hoist which had been the last word in modern labour saving when installed in 1927, taking the coal from outside via a hatchway and conveying it on a belt up to the hoppers which fed the furnaces. In the grimy shadow of this machine a small access door was let into the floor and led to the tunnel's mouth.

Between them Leon and Felix had a system of warning signals which would give the boy time to drop through this panel and crouch in the hot darkness with the tube of blazing gases shuddering by his ear. These included a certain way of rattling the No Admittance door handle and, for real emergencies, dropping the word 'stokehold' into conversation which meant Leon and a peremptory guest were about to come through to the boiler room. As it happened, this extreme measure was seldom needed and only twice in earnest, once being when Dr Anselmus demanded to know exactly how decrepit the boilers were and to inspect them for himself. The second time was early one morning after a heavy air raid, one of the last in the war, when a German officer and a squad of soldiers came to the Botanical Gardens looking for survivors of an American aircrew who had bailed out of their stricken B-17 over the city. They made a thorough search of all the outhouses, poked among the plants in the Temperate House and then came to the Palm House, obviously dispirited. The officer quizzed Leon about parachutes. 'The stokehold – you'll need to see that, I presume?' said the gardener loudly, throwing open the door with fine indifference and disclosing a neatly swept space with highly polished pipes and gauges. The officer glanced flintily around, said 'Good work' and gave no order to search. He and his men drove off and never returned.

With these measures working Leon tried to coax Felix out into No Admittance. At the first sounds of a visitor to the Palm House, though, the youth would scurry back into the boiler room. What combination this behaviour represented of shyness, shame and fear Leon could not judge. At any rate Felix quickly turned into a reliable boilerman, learned to operate the mechanical feeder and seemed to take pleasure in keeping the room swept and neat, polishing up copper pipes which had oxidised to a dull mahogany. Now and then he even washed clothes for both of them. When early in that final winter the coal stopped Leon would drag his lopping spoils into the yard, lock the door into the Gardens and set to work with axe and saw. It was several weeks before he could induce Felix to take a step outdoors, still longer for the boy to acquire the confidence to work there, sawing and stacking. At the least noise he would bolt indoors and cower by the entrance to his hiding place whence the gardener had to coax him, shaking. Yet under this furtive regime he appeared to be recovering well, though still unable or refusing to speak. One day, to Leon's delight, he made himself a catapult and, sitting on the back step, began to knock the odd thrush or sparrow out of the branches of the copper beech which partly extended over the yard. These morsels supplemented their scanty diet. The ornamental fowl had long since gone from the tarn but Leon, who as a child had learned fowling in the marshes around Flinn, had netted the shallows and sometimes snared an incautious wild mallard or oystercatcher at dusk. Quite early in the war he had cleaned out most of the Gardens' squirrel population, trapping them by using cypress cones as bait. He then stuffed them with pine nuts and a sprig of rosemary before roasting them. They had been delicious. The occasional squirrel was still to be seen, having come in from the park across the way; but maybe the war had made them as canny as it had made people for neither he nor Felix caught any more.

Thus weeks lengthened into months and a gingerly domesticity rooted itself on the narrow frontier between the temporary and the permanent. It was as if nothing could be decided until war and winter both ended. Emergency was not subdivisible. The times were radically disrupted; no peculiar circumstance could disrupt them further. It was a way of surviving which had its own strange stability, and often at night in the boiler room's warmth the glow of fireboxes and the sighing of the flue extended timelessly in every direction. It was then that surviving was indistinguishable from living and might happily have led nowhere else. At other times when wind and searchlights whipped through the leafless branches of the beech outside and the furnaces devoured their mixture of hoarded coal and scavenged timber, the boiler room filled with a ferocious, dense roar which made the walls shudder like those of an engine room in a ship under full way and racing towards its own destruction on an uncharted reef. Hot pipework, scorched lagging, feathers of escaping steam, the grind and clank of the automatic hopper: all were part of a power which was surely being translated into forward motion. Leon expected to hear above it the seesaw whine of harmonics as gearwheels and transmission shaft went in and out of phase with each other. On getting up and going into the darkened House he would be half surprised to find it silent, its unmoving ironwork anchored deep in urban soil.

In the war's final month the searchlights in the sky above the city grew more and more haywire. The gardener would stand beneath the palms and watch the beams swoop and skid as if they were unable to remember what they were looking for, no longer capable of concentrating. One by one they failed or were shot out until there was only a single beam left. Possibly its aiming gear had been damaged for instead of pointing up into the night sky it swept impotently around over the rooftops like the intermittent beam of a lighthouse. Its whizzing white passage above the Gardens distressed him. '*Steena*,' it sang as it whanged overhead and vanished behind the trees. '*Steena*,' it reappeared. Two nights later the House drummed to a low frequency shaking and the sky glowed vermilion. Evidently the searchlight was hit and further crippled, for although it remained alight the beam froze as it passed overhead, coming to an abrupt stop in mid-sweep so that its lower edge just caught the weathercock on the Palm House's dome. The searing brilliance pinned the ship like a moth to the sky, leaving Leon benighted in a penumbra below. For ten endless minutes the golden galleon flared on a black sea, '*eeeen*', so the gardener, staring up through the roof with tears glistening on his cheeks, covered his ears with his hands to shut out the persistent keening. Then the light went out for good and the freed ship vanished, the noise stopped, and a week later the war was over.

As a squid-cloud thins and the water transpares, the fog and mania drew apart and everyone suddenly saw with awful clarity what they had been and what they had done. There was nothing for it but to rejoice. Stygian camps emptied and people went back to dying in ordinary untainted traffic accidents, to falling off alps in the normal course of pastime. For others the camps never did empty and they never completely came out of hiding. Leon did not triumphantly disclose the ingenious bolt-hole beneath the boiler room, nor did Felix run for cover with any less urgency. The months passed, the transients departed, the population shook down. Now was the time for citizens to re-register, for lists of voters to be re-compiled, for claims to pensions to be established, for all kinds of aberrant and abhorrent recent behaviour to be amnestied or amnesied. But Felix did not emerge, or Leon didn't allow him to, or wordlessly they agreed to prolong their liminal predicament for reasons of their own, still subsisting on one man's rations. Was the boy too ruined to contemplate returning to the world beyond the wall? Was grieving for a brief manhood to be assuaged indefinitely by half-life at the edge of a spurious jungle? Suppose the gardener kept warning him that gangs like those of muzzle-face still roamed the unpoliced streets, snuffling out unfinished business?

At night Leon still wandered his private jungle and sought his plants' advice but they could tell him nothing he didn't know. Rather, they had a habit of indulging a querulous preoccupation with their own lives which calmed him and drew him back again from the harsh and hollow-stomached transactions beyond the garden wall. Among man's immemorial consolations is undoubt-edly the company of green and growing things, no less than the melancholy comforts of scholarship. So it was that his plants had taken characters for themselves, speaking as individuals on a variety of topics. One of his favourites was *Encephalartos*, the ancient cycad which had partially appropriated the tone and manner of Professor Seneschal, a venerable Fellow of the Society and a world authority on gymnosperms. Its heavy head hung loosely in its collar and its captious asides pleased Leon as he paused to check that the soil was not too damp. 'Turned warmer since 1908,' it remarked one day. 'I put it down to the glass. Not such pretty light, this modern stuff, but it's thicker quality. Holds the warmth better . . . And who might you be, young man?'

At any opportunity, indeed, Encephalartos altensteinii *seemed prepared to indulge tetchily in the comforts of his own scholarship, airing his theories for any passer-by:*

'Wars?' he said. 'I've seen them come and go. This last has been the worst so far. All that banging and crashing at night with great flashes of light and what happens? *Draughts.* Holes in the roof and damn great draughts cutting through the House at every angle. If it hadn't been for that new gardener's boy they've brought in – what's his name? Leon? – we'd have all of us frozen in our beds. As it was my cone became quite numb and such things are no laughing matter at my age. But he turned up the heat and mustered a gang and soon had things back to rights. The palms, of course, preserved their usual lofty disdain. Anybody here would testify that there's not a malicious fibre in my being, but frankly I shouldn't have minded too much if one or other of the palms had got a little smack – say a piece of steel in the head, nothing too fatal but enough to wake its ideas up a bit. A good stiff jolt to bring it back to reality, if you like.

'You'd care to hear my theories? Bless you, I'm flattered.

129

Though I do say it myself I have, I think, one or two to offer. What you say is perfectly true – age does lend a certain weight, I find, to one's opinions. There's a fellow comes here from time to time who pokes rudely at me and fondles my parts – calls himself a professor, too, quite disgusting – Seneschal, that's his name. Claims to be an authority on me and mine, or "gymnosperms" as he calls us – and no, Professor Seneschal, we're not much flattered by your attention. The insolent monkey claims my noble race of cycads is *primitive*. I fear his unappealing little brain automatically equates the ancient with the unsophisticated. Like so many members of his species he sees himself as the culmination of millions of years' evolution and thus fancies himself as *perfected*. There he stands, the great Professor Seneschal, the perfect example of his perfectly evolved species. Racial purity in person! From which position he deigns to examine my own genus and declare it imperfect. He knows quite well that cycads have survived practically unchanged for about a hundred and sixty million years longer than his own miserable species ... I do beg your pardon, but you know what I mean – a rhetorical trope, merely. I'm informed that the entire evolution of the human species via the apes can now be considered as having been compressed into the last six million years or so which I'm afraid makes you by comparison a lot of Johnny-come-latelys – again, no offence. But explain if you can how, unless it's from an innate racism, Professor Seneschal can look at a family which has survived intact all the changes and vicissitudes of a hundred and sixty million years and still see it as *primitive*? Surely it is proof of extreme evolutionary sophistication? His kind have been obliged to go from trees to trousers in a wink of time whereas we cycads have needed no such desperate measures. Does it not argue conclusively that it was we who were already perfected, having no further need of change in order to survive? None of these embarrassing transmogrifications for us: shedding tails and shedding hair and, come to that, shedding blood. Scarcely a dignified history, if I may make so bold.

'But I digress. I haven't forgotten that my real subject is the palms. However, it was necessary to "set the scene", as it were, because we now reach the point at which Professor Seneschal and his cronies draw from their already erroneous hypothesis their most opprobrious conclusion – to wit, that far from being a clear and perfected race we cycads are in fact muddled and ambiguous as to our identity, that we have not yet "decided" whether we are "really" palms or conifers. It's like saying the Professor's problem is that he has failed to make up his mind to be either a chimpanzee or a fruit bat, though someone more malicious than I might suggest the choice had already been thrust upon him. In any case he says our leaves are reminiscent of palm fronds while our beautiful cones resemble those of fir trees. Oh, the vulgar fallacies of these racist evolutionaries! *Post hoc ergo propter hoc!* And this same grotesque logic is somehow expected to build into a steady intentional line of descent, culminating in the great Professor himself! Under duress, then, I might well agree that his hands had a remarkable similarity to those of a chimpanzee and – I have this on an authority whose identity I cannot divulge – his gonads bear a considerable resemblance to those of a fruit bat, erectile tissue and all.

'The palms? Well, as a member of a race which can draw collectively on the memories of a hundred and sixty million years, I can inform the Professor that it's perfectly meaningless to go on about who derived from what and when. Here we all are, are we not? The fact that there are, undeniably, palm trees in this world whose fronds might be thought to have some faint similarity to our leaves is scarcely a reason for accusing my kind of ambiguity and muddlement. It's insulting. Besides – and here's a pertinent question for Herr Doktor Professor –

what's wrong with ambiguousness in any case? There's nothing in this world which is not ambiguous, not one single thing which could be said unequivocally to represent "reality", whatever that might mean. My word, one despairs at the lack of intellectual sophistication on the part of some of these newer – my apologies again, dammit, but I'm sure you'll forgive my heatedness. This dreary simplistic way of looking at things gets me on the raw, I'm afraid.

'The real problem with the palms derives largely, in my view, from their crude height. This casual fact of nature has led directly to all their faults of character. I'm sorry to stoop from the level of scientific discourse for a moment to that of mere moralism, but anyone in this House would readily agree with this opinion. To borrow the repugnant idiom of the times which I've heard bandied about by recent visitors, the palms have a tendency towards a "Master Race" complex. More unfortunate still, it's made worse by the attitude of *Homo sapiens sapiens* (too wise by half!) which merely encourages the palms' belief in their own superiority. I've made this a matter of some study so you won't find me short of ammunition. What? Oh very well, then, chapter and verse. Linnaeus, who described many of the more than 2,500 species of palm, called them the princes of the plant kingdom since they supplied *Homo* with food and shelter and clothing. This is notoriously not the behaviour of most princes, but we'll let it pass. He also pointed out that the etymology of the name "palm" derived from that of the palm of the hand since the fronds reminded humans of their own fingers. Linnaeus was, of course, a man himself. Any plant meeting with mankind's favour is accorded royal status! So much for scientific objectivity. Such childish hierarchies! There's also a glaring inconsistency here. We cycads are considered "muddled" because we remind man of both palms and conifers. Why, then, isn't *Homo* equally muddled because palms remind him of himself? Why indeed.

But it gets worse, as this Leon fellow's readings in the Society's library will confirm. If you turn to the *Deutsches Magazin für Garten- und Blumenkunde* for 1872 (volume 25, I fancy), you will find the following pieces of dotty anthropomorphism, which I'll take the liberty of doing into your own language to save time:

'The palm tree resembles man in its straight, upright, slender proportions, its beauty and its separation into two sexes, male and female. If its head is cut off it dies. If its brain suffers then the whole tree suffers with it. If its fronds are broken off they will no more regenerate than will a man's amputated arm. Its fibrous bark covers it as a man is covered with hair.

'This is lamentable stuff, to be sure, and we need hardly bother to spike the weak points in such analogies. Separation into two sexes, forsooth! Most palms are monoecious, are they not? The same plant bears both male and female flowers. No ambiguity there, of course; oh no. (*Our* male and female cones, I'd like to remind you, are borne on separate plants.) And as for the "fibrous bark", I'd always understood that the whole point about *Homo*'s alleged superiority was precisely that he was *not* covered with a pelt of hair. It's clear that Professor Seneschal and his ilk still unconsciously think of themselves as apes, no doubt from having been apes far longer than they've been men. But let us proceed:

'The palm's distinguished shape is superior to that of all other plants in its noble bearing, as are its deliberate striving to reach the skies, its nourishing fruits, the materials it supplies for clothing and shelter, and its airy crown swaying to the least current of air whose rustling passage led man to believe he was listening to an invisible being.

All these combine to create the impression that the palm tree embodies a higher being: if not an actual deity then surely its dwelling place.

'Gentlemen [said *Encephalartos* with a lecturer's at-a-loss gesture], I ask you. With all this sheer tosh talked about them, is it surprising it's gone to the palms' heads? When those passages were written the palm – in however stunted and ignoble a form – had become an essential ingredient in any bourgeois household, whether in drawing room or conservatory, as several of the species in this House bear witness. (One searches in vain, I submit, for anything *princely* in these runts and dwarves.) The palm was thereby reduced to a mere cliché of the exotic, a symbol of the longing which urban man felt for a rustic and supposedly spiritual self he had lost somewhere in the past. Oh dear, oh dear. One really does despair. All I can say is that so far as anyone in this House is concerned the planet had been getting on quite well without this sort of pretentious prattle. Before that, palms were just tall plants, and nowhere near the tallest. Nowadays it appears they're actually the nests of gods, mainly because they remind human beings of themselves. And we cycads are supposed to be primitive? Words fail me.'

For once, this turned out to be true and *Encephalartos* relapsed into his customary pithy gloom.

SEVEN

The Gardens are being dug, weeded, bushes trimmed and tied. The lawns have been cut and young men stand on wooden edging boards driving half-moon blades into the straggly turf to produce crisp lines. Others pull rollers or, crouched in potting sheds, laboriously stencil fresh signs and labels to replace those faded to illegibility. There is no shortage of able-bodied help, for the economy is not yet back on its feet. The currency is unstable, the black market thrives: Swiss watches, cameras, nylons, scent, cigarettes, spirits; but also butter, petrol, paraffin oil for heaters, meat, coal, eggs. Any work is better than none, a pittance preferable to no income. Assets are gradually unfrozen and members of the Royal Botanic Society return from visits to London and Zurich having retrieved funds judiciously salted away six years earlier. Their bequests and loans not only turn them from Members into Fellows but enable the Society to hire abundant cheap labour for the Gardens and to put in hand repairs to its devastated seventeenth-century seat, the beautiful mansion at the far end of the grounds . . .

Not true, any of it, apart from the black market. Wars do not end as neatly as chapters, nor does regeneration follow on their boot-heels like spring. Nothing is clear. In the listlessness of convalescence everything is lacking, uncriminal energies in

says they've got about enough money to keep us on our present salary for the rest of this year. Two years if they don't take on any of the new men we need.'

'Something'll turn up.'

'I spent yesterday with Jan nailing up the front doors of the house and putting up what shutters are left. They haven't got forty thousand, not anything like, so the place'll have to wait. It'll be all right so long as the weather doesn't get in. The roof's sound, at least.'

'Something'll turn up.'

Since that morning months had passed and the gulf Leon had felt opening seemed to have closed again. The boilers throbbed loyally, the gravel crunched firmly beneath his flapping galoshes, the plants creaked with growth and the night people were trooping in to gossip and shelter and admire his blooms. Better still, they were paying for the privilege, nominal entrance fees whose scrupulous surrender by Leon touched Dr Anselmus and made him still sadder since he knew things his famous stove house expert did not. But then, everybody knew things Leon didn't. The princess was no exception, with her Lancôme scent and flirty predictions. He listened to their gossip but the rumours never quite touched him. They hung about like cobwebs in an untidy bachelor's house, so familiar he no longer noticed them. That is, until one candlelit night when, in the grotto behind a stand of bamboo, he came face to face with the spider. He overheard a conversation among a group gathered around the night-flowering *Cestrum* whose slender yellow-green flowers they were sampling.

'I say, Bettrice, try this one . . . There. Isn't that divine?'

Her 'Mm, yes' mingled with 'Make the most of it' from a second male voice.

'But surely they can't?' said the woman. 'Legally, I mean. Part of the nation's heritage. You can't sell off a public garden.'

'That's just what they're wrangling about, whether it's actually part of the University and therefore public or private. Weren't you there when André was saying all that about the city council getting the estates department to come up with a watertight plan?'

'I never listen to what André says, darling. He's always using phrases like "watertight plan".'

'Well, all right, I grant he's a bit dreary. But he's in the know.'

'And "in the know".'

'I'm not doing very well.'

'Not if you're hoping to sell me on André's intellect, no. If you're trying to convince me he's been eavesdropping on City Hall gossip you needn't bother. We already know he does that. *C'est son métier*, after all. The man's a journalist.'

'They have their uses. He might at least ensure this whole business gets aired before it becomes a national scandal. This isn't a satrapy any longer. It's supposed to be a democracy again. I like to know what's being done in my name.'

'In *your* name, Charles?'

'He's right, Bettrice,' said the other man. 'It's all very grand to form coalitions and governments of national reconstruction and invoke crisis and emergency and so on, but you've got to watch these people like a hawk. This place is a plum.' ('Hawks? Plums?' Bettrice could be heard murmuring.) 'How many acres, do you reckon? Can't be less than ten, surely. Imagine: ten acres of verdant real estate this close to the centre of town. And calls on all sides for mass new housing as well as these grandiose plans of theirs for commercial hubbery – "entrepôt status" or whatever the cant phrase is. That means a lot more people, a lot more shops and offices. It's the exact moment when those buggers with the powdered jowls who survived the war at a profit begin casting around for likely sites for land deals. You yourself said the other day your horrid little landlord had just snapped up that entire bombed street. The one with the Lutheran church.'

'I don't like this at all,' came Bettrice's voice muffled in petals. 'You try, Charles. Talk about exotic. It's sort of druggy, as if it's trying to anaesthetise you. Isn't it? See what I mean?' There was a masculine grunt. 'Boring old plots and conspiracies, then.'

'Of course. Fill in the blanks yourself. On the one hand a choice piece of land and a national need for building sites. On the other a bunch of botanical dodderers, dons and professors and women with tweed skirts and scratched wrists. Stony broke, the lot of them. Can't even reopen their own headquarters because they can't afford to repair it, while their grounds go on looking like the aftermath of Stalingrad. Even this Palm House, which is a real gem in its way, looks pretty tatty outside. Now of course the Fellows and professors and whatnot will have some fancy parchments locked away which no doubt contain phrases like "inalienable possession in perpetuity". They've also got a government which claims it hasn't the money to bail them out but which by magic could probably afford to *buy* them out. It would just be dolled up to look like an act of principled generosity. They'd offer an alternative site twice as large and far enough outside the suburbs to be properly rural, gift of the nation, blah-blah, even more inalienable and even more in perpetuity, tax-free status for the Society and the odd bizarre right such as fifty tons of free manure a year from the Royal stables and a hogshead of beer per gardener. Authenticity. The nation pays to transport the whole caboodle, the King signs the charter his predecessors must have failed to sign for these premises, and even before the ink's dry the air's full of flying bits of gentleman's bespoke pin-striping as this place gets carved up.'

'All that, yes. Plausible enough. But surely you can't *transplant* . . . I mean, can you actually move a place like this? What is there? Just plants and air.'

'Who knows?' This was Charles's voice. 'I believe every word of it. A palm house, well, it's just a lot of old glass and ironwork, isn't it? A thing like that wouldn't stand in their way. He's right. They'll offer to build a modern one out wherever, brand new heating, all Vita glass or whatever the stuff's called. Anyway, what about the docks? You know where those refineries were on the island before the RAF bombed them? They're talking of building a completely new terminal away on the estuary and turning the island into a dormitory town. Something else to look forward to. We shan't know the place. And the point is, we live here. We should have some say ... Do you think this is mould or are these leaves naturally blue?'

It entered Leon's awareness that they must have reached the *Chamaedorea metallica* which he had hand-pollinated so it had fruited the previous year. He shifted his position and immediately felt the coursing of blood to limbs forgotten and frozen. The pit had opened again and into his mind came no words but a wash of black solvent whose acrid flood nothing could withstand. Not just the Palm House but a succession of unidentifiable solidities fell to driftwood in an outward spread of concentric rings. It was not to be stopped. Under a clay-coloured sky baulks of timber trundled in the surf or lay stretched like bodies at all angles on the sand. After all there was to be no escape. It lay beneath everything, eroding, undercutting: fish oil and smoke and frozen hands and an absence too huge to be named.

When the visitors left they took with them much of this turmoil of dissolution. When he was once more alone with his plants and the candle flames burning steadily in the dark a calm resolution possessed him. He made a thoughtful round of his night blooms. The scent of each recalled its history, reminding him of hours of tending, of watching and sniffing and touching (for the texture of leaves, tumescence of cells, stiffness of vascular bundles tells much about a plant's health). It brought back memories, too, of scrounging and sawing and hauling; of rising five times a night to replenish inferior fuel in boilers which would have stayed in happily on a couple of hundredweight of good coal. Of Felix, and whatever crumbled within him at the thought of discovery and endings, of draggings out into daylight's jeering scrutiny. Of standing alone on this very spot on terrifying nights with the searchlights whanging overhead like crazed lighthouses. He longed for order, or at least for a disorder which had become permanent. '*Sprrixx*,' he breathed, and saw sunlight flashing on bicycle spokes, the tiny beams glittering round and round. The dark dissolve might reach inland to that point, but there it had to stop, held for ever at bay by those twinkling wheels, *sprrixx*.

Well then, he would fight. Which was to say (feeling the drowsing power of growth encircling him, any rootlet of which could lift concrete) they would fight. Or resist. Or intrigue or do whatever one did to get one's way. 'We took on a gang of pariahs with knives. What are a lot of soft men in suits?' he asked the plants as he paused and strolled, stroking leaves and caressing stems. 'Nothing,' he clearly heard them reply. 'Anyway, we have Dr Anselmus on our side,' which was surely true. A powerful ally indeed. The Society was internationally renowned; it was inconceivable they would ever agree to the sort of plans he'd just overheard. A garden was not something one could move, after all. It took years to grow into its shape – in this case centuries. Even if in some imaginary world every plant and tree could be transported alive to take root infallibly in a new site it wouldn't constitute the same garden.

'And what then?' drawled the Italian chargé, fitting a cigarette into his oval holder somewhere inside the gardener's brain. 'A different work of art, that's all. An exquisite garden like this is a little landscape, and a landscape is *constructed*, put together with wit, sensibility and artifice for aesthetic and symbolic ends. "Nature", on the other hand, is brainlessly aleatory. Look how randomly she plonks trees down in just – I do beg your pardon,' as Leon's leathery hand reached out for his prize. 'Would you, I wonder, be making a collection of these?'

But Leon didn't want a different garden, he wanted the same one. Nor did he want a newer or improved Palm House. The instant he had first set foot in it as little more than a boy he had recognised that it was tuned. That was the word. He had once overheard a night visitor describe how one could make the most perfect facsimile of a Stradivarius violin but that a good musician could always tell from its sound it was not the genuine article. It didn't matter how carefully one chose wood from the very grove Stradivarius had used, or analysed the chemistry of the varnish and reproduced it exactly, or even strung it with gut from descendants of the sheep which had supplied its original. The tone would always be different. Apparently it had to do with changes taking place in the entire fabric of the instrument in response to two or more centuries of constant playing. Infinitesimal molecules of wood lined themselves up like iron filings around a magnet's prongs . . . something like that, anyway. But tuning was the image which most exactly described how the Palm House felt. All that carefully tended growth over the years had somehow harmonised the whole structure. It had all bedded down just right and the glass let through exactly the right quantities of the correct rays and the weathercock's shadow traced the right path.

He blew out the candles in his slow ritual and paused by the *Utotia mirifica* that dim Bettrice woman had so disliked. She must have a nose of iron, he thought, sipping at a bloom. 'Anaesthetic', indeed. It was like taking a gulp of genever and saying it tasted drunk-making instead of holding it on the tongue and breathing out, letting it slide down a bit and breathing out some more, a whole palette of subtle taste shades distinguishing themselves one by one. Of this pale flower she had snorted up its vertiginous purple but had missed the vanilla and chypre and the elusive breeze of brisk green energy. On impulse he did something so rare for him he could almost hear the House fill with gasps of astonishment. He picked the bloom and, having completed his round, approached the slight dark figure meekly outlined in the doorway of No Admittance.

'No change, my Felix, no change,' he said, presenting the flower.

The young man took it and held it to his nose, head bowed. It was quite impossible to tell from his posture whether it was merely demure or else an expression of profound sadness.

'No end,' said Leon. 'Rely on me, no end.'

These are terrible words for any young man to hear, particularly when he has been agonisingly ransomed from what had previously seemed like a possible life. After all, what did it mean to be rescued? What had been restored? (The dark puddle at the foot of the wall gleamed for a moment like a sea separating rescuer from victim, the victim from his previous self.) Thereafter his life would begin again shakily on a barren, unknown island which he might or might not decide to inhabit, an indecision which could prolong itself to the grave.

It could only be guessed how much Leon had told Felix as he talked him through shock and pain and delirium, hour after hour, though the boy had surely been in no fit state to remember tales of another's life when his own was at the brink of dissolution. On the other hand he may have attained that point so easily reached drifting in or out of sleep when the entire fiction of one's life thins to a thread which can become entwined with almost any other version and seem no less real. Thus the voices from a bedside wireless may entangle themselves in a waking dream, for stories have an affinity for one another and merge at the least opportunity. Each day marks fresh hours of effort to keep pure and clear the life story one has inherited from yesterday. Does this not explain our monstrous preoccupation with courtroom dramas, so often pawky and sordid? As we watch the accused racking their brains for the right narrative braid, the right yarn which will lead away from guilt and towards acquittal we acknowledge our own wrestlings with alternative identities, which given half a chance (such as panic) so readily anneal themselves into a life we have never had but which everyone else seems to recognise as our own – an alchemy which quickly turns braid to hemp. It was hardly likely that Felix's life before that fateful day had resembled the gardener's; the man was surely too anomalous and singular. But supposing the boy's rescue and convalescence had plaited into his history new, overheard strands which were not wholly alien? An orphan, then? Sooner or later almost everyone becomes an orphan. An aching loss? Most people nurse one of those, too.

Perhaps after all Leon had talked unheedingly, staring not at the bruised, slit-eyed face or seeping moss pad but at one corner of the mattress or a spot on the wall, talking maybe to the unseen audience of plants. And maybe the gypsy, hollowed into an echoing shell by pain and creeping knowledge, had rung with his words until they began to describe himself. And there again perhaps Leon had really been addressing a bronchial child gasping for breath in a cottage hospital bed who, by sleight of circumstance, now lay on a blood-soaked mattress in a boiler room. *No change.* What faith was being kept, then, locked into repetition? *No end.* Could Felix sense himself being dissolved, his own loss and pain hijacked by a stranger to blend into his? And had his language been stolen too, as he lay on the floor watching tongues of flame? Stolen and given over to shrubbery, maybe, so that his saviour-captor would ever afterwards listen more attentively to mere plants than to him? The injustice of falling victim is exceeded only by the assertion of rescuer's rights. The injured's desire for amends, for compensation, is swamped by the healer's expectation of reward. Money? Nothing so crude. Just boundless love, and a bemused obligation to fall in with a stranger's fantasies. So what must it have been to come up on one elbow on a mattress stiff with your own blood and feel yourself falling into that harsh mouth bent solicitously above you? Mouth? A face, body, an entire being, full of a desire which can never be kissed away. For the moment is long past when the right kiss at the right time might have freed this terrible fond man.

Now, in times of unease, with his own night people shedding rumours of change like a sinister perfume, the gardener could only issue blank denials. They might take the form of an impassioned speech in the Palm House's defence (not yet delivered but gradually being honed and refined before his leafy and attentive audience) or of a single flower plucked and presented to a baffled youth in earnest of some ancient covenant the boy had never signed. Passive and windguided he might have been, this gardener, and weakly skewed with loss; but what impassioned resolve had it taken to construct an entirely private life in the heart of a public garden? Was such a man suddenly to relax his grip, as rotten putty releases a cascade of glass? A survivor, then, drawn to another, even if by a love too implacable to be called affection, or by an affection too voracious to qualify as love. Long ago this survivor was himself a boy, who had stood in fishy dungarees with his pale hair flailing a cheek, nearly invisible among vast gestures of land and sea and sky. Then, he had affirmed a new pact with an inseparable companion to whom he had already sworn his lifetime oath and with whom he daily walked, ate, slept and talked: that whatever happened and wherever he went he would never rely on anyone else.

Twenty years later he simply said 'My Felix' and, a protective arm about the thin shoulders, steered a mute gypsy holding a flower towards a boiler room in a postwar city.

Utotia mirifica, *the flower which Leon had picked, was remarkably philosophical about its own beheading:*

'One of the lotuses – who has since gone to shed her light in what's probably a quite dingy diplomatic apartment – used to say she tried to cultivate a spirit of constant astonishment. This, she'd been told, was the correct attitude for facing the world. She was right, wrong only in thinking it needed cultivating. Tonight constant astonishment came to me of its own accord and won't leave for a little yet. To have one's neck deliberately broken by one's own gardener is a shock, and although not actually painful has left me with a feeling which goes beyond pain: that of the most desolating separation, of being literally torn away from one's parents without so much as a farewell. My brothers and sisters were coming into bud even as I bloomed and it'll now be up to them to be "exotic and druggy", as one of the night visitors described me.

'Now that the original shock has diminished I'm beginning to feel honoured. To be singled out as a special gift is flattering, even if it means an early death. It's true I might have lived another week or so had I not been picked: a week of wasting precious pollen grains in powdering a succession of huge, blind, white, oily noses shoved violently in among my stamens. Then the noses would have switched their attention to my unfolding siblings and a day or two later I should have been dead-headed. So it would come to the same thing in any case. But if I lose a few days by having been chosen in this amazing way I gain immeasurably from being caught up in the economy of homage.

'The *economy* of homage? But I'm not sure what else to call it. At its simplest homage is a unilateral act – of acknowledgement as much as of love, of obedience no less than praise. So the gardener picked the flower which he himself had planned, sown and raised, and presented me to his damaged vagrant in an act of homage. But it goes beyond that. It has to include a constant sense of . . . of astonishment, really, that the gardener too is humble before his plants, and we before our gardener. "There ought to be someone to thank" is a feeling I've never been without even though I know perfectly well there's nothing to thank except contingency which, in the absence of anything else, comes to seem suspiciously divine. Being snapped off at the neck as part of a transaction which expresses this feels, as I say, like an honour. The gypsy was touched by the gesture: I could feel it by the way he held me and put me in a jam-jar of water in the centre of the table in No Admittance.

'The more I think about it the easier it becomes to read an unintended accuracy into that phrase "exotic and druggy". These, too, are people who are going to die, and even if they never expect to glance up and see a slow drift of angels eddying among the wrought-iron something of that knowledge can leak out of them in their most casual asides. Exotic has to mean more than just coming from outside or outlandish, else familiarity would reduce everything to the humdrum. Yet this doesn't happen in the Palm House any more than it happens with the greatest art. No matter what taxonomies are used to tame us, to hold us in the direct line of scientific sight so its beady glare can focus and refocus on whatever of our attributes has a passing interest, we're never quite there again, are never precisely the same. What could be more hackneyed than a rose? But what more elusive, since it never stales for long?

'So a conclusion is forced upon us, very simple, very hard to accept: that everything is exotic and eventually incomprehensible. Our gardener is almost alone in perceiving this. None of the others do: not Anselmus, nor Witte, nor Seneschal, nor the motley assistants. One of the few visitors to have more than a glimmering is that Italian chargé, of course, but it makes him uneasy and he has to hide it beneath effete badinage. But our gardener knows; and no matter that the tamarind at the far end of the House refers to him as a sort of failed priest acting out a displaced love, it's still a form of homage. Personally I don't agree with that interpretation, which strikes me as facile and modish (the tamarind's still young, of course). Our gardener's a horticulturist through and through. Yet undoubtedly he feels the mystery and in his muddled, wilful way knows nothing can diminish it – that it alone merits the attention of a constant intelligence. He's sad to fail so often. Sad? It's his greatest remorse. Sometimes he suspects he has held Cou Min's shadow tiny in the centre of each pupil in order to block his sight. It's safer to gaze at the past casting its lovely shadows than to contemplate the present, and certainly the future. He knows it's an evasion. But what counts for him is the homage. To what, though? To whom?

'And so I'm expiring fragrantly but not unhappily in my glass jar of water, caressed by the gypsy's gaze as he squats by the table and lowers his chin on to folded hands a mere eighteen inches away. There's great pain in his eyes and every so often they flood slightly as though he would weep if only men and gypsies were allowed to. I can do nothing for him except be the gardener's gift and exhale astonishment steadily into his face in the hopes that he will catch it too. This is the astonishment which the visitor called "druggy" because she had expected something familiar, sweet and safe – a tropical rose, perhaps. But my scent unnerves. It wasn't designed for you, gypsy, pretty lad; but if you pay it heed even as I pay you homage you might learn things.

'Meanwhile, I've been learning things myself from this new perspective of being up to my neck in a jam-jar. I've now been separated from my family an hour and I have to report that the original desolate feeling of separation has considerably faded. To be truthful, except as images in my memory they've effectively vanished. There's a certain reckless bravery in being able to ask: do my father and mother, my brothers and sisters, my closest friend really exist? Or have I invented them to fill the role of parents, siblings, friend, which the world demands we supply in order to become socially visible ourselves? No doubt they're still out there somewhere in that distant land beyond the door, but that part of my life's clearly over. Now there's only a face, chin on fingers, an unspeaking mouth, and dark eyes brimming with anguish.'

EIGHT

One afternoon the princess said:

'Your lotus plant, your present to me: it's doing well. Always in flower. It reminds me of home. We call it *basimbun*, which means calm or calming.'

'Not very original,' said Leon testily. 'How many flowers are noisy or irritant?'

'We have several of those,' she said, undismayed. 'In most cultures there's a language of flowers, I believe. At any rate we have in our forests a thin, tall plant with a big, straggly yellow head which turns according to the sun.'

'A sort of sunflower, I suppose.'

'Only in a negative sense. This plant turns consistently *away*. Our name for it means "positively enraging".'

Leon was surprised by the adolescent thrill it gave him to discover he was being flirted with. Lately the princess's mode had been confusing him more and more. What could she possibly want from him? She a beautiful foreign lady of the highest social caste, he a mere gardener. Rather a good gardener if he said so himself, even quite learned in his subject, but scarcely high-born. (Now and then he could still experience a fugitive olfactory vision, a nasal illusion when somewhere between nostril and brain a drifting corpuscle of scent lodged for a moment

the assistants he commanded were variously watering, sponging down leaves and raking out dead material in various parts of the House. His main occupation at such times was supervision since all the staff were new, in two cases being little more than casual labourers. A sign of the times indeed. Such a thing would have been unthinkable before the war. It was one more of the countless hierarchies to have been destroyed and needing laborious reinstatement, since how could there be profession without apprenticeship? Meanwhile one had to muddle by as best one might until a more rational world emerged. Like many others beyond a certain age Leon had vaguely expected things to revert to a prewar normality once hostilities had ended. That this clearly wasn't happening had left him disgruntled – reactionary, even, with a smear of naivety.

'I've just come from Dr Anselmus,' she was saying. 'He knows and approves of my intention to speak with you. You need have no fear on that score. I trust you don't mind?'

'No,' he said. 'It's just that I don't feel I can do you justice. What is there I can tell you? Everything I am is what you see here – ' he lifted his hand once more to indicate the steamy cathedral into whose silence fell the pit-pat of drops, the mutter of voices and stray clink of tools. 'And I'm ashamed of it. Truly ashamed. Almost nothing is as it should be. I can't get the right plants, I can't get the right staff, I can't get paint or my new boilers.'

'The war,' she agreed dismissively. 'Your problems are no different from anyone else's. Things will mend. Just at the moment what's inside this Palm House is not as important to me as what's inside your head. What I need is information. Perhaps I'd better explain that I'm my country's cultural attaché. You knew that already? No, well, I am. We're a poor nation though potentially very rich. We have great natural resources such as minerals and timber and tropical products so we're eager to promote links with the advanced nations which will lead to trade and development . . . Do I sound like a diplomat?' She laughed with surprising girlishness, a hand flying up briefly to cover her mouth. 'I have to make speeches, you see. "Eager to promote links." Our government's policy is to select those aspects of Western culture and technology which can enhance our own . . .'

What she really wanted was to know about stove houses. They were, she had assumed, quite a new thing, a bright idea of modern science. Leon assured her that the notion of putting plants under glass to force or protect them went back at least to Roman times when they had first learned how to cast glass in sheets. The princess seemed vague about Roman times.

'Say two thousand years ago,' he told her.

'But surely . . . ?' She looked about her and smiled blankly. It was only then he began to perceive how little idea she had of European history and, indeed, of chronology generally. With an autodidact's relentless enthusiasm he began to set her straight. Of course this Palm House wasn't Roman; it was actually built in 1860 . . .

'You keep mentioning science,' he said, 'but even that's quite recent, really, especially anything to do with plants or botany. These Botanical Gardens are only about a century older than the Palm House, you know. It wasn't until then that botany became a separate discipline. Not long ago at all. Before that, this was a physic garden full of plants for herbal medicine, which was the only kind of medicine there was. There were dozens of physic gardens all over Europe by the seventeenth century, mostly attached to the medical schools of universities. You wouldn't have found a gardener in charge of a place like this. He'd have been the professor of medicine.'

'Like Dr Anselmus, perhaps?'

'Oh, he's not a medical doctor, he's a proper botanist.

Botanists began taking over when it became a real science and the first systems of plant classification were invented. An ordinary medical doctor wouldn't have a clue about running a place like this. I'm a hangover from the past, really, since I've no formal qualification. It couldn't happen nowadays, no matter how good you were. From now on you'll need to be qualified before they'll even let you pick up a hoe. But two hundred years ago it was a completely new science which more or less coincided with the great voyages of discovery to parts of the world like your own, when they began bringing back all sorts of weird and exotic plants and animals. Weird and exotic to us, I mean. Pineapples and coconuts and things. You'll have noticed the weathervane up there? The ship? That's to symbolise how dependent all botanical gardens were on supplies from distant places. Or so I've been told,' he added.

'So that's why they built palm houses? To grow plants from hotter climates?'

'It was a mixture of reasons, things which all came together. They'd already built orangeries back in the seventeenth century so they could grow Mediterranean fruit in northern Europe and that led to the idea of greenhouses, which consisted more and more entirely of glass. Obviously the next step was to install proper heating rather than just lighting a coke brazier on frosty nights. Then the new industrial technology began coming in, especially in England: boilers and cast iron pipes and so on, and the first efficiently heated greenhouses became possible. Until then they could never have built a place like this.' As he indicated the curvilinear roof overhead ecclesiastical imagery deserted him for once and he saw the structure as the upturned hull of a huge, delicate vessel beached after its last voyage. 'They couldn't get the strength, you see. Not until they'd learned how to make ironwork of high enough quality. The central problem of glasshouse construction', explained Leon with the pleasure of a hypochondriac asked to recount his symptoms, 'is how to combine maximum light with greatest structural strength. The problem fascinated them in the early nineteenth century. They had this constant stream of tropical plants arriving and wanted to propagate them. Obviously, to grow palm trees indoors you need a pretty large building. Up until then they'd relied on wood for construction, but of course it rots in a hot damp atmosphere. It had to be either oiled teak or red cedar, and they were expensive. Now, if you have to use wood for your ribs and glazing bars they also need to be thick enough to support the weight of the glass, and the thicker they are the more light you lose. Even so, you could never build a place this size in wood. But once the English had discovered how to make light, strong structures in iron it solved the problem. You only needed quite thin supporting pillars inside, too, like those along the aisle there. And even they double as drainpipes. They aren't solid, you know.

'So now you had your structure. The other problem was the glass itself. You'd be surprised how long it took them to discover how to make sheet glass of any size. They simply couldn't make a really large pane of decent glass, and you need the best glass in a greenhouse. Any bubbles and flaws act like little magnifying lenses and burn the plants. They're also weak spots, of course. You imagine the effect of a good clout of wind on an area the size of this roof. Tons of air suddenly loaded on to tons of glass. And there's suction as well as compression, especially in those summer storms when the atmospheric pressure drops with a bang in between gusts. At that moment the pressure inside the house is much higher. If your glazing's weak it can blow out half the panes. Even if it's good glass but poorly cut, the lumpy edges can nip the glass unevenly and set up stresses which'll crack it just like that in a decent breeze.

'In those days what held up progress here, as in England,

was the tax our government used to levy on glass. The makers were taxed on the weight of glass they sold but had to charge their customers according to its area, so of course they made their sheets as thin as possible. That meant it was too weak to be made in large panes. That's why until the mid-1840s ordinary houses – and especially glasshouses – mostly had small window panes with a lot of glazing bars. When the tax was repealed the English built their Palm House at Kew Gardens outside London. You've seen it, I suppose?'

'No, I've yet to go to England.'

'I've no desire to travel,' admitted Leon, 'but I'd very much like to see their Palm House. I know it well from photographs and plans, of course. Every horticulturist in the world does. It's the greatest of them all.'

'No desire to travel?' she took him up, casually muffled. 'No curiosity? Still none?'

'I stand by what I've already said. Not on my salary. There's also a difference between being curious and being determined to go. If by magic I woke up one morning in India or Africa or your own country I should of course be interested to see things. I suppose I would on the moon, too. It's the thought of such distances I don't like. I should never be sure of coming back to the same place I'd left so long before. I mightn't recognise it quite, or it might have moved a bit so I couldn't find it again. Stupid, I suppose.'

'I'm sure there'd be ways around such problems,' she said, 'provided you had enough incentive. So tell me, how would one go about building a place like this nowadays?'

'A palm house, you mean?' He was clearly surprised. 'Oh, you wouldn't. It's an antique. It'd be like building a new Gothic cathedral. These places belong to the last century; you can't rebuild the past. What would be the point?'

'What was ever the point? Propagation, you said.'

and re-exported to Ceylon and Malaya. It virtually destroyed Brazil's rubber trade. They were ruthless, the British, like the Belgians; ruthless and inventive. At the start of this century our own King came here to these Gardens and stood in this very House to make a speech about the grand purpose of such places. He really came to see the new heating system he'd paid for. That's the system I've still got,' added Leon, 'so you can see the problem. Boilers nearly half a century old. Small wonder we limp from one crisis to another. Anyway, you've presumably noticed the plaque.'

'Plaque?'

'On the wall by the main door. That bronze thing. Needs a good clean, of course, but I haven't the men to waste on details.'

He led the way to the entrance and the princess saw that what she had always taken for a black hatchway, an access to some arcane piece of plumbing, was no mere metal panel but a commemorative inscription fixed by four magnificent bolts to the brickwork. "A National Garden," she read, "ought to be a centre for receiving stock and, in turn, for aiding the Mother Country by supplying everything that is useful in the vegetable kingdom. Medicine, commerce, agriculture, horticulture and many lucrative branches of manufacture can benefit from the adoption of such a system. Thus by care and diligence Man may multiply the riches of the Earth."

'A fine piece of mercantile and nationalist rhetoric,' he agreed, watching her face as she read. 'There you have the energy and spirit of the nineteenth century. And there you also have the end of the great era of glasshouses. The King didn't know that, presumably, but they were doomed.'

'But why?'

'Partly they fell out of fashion. Mostly because the world was changing. They may still work as living museums but they're inefficient in terms of purely scientific work. Propagation needn't involve growing palm trees to their full height. According to Dr Anselmus it was the First World War which really put an end to them. A good many glasshouses were in private hands but their owners couldn't get the coal to heat them. A magnificent one came down not far from here at Marby. It was derelict, the plants all dead. Perhaps the best of all to go was in England, the Great Conservatory at Chatsworth. That was a wonderful building, wonderful. Its central dome was two feet higher even than the Palm House at Kew. Built in 1836, a whole decade before Kew, it was full of mature palms as well as bananas and ferns and orchids and an unrivalled collection of aquatic plants. Interesting construction, incidentally. Ridge and furrow design instead of smooth walls and roof. Like magnified corduroy. It was an old idea for using all the available light as the sun changed its angle. But it needed a ton of coal a day to heat and in wartime they weren't entitled to have it. Preserving tropical flora was not a work of national importance – one of those bureaucratic phrases we've also become familiar with over the last few years. Different war, same problem. That First War, though: it ruined any pretence that there could be peaceful commercial competition between nations. All trade is war and glasshouses aren't built for wars. Anyway, the British pulled down Chatsworth Conservatory in 1920. They say men wept as they did it. Forty-eight iron pillars each weighing three tons on either side of an aisle wide enough for a carriage and pair. I wish I'd seen it before it was too late.'

She watched as he stared out through the paned doors at the snow. How very differently occidentals acted when moved by something, she thought. Instead of bursting into laughter they became quiet and deliberately reduced themselves to a kind of elegiac nakedness. Still not used to it she was slightly repelled, or at least ashamed on their behalf. This man talking about a long-defunct glasshouse might have been a child mourning its mother. It was quite unfathomably inappropriate to treat things as if they were people. Once again she saw a river choked from side to side with children's bodies, the dead puffed up in the water's face.

'But we took in several of the Chatsworth plants,' he was saying. 'That *Encephalartos* you saw me hitching up the other day is the best of them. Ah, we've got plants here from all over Europe whose original houses are gone. And now this latest war. I'm told half the great German houses are down. Bombed or starved out. Times like these, it's the civilising things which go to the wall. Gangs of children roam our cities like packs of dogs, you know. Stealing, black marketing, selling themselves to soldiers for food, living in doorways. Who'd dare to claim that keeping a lot of plants alive took precedence over feeding them? But if you look at history you'll soon see that's a false question because there are always the hungry and the homeless. The human casualties of the industrial revolution didn't for a moment stop them building places like this.'

At length she said, matter-of-factly, 'You know a lot.'

'The history? Book learning. I'm interested. If I were an engine driver I'd want to know the history of steam engines. Aren't you the same? You couldn't do your job without knowing the history of your country, I suppose?'

She didn't reply except to say, 'Well, history. What about the future? Your own? You've just described the place you work in as obsolete.'

'Only out of fashion. Not useless at all. As Loudon said, "A greenhouse is entirely a work of art." He meant artifice: that it's a matter of human ingenuity and aesthetics to create a completely artificial enclosed world. Nowadays people use the word artificial as though it always meant fake, something ungenuine, not real. What could be realer than this?'

Nearby, a man in shirtsleeves stood on a pair of steps and was sponging the undersides of a banana's broad leaves. Not twenty feet away in another world a humped flowerbed lay like a corpse beneath snow criss-crossed by the tracks of birds.

'It's just very unlikely.'

'Isn't it?' he agreed with pleasure.

'But I've been hearing things. People say a new spirit's emerging, that science and art must pay their way, that from now on places like this will have to justify the money spent on them because there are so many priorities. Food, housing, jobs, health, reconstruction everywhere. I've heard there's even an argument about the future of these Botanical Gardens because the land should belong to the city. They say it's old-fashioned and undemocratic to have a place of minority appeal taking up valuable land. They say.'

'Utter nonsense,' said Leon sharply. 'Oh, I've heard the rumours, of course' (how easy it suddenly became airily to dismiss the murmurs which, voiced by candlelight and among conspiratorial leaves, had so recently left him panicked and hollow), 'everyone's heard them. There's nothing in it, I assure you. History again, that's how I know. The whole history of city planning since the industrial revolution has been concerned with how to give people access to open spaces. Garden cities and city gardens. Parks are fundamental to cities. The Botanical Gardens aren't the city's to sell, in any case, and since this Palm House is the last of its size in the country and one of a dwindling number worldwide it's a national treasure and couldn't possibly be under threat. We're incredibly lucky to have survived the war. We're certainly going to survive peace.'

'I'm told dirty air will be an increasing problem. The glass becomes filthy and the light can't get in.'

'Of course it's a problem, especially when people use low

grade coal. But that's a matter for government legislation, a clean air act or something. Stop people making smoke within the city confines. Don't ask me,' he said with sudden dismissive vehemence. 'I'm not a bloody politician, I'm a gardener. I just want to get back to my plants.' He turned away and lifted an edge of split bark with a thumbnail, looking for pests. 'Mealy bugs,' he said in disgust. 'That's what comes of talking instead of spraying.'

The sudden change in the conversational temperature apparently left the princess at a loss. Then, as if it determined her to be undiplomatically blunt, she said:

'As I said the other day, I may be going away. A new job. Recalled home. So I'll make my offer now. Thanks to this place, and thanks mainly to you, I've decided on a grand project. I want to build a glasshouse for my own city, but I want it to be of a completely new kind. Instead of a hothouse I want a cold house. My idea is to plant all the things which can't live in the tropics – all those daffodils and little bulbs which like the snow, your soft fruits, the raspberries and redcurrants and – what are those hairy things called? – gooseberries. With the most modern refrigeration I'm told we can even make real snow. Wouldn't that be piquant? Crocuses poking out of snow inside as mangoes ripen outside? It's a . . . a delicious reversal. Real artifice, don't you think?'

His back was still turned but she saw his hands were still. His jacket's drape remained lumpily impassive but maybe (she thought of an expression in her own language) maybe ears were sprouting from his shoulder blades.

'So,' she persevered, 'I want you to come and take charge of my dream for me. Nothing will be spared in materials and labour. Everything will be put at your disposal. Architects will work to your own design if you want. You'll choose the plants, the layout, everything. The project already has our government's backing as a matter of national culture with educational and scientific significance. You can name your own salary within reason. There. Think about it and give me your answer soon. You admire this man Lyddon? Lyndon? Loudon. So now you have a chance to be Mr Loudon. I don't think,' she added softly, for one of the assistants had moved his steps closer to where they stood and was trying to unseize the worm gear controlling a system of rods which opened the clerestory louvres, 'I don't think such a future can be found indefinitely in your present position. Polymethyl methacrylate,' she said unexpectedly. 'My scientific adviser tells me it has been used with great success for aircraft windows. I think they call it "Perspex". Maybe my cold house needn't be a glasshouse at all but a thermoplastic resin house, properly up-to-date. Lighter, stronger, bigger. Fewer condensation problems. As you can see, where you've been thinking of history I've been considering the future. You and I will, of course, be working very closely.'

Absently his thumbnail resumed running up and down the flap of bark, squashing the powdery scale insects and leaving a brownish pus.

'Very closely,' she repeated. 'And I think you'll find there's less standing in your way than you'd imagine.'

When he half turned to answer her with a piercing suspicion he found she had gone. Instead, shocked, he saw Felix lounging in the doorway of No Admittance only ten or twelve feet away. There was nothing in the boy's stance of the timid night creature caught by daylight. This sudden unilateral betrayal of their secret, the casual boldness, nonplussed and frightened him as much as if he had heard the first bulldozers starting up outside. Hidden things were advancing, slightly beyond his present horizon. More immediately, the men would see, the assistants nearby. Wasn't one of them up in the clerestory with a panoramic view of the House? Arms outstretched, extending

the concealment of an imaginary cloak, he began a lurch towards Felix, a gauche shooing, at the same time hunching himself as though his own body were the boy's, willing it into invisibility. But the breath he drew to whisper a fierce command caught in its own phlegm and set off a fit of coughing which stopped him in mid-step. Pain in his chest hacked and racked while his indrawn whoops filled the House. Convulsively he pressed the insides of both arms to his rib cage, a hand glistening briefly, wet with burst pests or spittle. The familiar crazed reds and blacks filled his eyeballs as he sank to his knees at the feet of the gypsy who remained in the doorway, looking down at his fallen befriender as he rocked and fought for breath.

When at last the spasm subsided Leon slowly raised his face. His forehead was stuck with chips of gravel and his cheeks were wet with tears. Weakly he drew a sleeve across eyes and nose. Then for the first time Felix smiled. He put out a hand and helped the gardener to his feet. As he did so the princess spoke from somewhere behind Leon.

'We really must do something about your health. You're much too young to be ill. Besides, you'll be needing all your strength.'

Her footsteps crackled daintily away and at last he heard what he faintly knew he had missed hearing before: the familiar double squeak of the entrance doors closing behind her.

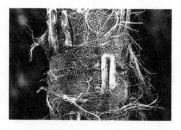

Outside, the dark day closed and drew down its snows. Once the assistants had left Leon bitterly set about preparing for his night visitors. The boldness of Felix's treason was too wounding for him to dwell on. He seemed hardly able to think coherently, aware only of a fatigued dread of sooner or later having to confront the gypsy. Bending to pick up a horned nut beneath a Strophanthus divaricatus *he was arrested to hear a monologue startlingly congenial to his own mood:*

'Our princess may be desirable but she's touchingly ignorant all the same. Did she really think this place was built by the Romans? Still, we're all foreigners here, and how much do we know of her own land? Nothing.

'Do we want to? It feels like a myth: the forests and butterflies all dreamed, so that as long as we can believe in them we go on planting and coddling and growing their counterpart here, this yearning effigy. But imagine if we actually went, the terror of the journey! Imagine if the dream began fading when we were halfway there while behind us were abandoned ruins! We should be left with nowhere to alight, like a mournful giant albatross cruising the tradewinds for ever above a wrinkled ocean.

'Why this, why that? Why can't she take us in her arms? It's all slipping away for lack of clarity. Maybe after all she has a Chinese husband. The heart's like a nut: the beginnings of a forest crammed into a shell, celestial butterflies and all. We carry it for years. Sheer loyalty. Between our fingers every other damn thing sprouts, bursting up under the constant patter of warm drops. Only the nut with its stupid clenched dream sleeps on, hardening as time passes. Once it was enough to know it was there. Suddenly there's wrecking in the air and now it all feels too long ago to help, too private for such public events.

'We ought to break her. We ought to give her something she won't forget. Going away, is she? They all do. One after

another, they go. What's that if it isn't betrayal? If it's not being continually abandoned? All that Paris scent and gliding around in furs. Actually, we wouldn't mind just once seeing her face pushed into the mould, her lovely nose forced to breathe peat dust. Not revenge but justice. And what, instead, do we give her? Lectures. Lectures! The first resort of the self-taught, the last resort of the lame.'

NINE

The passive, the windguided who – like Leon – move at a
slow drift through whole clutches of years are most likely to
fake up, retrospectively, a narrative to cover themselves with
spurious intent. The career landmarks of *And then . . . And then*
don't adequately describe their lives. Had Leon been obliged
to look back over his thirty-three years and describe their course,
there might only have come to him the moods associated with
certain events if not the events themselves: whatever indelible
indigo had welled out of endless wanderings along a solitary
shore, constant planting to see what might grow, his head all the
time coming up and his eyes fixing on nothing as thought walked
away from him down a familiar corridor and he unresistingly
followed. What might characterise such repetitions? Neither
a hunt nor a chase, maybe: more methodical than the one,
in slower motion than the other and altogether less gallant
than a quest. And the object sought, the ostensible Cou Min
so often summoned? How could she not suffer a marvellous
fate, a transformation like that a sapphire undergoes when it
emerges from the ground looking for all the world like a dull
chunk of gravel but which, trundled round and round in a tub,
loses its irregularities and becomes smooth, taking on lustre and
its own colour? Finally the craftsman cuts and polishes until a

gem sits on a piece of velvet, the diminished but sublime ghost of its crude ancestor.

When Leon thought of Cou Min, as he frequently did, it was the jewel he mostly saw, a hallowed thing made smooth by constant handling. Very occasionally she ambushed him in a raw manner of her own, provoking a jarring discontinuity. At those moments her figure sidestepped the tragic tameness he had assigned her as if his great passion had happened to another person entirely, or maybe to the same person but in a different life. Even eighteen years later a trap could still spring and drop him out of the diurnal world of stove house gardening into a melancholy pit. It happened one day when he was sowing five trays of assorted spices, three of which he planned to turn over to a colleague for raising in the Temperate House. The cumin seeds' dry rattle in their packet, the fleeting image of a live organism encapsulated in a husk ready to be awakened, the play of names which could mean nothing to any but one man, precipitated that man through a hole where he was caught and held a long moment, seeing another world and another time, his deserted hands frozen above a tray of leaf mould. Now and then he yearned to be free of her, to slough off her memory and escape. More often he adored her abiding centrality: the unseen attractor around which his life could revolve. It is some people's luck to find a way of remaining true to their first passion, a hidden faithfulness which survives, that endures even happy marriage to a stranger and a lifetime's displaced love. There are others who, having survived the scald, can never put it out of their minds and are forbidden all compromise. Like anyone they may be plastic in their daily affections, opportunist in their desires, but they grip at their heart something which renders all else casual, temporary, unreal; and sooner or later – in the nick of time or, painfully, not – it surfaces like a deep-sea creature and lovers break up and marriages are annulled. Leon's case was simple: better no-one than not-her, a proposition that extended itself into a more general idea which ruled his days, that Nothing was preferable to anything on the wrong terms.

Thus the windguided, the passive man: who neither hunts nor chases but maybe searches in the patient doleful manner of one hoping he will recognise what he was always looking for if ever by chance he were to find it.

The evening of his uneasy conversation with the princess and of Felix's melodramatic self-revelation dragged interminably. For the first time he saw the night people as intruders and wished they would leave him to his House and plants, to his provocative lodger on the other side of No Admittance. He thrice confiscated the chargé's cigarette, eliciting, with his claimed need for nicotine as a pesticide, a dandyish and acerbic 'Oh nonsense. My dear sir, it piques you to be punitive. Terribly exciting in its way but if you really wanted nicotine so much then instead of gathering it in tiny amounts – one slapped wrist at a time, as it were – you could surely have grown tobacco by the bushel. You could grow anything in here. Opium. Hashish. Babies, probably, if you knew how to sow them.' Laughter, not all of it easy. In darkest manner Leon informed him that until the war the Customs and Excise people used to give the Gardens regular bales of impounded tobacco for burning in fumigators. It was the war which had upset the supply. Furthermore, it was as much as his job was worth to be caught growing illicit or dutiable plants in any but specimen quantities. This ponderousness raised a wilted eyebrow but no riposte. Eventually the door gave its last squeak and he shot home the bolts even while the yellow candlelight still showed a hunched back skidding away beyond the windows along the glassy path. The man fell heavily but he didn't reopen the door, listening instead to the sounds of friends rallying around. The stray beams of their torchlight outside pattered randomly across

the tropics within. Soon these too disappeared and he was left to do his ritual nightly round.

Something is happening to me, he told his plants as the candle-tongues sizzled between his licked fingers. I see now what I've made of this life, this one flash of light on a black sea catching me for an instant before it sweeps on for ever. All my passion's in vain. I've never discovered what a satisfactory outcome would have been. To be loved in return as the rock loves the limpet for needing it? Dumb sucking? No; surely my purpose is altogether grander? Down on Palace Square (he told the night-flowering climber, *Nyctanthes arbor-tristis*) there's a clockmaker – or there was, before the Nazis took him away and stole his stock – who made beautiful brass clocks. You could watch their works, how the little wheels whizzed and clicked. Instead of putting windows in the sides of the cases he used to place a glass bubble over the entire skeleton. At once this produced a different effect. It became a display. No more of the mechanism was actually visible but it set the whole clock apart as a self-contained world so that passers-by outside the shop window could reflect on it and be reflected in it. That's also why the instruments in the Royal Science Museum are so fine. One way and another they're all behind glass, either individually cased like clocks or together in cabinets: isolated, held up as examples of pure function which itself reveals the designer, the maker, the mind. Are the laws of physics universal? I sometimes ask the scientists who visit this House but they can't agree, apparently, though most seem to think they must be. Look at a working clock beneath its glass dome, then, and you're seeing a fragment of the universe, motion and energy and energy's decay . . . Before they took him away they smashed his hands with their rifle butts. It pays to make sausages and shut up. The light sweeps on and never returns.

Are you still listening? In my Palm House we're inside

the clock itself, watching the growth, feeling the affection of living, sniffing the decay. I can't imagine why some people remain unmoved, but most respond. Even those who scarcely notice plants when they're outside in the open air will pay attention once they're enclosed in glass and properly arranged. It's remarkable. Some things only become visible if you put glass over them, and the more ordinary they are the more this is true. What visitors see in here is the universe on display, the Earth's history and their own evanescence, and they know it.

But (he stroked *Nyctanthes*' leaves) something is happening to me. Now and then I lose sight of the universe and just see myself, a freak displayed like a specimen in this marvellous bottle. Now and then I know what the palms feel as they press their fronds up against the inside of the dome. I must break out if it kills me. But how? The obvious thing's to accept her offer. Follow the princess to her fabulous land. Become her tame expert. Design a world for her where I could strut and cough in the artificial chill among beds of narcissi. My bank balance would grow with the crocuses, the snowdrops, the winter aconites like ruffed buttercups, the pear trees, the little grove of sallows I'd like to plant at the centre. If I were homesick I could construct a seascape in one corner – no expense spared, didn't she say? – and try to get rock samphire, sea holly, thrift and spurrey to grow. And meanwhile she . . . ? Would I become her servant, once on her own home ground? Her confidant? Her teacher? Lackey and lover? Or just lackey?

Nyctanthes arbor-tristis replied not a word. In the semi-dark Leon could hear only the dripping of water and his heart valves' creak. Really, candlelight was the perfect illumination for a palm house. It was a surprise that enough light drifted upwards to sketch faintly the structure's outlines: the cast iron spiral staircase which twirled its lacy texture of holes and patterns towards the gallery in steps and risers and balustrade, the arching ribs far overhead on the edge of visibility between plumes and fronds and feathers. Warmth seeped up his trouserlegs from the gratings underfoot. This was his home, there could be no doubt. Anyone might wish for a home both benign and mysterious which comforted and sustained even as it enclosed a tendril of the raw universe.

I don't want to see the real tropics – he confided to *Nyctanthes*.

How could one be rational when there was a suggestion of bulldozers and treason in the air? Dr Anselmus had never been other than a staunch ally who, Leon recognised, had championed him practically from his start as apprentice glazier. What could he be talking about with the princess? Of course it was true that, finally, Dr Claud Anselmus was Director and Leon was an employee, and directors and princesses could consort and chat and plan together where directors and employees could only exchange quite formal, technical opinions even though they had known each other sixteen years. That was how things were. But he made a vague, timorous resolution to have the matter out as soon as he could. Didn't he have his own plans on the Society's behalf? Wasn't his Palm House becoming a popular attraction instead of the uneasy and virtuous cross between fossil and museum which it had been before the war?

Just then his attention was caught by a movement above him, framed by the banyan's aerial roots. He froze, the candle he had snuffed sending up its greasy wisp of expiry between his fingers. Nothing moves in here, he thought. Only at the height of summer with all the louvres open do the larger leaves begin their wobble and single fronds whir like lone propellers. Tonight the windows were tightly shut, the muggy air unmoving. A sudden shower of drops clattered through the long leaves of a fishtail palm. Had a darker shape momentarily swung along the deep grey roof, up there where snow muffled such light as was reflected from the clouds above the city? Although capable of rash acts of passion which might pass for bravery Leon had preserved much of his childhood timidity. Not afraid of the dark as such, in certain moods he was apprehensive about his own capacity to frighten himself. Now the lacquer of competence and authority, which the night visitors always applied to him in a shiny coat with their questions and banter, swiftly thinned to nothing and dripped away like sweat. Was it perhaps one of those same night people who had purposely hidden so as to be locked in? And with what stealthy design? The war with its street gangs and inventive brutalities was still too recent for survivors not to remain fearful out of sheer habit. He stayed, therefore, breathing as shallowly and quietly as lungs and chirruping heart would allow. A scuff of sound, a hiss as if skin were sidling through leaves reached him now from all parts of the House. Even acoustics conspired to deceive.

'I know you're there,' he remarked, courageously offhand.

Silence. He hardly knew which to fear more: the arrested moment continuing indefinitely or a sudden blaze of electric light and roisterous cries of 'April Fool!' or similar joviality as a band of pranksters leaped out around him and burst into laughter. As the silence lengthened he began to have wilder thoughts. Some animal – a monkey, perhaps? A *panther*? – had escaped from the nearby zoo and homed in on this only other possible habitat. He had recently heard they were restocking the place with animals collected from wrecked German zoos. 'Indefinite temporary loan' was how the newspapers described it. There was also the shipment of plants he had ordered in 1939 and which had arrived just that afternoon. There were three of them, crated and swaddled in sacking for their long journey from Polynesia, and he'd only had time to unwrap the *Gnetum*. This was because Professor Seneschal had capered and dithered around it since like the conifers and cycads it was classed as a gymnosperm and so was apparently irresistible to the old idiot. But the other two

– the *Pandanus odoratissimus* and the *Pritchardia pacifica* were still unwrapped. Why mightn't some snake or sinister monitor have awakened in the crates and even now be sliding its way towards him?

Without a sound the remaining few candles began going out. They did so in no obvious order and he was always too late to focus on whatever it was that extinguished them. All except the last, of course, which he watched with fascination as though his feet were clamped to the grating beneath. Much later he realised how easy it would have been to distract his attention from this last candle: a handful of gravel thrown a second before its flame could reveal the face. Instead he watched a bare arm emerge from the greenery, hand cupped like a cobra's hood. It struck, and all was dark. And in that moment Leon knew the arm even as he couldn't guess the purpose.

'Felix!' he called. 'What is it? What are you up to?' His words fell like pebbles. 'Is this a game?' When the question had echoed in his own skull long enough to irritate him he at last moved, impatient with further hiding. He walked back down the aisle to where the main light switches were. He felt for the teak box screwed to the end wall, opened it and smacked his palm down over the rows of toggles. Contacts clicked, relays closed, the dark remained. Had Felix, then, removed the fuses? These were in a similar box inside his own quarters. At that moment something struck him lightly on the shoulder blade and fell to the gravel. He turned and crouched in the faint monochrome, patting the ground until he found the missile: a round object the size of a golf ball, an unripe seed pod he could not immediately identify.

'No, Felix,' he sternly told the hot spaces before him. 'Stop that! It's gone beyond a joke. Not the plants.' A second object struck No Admittance with a hollow knock. 'Did you hear what I said, boy? Have you gone mad?' But again his own bluster burned in his ears and enraged him with its impotence.

He walked along the aisle to the point from which he judged the missiles had been thrown. It was hopeless to be moving into deep bulks flawed by only the dimmest mercuric sheen of snowlight, sensing that they closed behind him once he had passed. Leon, who knew every inch of his domain, soon passed into unknown territory. Never before had he been so aware of the heat, pressing and yielding and dripping as though by merely leaning his body against it, moving into its illusory resistance, he could squeeze actual water from the air. He shed his jacket, suddenly heavy and sodden, then his galoshes. Now in silence he squatted beside a tall shrub and again caught movement above him where none should have been. Felix was up on the clerestory walkway.

Hoping to cut him off he made his way at a silent semi-crouch along the track to where the spiral staircase rushed upwards on wings of iron. His naked feet doing likewise he found himself in the jungle's canopy, wheezing, heart clicking in his throat. Now his prey was surely trapped, for although this main landing crossed the House and linked the two clerestories there was no corresponding gallery at the other end. There had, he knew, been architect's plans for one but for some reason it had never been built, perhaps further evidence of the builders' ambivalence about the place's true function. Church or glasshouse? Temple of nature, maybe. At any rate only three sides of the rectangle remained viable upstairs. Down one of these the temple's presiding spirit, the master gardener, now pursued his quarry, his rogue secret, hoping to suppress, capture, stifle it before it could escape. From the faint signs of movement at the far end of this narrow walkway he knew his stratagem was working. Felix was cornered now, up under the curved panes. Unless he tried a suicidal climb across one of the spans to the other side there was no way down. At which moment the dim snowlight fell with muffled gleam on a torso, washed in the smouldering chemicals of panic and desire, before it sprang outwards with simian carelessness. Instead of the expected sound of a body hitting a plinth thirty feet below the pursuer heard only a sharp swish of leaves and the creak of wood bending.

This savage, accomplished leap at once bridged the gap between Leon's knowing and refusing minds. Just as only an agile climber could have severed the banana's flower, so only Felix could have judged and made that jump into space. He must have had bad luck indeed to fall into the hands of a dismal gang of street louts. His splendid litheness had been caught unawares, probably dog tired and asleep in a doorway. Only in this way could so skilled an animal have been dragged down by an urban pack. Now he was loose and roaming the dark spaces below, pupils dilated to full night vision. But what was his plan, his purpose? To mock? To tantalise? What imaginary grim crime could this fond vandal be repaying? Leon, who had retraced his steps, stood uncertainly at the head of the winding stairs. Suddenly the forest at his feet contained real menace. Too much was opaque. He remembered the cleanness of the cuts in the flower stalk and tree bark. A very sharp knife precisely wielded. He knew nothing of madness except being able to assign it conventionally to unkempt souls who gibbered in public places (and who had largely disappeared under the German occupation). He wondered whether Felix might genuinely have taken leave of his senses. The boy had made a remarkable recovery from his injury and in the months since had been docile and tractable. Affectionate, he thought; of course Felix was affectionate. They had shared too much, too much sacrifice and fear and mutual indebtedness for there not to be affection. And hardly a firelit night had passed without the boy's wordless accommodation. But were there not things more important than words? Dumb of mouth didn't mean dumb of gesture, still less of brain. Without speaking a syllable Felix had mastered the heating system's idiosyncrasies. He was no prisoner, either. Had he wished to leave he could have walked out at any time since the war's ending. So what was happening now?

Such novelistic representations of a pondering mind did not, of course, enter Leon's, though all were more or less thoughts he hadn't put into words at one time or another. He did, however, stand in indecision, fearful of going down. The heat was extraordinary. Surely the temperature was too high? The ironwork was hot to the touch, slick with moisture. The pattering of drops was a light shower passing over a forest, lost and primordial and extending far into the distance. He was aware of these events' sheer wrongness. The botanical world was holding itself apart from the crude human plots and motives being played out among its trunks and leaves. It was retreating. '*Shuuuff*,' sighed the gardener without knowing it, but no charm worked. He was left with no alternative but to go down, to play out this doltish piece of theatre.

'We're stopping this at once, Felix,' he said as he descended, speaking conversationally down into the threatening arena. He had just decided that light was the most important thing. Playing cat and mouse in the dark with a demented street arab was absurd. How could he, a man of his professional standing, have been drawn into this game even for an instant? He should have gone straight to the fuse box where he kept a torch. He would now do just that, relying on the armour of rational behaviour to get him along the aisle of the Palm House – *his* Palm House – and through No Admittance. After all, Felix wasn't chasing him, and of course was being mischievous rather than murderous. Purposefully he stepped to the ground and walked back along the aisle, making no particular attempt to watch or listen. Reaching the door he found, with the sense of having known in advance had he only been able to put the thought together, that it was locked.

Reduced once more to bluster he rattled the handle angrily. 'Damn you, Felix! Come on, open up. I know you're in there.' But by the steady pattering at his back, by the chirp and murmur of unseeable things, the vacant bark of his own voice, he knew there was nobody in the rooms beyond and that just now they were part of another universe. On the far side of the door lay a utilitarian realm of sinks and cupboards and boilers. It was in the world behind him that an outcome awaited. (Somewhere just out of sight and at some other intersection of time two figures stalked each other through a dream forest, two animals in human guise driven out of their wits by hunger or hatred or pure inaction. Whatever was in their hearts tugged at each other with the power of a moon's gravitational pull. Wordless, blind, and irresistibly attractive, it turned them into archetypes or candidates for war.)

Absently Leon undid his belt and stepped out of his fatigue trousers, shed his underwear and stood naked in the tropical heat. Then he walked quickly to the place where he kept his spraygun and a few tools, including a couple of old but well honed pruning knives. The syringe was there, as were the hank of raffia and the jar of cigarette ends, but his stealthy hand could find only one of the knives. He tried to remember when he had last seen both together. The assistants were always using them, dabbing them down on ledges where they worked and forgetting to bring them back. One could have been missing for a week without his noticing – since before *Myroxylon*'s bark was cut, in fact. How often must Felix have got up in the night to stoke the boiler, waited until Leon had gone back to sleep and then prowled the leafy sanctuary beyond the wall, learning where everything was, planning this very event? No; that was surely too intentional, too contrived and silly . . . Nevertheless, he hid the remaining knife and as an afterthought wrapped a yard or two of raffia about his own waist. Thus clad he stepped forth, unarmed but robed in the full majesty of the jungle.

Far away it was snowing again on the sleeping city so that before first light next morning the early trams all over northern Europe would moan softly across unbroken sheets on invisible rails like icebreakers opening paths across the Barents Sea. The Palm House had meanwhile fallen out of this continuity, or had floated free of it. Trapped in their bubble, this gigantic Wardian case, drenched in heat and breathing the humid stew of molecules – foetor of gums and mulch, resins and mould – Leon and Felix stalked one another. Each had his particular advantage: Felix a youth's agility and night vision, Leon his wiriness and peculiar memory for sound. The boy who had once distinguished between the noise made by wind through marram grass or samphire was the gardener who could make inspired guesses in the dark as to whether the sibilance from near the staircase was that of a body pushing past sugar canes or pandans. Though the night sky was uniformly clouded the available light did vary slightly from one part of the House to the other. Like many glasshouses built in these latitudes it had been oriented roughly along a north-south axis to take advantage of both morning and afternoon light. Accordingly the western transept felt the day's last warmth and was also slightly protected from northeasterly winds. Here the panes were freer of ice along their lowest sections, admitting more of the snowy gardens' dim blanch. So it was that Leon, moving towards the screwpines, caught his first full sight of Felix. He was standing at the edge of a path with his back three-quarters turned to his pursuer in an oddly meditative posture, head bowed, arms loose at his sides. It took the gardener a long moment to perceive that Felix, too, was naked. Just then the outline of the downcast face, slender figure and inky fall of hair froze Leon with something he could not name. Trying to imagine what that sidelong musing might be seeing he thought of the water tank into which the visitor's child had recently fallen. He stared and stared in its direction to make out the least gleam of reflection and without seeing anything but darkness and more darkness. When he looked back at Felix there was only the crabby silhouette of *Encephalartos*. The boy had melted away, taking with him the impression of having been holding something desolate in his head as well as an object in one hand. A pruning knife, maybe.

So when a weight crashed on to his back, knocking him to the gravel, flailing the outside of one forearm against a brick plinth and numbing all the nerves in that hand, his first impression was that the boy had an accomplice or had split into two. For an instant he lay beneath the slippery weight and felt a peculiar rasping at the back of his skull. Then suddenly the weight was off him, there was a skitter of gravel, the wocking sound of a large leaf wobbling about its midrib, then silence. This strange attack brought on a mild bout of coughing as the gardener was climbing to his feet, but whether by means of fear or the vitalising damp heat he controlled it. The uncanniness of Felix's assault had shaken him quite as much as his impact with the ground. As he rubbed sensation back into his hand he wondered if the boy had really seen him reflected, however dimly, in the tank. In any case it was inventive and quite easy for him, once alerted, to have gone around the central stand of palms and come up behind.

Following an aural lead back to the bo tree Leon had his head abruptly grabbed, quickly noosed under the chin and drawn upwards so that he rose reflexively on tiptoe. Simultaneously he felt again that rasping sensation at his skull, in a different quarter this time, before the noose slackened and he stumbled involuntarily to a crouch. A light thud on the far side of the pipal marked Felix's departure from the tree. The tickling at Leon's neck was a loose length of raffia draped about his shoulders. He felt at his waist. No raffia there now. Evidently Felix had taken it during his first attack and had just used it to try to strangle him. Yet that made no sense because the boy had let go almost at once, immediately after that odd tugging and grating. He put up a hand and felt his skull. Great lumps of hair were missing. He ran both hands anxiously over his head. There was no mistake: ragged hanks had been shorn off the back and one side.

Leon's impatience with other people's physical vanity had always allowed him to be nonchalantly smug about his own hair which was, admittedly, unusual. Though unmistakably Nordic it was not a pale, flaxen blond but somewhat yellow – *golden* he might have preferred it called – as yet unmarred by a single grey hair. It flapped atop his tallish, gauntish frame in a distinctive manner, as well he knew. Its despoliation was upsetting and unnerving, a precise attack on a vulnerability he only now fully acknowledged. He moved nervously away from the *Ficus religiosa* through the leaves' long drip tips which brushed his face. He must keep moving; this was no place for idle meditation. He wasn't safe beneath any shrub which could support the gypsy's slight weight. Time passed. Heart sighing, he prowled uneasily, now and then fumbling at his head in dismay.

That he finally caught Felix was largely due to the boy's bad luck or ignorance. A sound had brought the gardener back to the general area of the first attack and, watching, he saw small repeated movements in the same patch of shrubbery. He smiled then, an excited, rat-catcher's smile. The boy had somehow blundered or dropped into a thick growth of *Acacia farnesiana*. Barefoot and barelimbed among its thorns he must now take each step with tentative, slow-motion care while crouching to disengage those spines already embedded. Oh, the cassia flower was a nasty one, all right. It grew all over Indo-Pacific littorals in dense mats high up the beach, the creepers of bushes which tangled into thickets against cliff faces (or so the book said). Even as he stole forward Leon thought off at a tangent, wondering whether the more excruciating counterpart of an emblematic crown of thorns might not be slippers of thorn. Reaching out a long bony arm from behind an adjacent bush he enlaced a handful of the preoccupied youth's own black tresses and yanked him out on to the path. He heard Felix gasp as his stumbling feet trod full weight on to the long spikes, adding to his own exultation. Vandal, mutilator, ingrate . . . Thief? That snouted dog-face, that scum gang leader (now a respectable bemedalled bureaucrat) had accused Felix of stealing, but Leon had never believed in the charge as anything other than metaphorical. Supposing the gypsy had made himself vulnerable, not by being caught asleep but by some imprudent proposition, some desperate suggestion? Supposing further that dog-face had agreed and then in order to swagger away with his pride intact had trumped up the charge of robbery for his cronies' ears? More still, mightn't that add a new, private twist to the idea of stealing from the gypsy ('let's nick his jewels')? Wasn't Leon (as he wrestled on the path with the squirming boy) really dealing with a common prostitute, street trash such as even now ought to be hanging around the occupying forces' barracks and pawing hungrily through the refuse barrels of mess and canteen? But Leon no longer knew what to think, lacked the time and spare energy to do anything but weigh his captive towards the ground at a brisk stagger, finally tripping him into a plunge half in and half out of the water tank, then all the way in.

At which Felix's struggles became galvanic with a non-swimmer's terror, interspersed with whooshes of air and water coughs. Leon was struck by how cold it was by comparison with the ambient heat, but it was after all groundwater and reached the

Palm House from the freezing universe outside. Still grasping the handful of gypsy hair he smacked the face repeatedly into the surface until Felix's struggles became weaker, then paused in his fury.

Kill or kiss? These are not human decisions when taken naked in a heated glasshouse in a delusory tropic beneath snow and in the aftermath of war. They are no longer even true alternatives for comrades in a shared prison. Strange indeed the land in which these comrades tracked each other to perform their spiteful acts of love, where playfulness might elide into murder without once leaving the same trancelike register and crossing no border on the way. It was then that half-starved Leon's strength became effortless and cost him not a cough to haul the cold eel beneath his hands bodily out of the tank and cradle it in his arms amid the plants' silence, in the heavy perfumed dark, while the slopping ripples died, leaving two thudding hearts. He walked with his burden to the newly turned earth at the foot of the tallest palm, *Cocos nucifera*, laid it on the ground and stroked the water from its quaking back. Then, drenched in the scent of flowers he himself had sown, for the last time he vented his muddled love into Felix in an act which was indeed the last thing he should have done and for which, having done, he leaned his brow upon the trembling nape and weeping begged forgiveness. Later, and for the rest of that night, no drops fell more heavily from the Palm House roof on to the waxy leaves beneath than those the repentant gardener shed by the boilers' hellish glow.

At dawn Leon went into the House to retrieve the hanks of his hair and smooth the soil at the coconut's foot before the first of the labourers arrived. As he raked over the mould his ears burned with guilt to hear the tree – evidently similarly unrested – let fall its sardonic remarks from on high:

'An intolerable night, quite intolerable, and culminating in a spectacle which prompted the thought that if one knew enough about it one would probably be disgusted. True of most things, no doubt. As it was, there was quite enough disturbance going on to make one positively cross. It's bad enough anyway to stand with one's head stuffed up into a glass cupola so that year by year the crick in one's neck grows worse. But to be deprived of sleep into the bargain by hubbub and commotion simply won't do at all. The militaristic excesses taking place outside this House until recently – of which I had, perforce, a grandstand (not to say perilously exposed) view – seem now to have been transferred indoors. This new, harebrained scheme of our gardener's to allow members of the public in here after dark is simply not on. We're not creatures in a zoo but a tender community which needs its peace and quiet. The dismal lindens and planes I can spy from up here lining the nearby avenue are presumably adapted to non-stop traffic noise night and day. They are low breeds with but rudimentary nerves. We are mostly not.

'In particular one can't imagine what our gardener thought he was doing tonight. They come and go, these people, becoming odder all the time. It was different in the old days. The one who planted me – Brunswik, did they call him? – was here until I was mature. He became old or sick or something and according to a conversation I overheard in 1913 they put him on a bonfire. Alas, poor Brunswik; we shall all come to it. But in the meantime one is disinclined to be hurried into an early grave by increasingly bad behaviour on the part of the very people who ought to be looking after us. What are they after all if not servants? There's been a good deal of rot talked since the turn of the century about egalitarianism, which as any fool knows is the thin edge of complete anarchy. It's pure drooling lunacy to pretend that all men are equal, just as it would be to claim all trees were equal. Certainly none of the trees in *this* House believes that. Under normal circumstances one would be only too happy to leave that sort of jejune ideological wrangling to the human element, but unfortunately it affects us too. Egalitarianism leads directly to hooliganism, as tonight's spectacle shows. It's precisely what happens when natural hierarchies are allowed to break down.

'I suppose if one is sixty feet tall disdain does come easily, but what is one to think when such things take place at one's very foot? Our gardener appeared to be wrestling with that strange child who is alleged to creep about in the dead of night committing unprovoked attacks on members of this House with a horrible little knife. One's first thought was that the gardener was inflicting some sort of punishment on him, though it's unclear why they both felt obliged to take their clothes off. Apparently humans need to climb on top of each other in order to punish, and the gardener was pulling this other chappie's head back by the hair so he was staring straight up at me. His eyes and mouth kept opening and closing and after a while it struck me as more a matter of enjoyment than punishment. But of course one never really has a clue about these creatures' facial expressions. They seem to register pleasure and agony in pretty much identical fashion. Maybe they're isomorphic forms of each other? It might be quite interesting to do a bit of speculative research on this: *Homo sapiens sapiens* is so inscrutable it might repay us to try and fathom him. At any rate these two worked themselves into a terrible state, completely wet and howling, all smeared with earth and whatnot. At last they went away, leaving me with the distinct impression that the man was sorry for having punished the boy. One simply can't imagine what goes on in these people's heads, it's so messy and unclear. In any case we all hope the little vandal learned his lesson.

'Enough of these creatures. That envious and acrimonious old cycad, *altensteinii*, has recently put himself in the position of deserving a sharp retort. One might overlook some of his remarks about palm trees just as one physically overlooks his frowsty head and obscene professorial neck – gnarled and twisted as it is and needing the support of a collar and wire. The name "*Encephalartos*", of course, derives from the Greek and means "bread-brain" – as unappetising a prospect as one can imagine. Certainly one is scarcely prompted to take sides on the question of his ancestry. That may safely be left to him and Seneschal with their conflicting theories of genetics, Mendelism, racial purity *et al.* As to whether he might, in another universe, have become either palm or pine remains a matter of indifference rather than debate. Speaking as a palm of not inconsiderable pedigree I'm happy to say I can see no remotest family resemblance – certainly not to *my* family, who unquestionably run to height and can hold their heads up without recourse to prostheses. No, all that claptrap can be sidestepped as just one more of those areas which attract lunatics as a flower bees: a mishmash of pseudophilosophy and pseudoscience which brings out the Professor Seneschals with their trunk calipers, their leaf gauges and their dotty botanometry. They're all as mad as each other. Linnaeus, de Candolle, George Bentham, Joseph Hooker . . . The presumption of these people! All ordering and reordering what they call Nature (note the capital) according to their own pet theories, with none of them the first idea. Humans! One despairs.

'The point lies elsewhere: to begin with, in *altensteinii*'s

189

allegation of what he calls our "crude height" having led to a "Master Race complex". It is indeed a small mind which resorts to such *ad plantam* logic and then attempts to back it up by appeals to some kind of notional popular vote. "Anyone in this House would readily agree with this opinion." If this is what longevity does to the intelligence one prays to die in one's prime. Besides, who wants to be popular? The very word betrays its egalitarian allure. One's interested in *thought*, not in worrying endlessly about being liked. Second, and far more important, is the issue of those tendentious quotations about how *Homo* turned coconut palms into objects of veneration – our supposed physical commonality with men's bodies, the deities living in our heads and so forth. All these quotations, incidentally, were cribbed straight out of the gardener's memory. *Altensteinii* never opened a book in his life. "Volume twenty-five, I fancy." What a hoary old schoolboy ploy that is! None the less there's ingenuity in the way he selected those particular passages. At first sight it might appear he was attacking *Homo* for what is, admittedly, preposterous and anthropocentric drivel. Gods in the hair, mystical emblems, men's whole abject desire to discern tokens of themselves as well as pledges of their own immortality in every damn thing they lay their eyes on. Why aren't they interested in anything other than themselves and their own deaths? It's most peculiar. *Altensteinii* appears to cite this stuff to make the same point about *Homo*'s foolishness but a second reading reveals his hidden argument, which is profoundly anti-palm. All that piousness about our noble bearing is undercut the moment one remembers that this is merely *man*'s opinion and manifestly not that of old *altensteinii*. Moreover, by his quoting a list of the ways in which we are useful to man we palms find ourselves in the patronised position of the servant whose services are suddenly discovered to be indispensable and is thereby accorded the status of holy fool.

'If it were harder to expose, *altensteinii*'s method might be described as cunning. Having bared it and left it where it lies, however, one draws oneself up with this noble loftiness for which we're apparently so renowned and turns one's gaze outward through the steam-blinded glass to speculate about more interesting things. The truth is that I'm a critic at heart, a didact, a lecturer, and it has taken me all this time to cultivate my skill. One more thing to guarantee my unpopularity.

'Dawn has broken over a landscape which in my heart I know to be utterly foreign. That's of no account; one's used to it while becoming ever more apprehensive of the moment when one's head bursts through the glass and out. Into what? That's the main preoccupation: trying to decide the nature of the world we're in as well as that of the world exterior to it. The first logically presupposes the second, but that isn't to say there might not be an infinite number of worlds out there. I can, for instance, easily see how the House could itself be subdivided by enclosing diminishing patches of soil under smaller and smaller glass shells. Indeed I can remember seeing just such a cloche arrangement used years ago to protect seedlings temporarily from the nicotine fumigations. But this raises a disturbing idea, which is that as one was able to look down at the seedlings under glass, taller than they by a factor of thousands, so it's possible to suppose a palm many tens of miles high beneath a roof enclosing half the sky looking down on oneself at this very moment. It's not a reassuring thought and leaves one's position equivocal, to say the least. Nevertheless it could be so, and the mere fact that I can conceive but not perceive it is no hindrance to its possibility. All perceptions – and notoriously vision – are easily deceived, as dependent on learned habits and expectation as on neural activity. I don't expect to see a greater universe *itself enclosed* enclosing mine, therefore I don't see it. I see only what convention tells me is the sky, dotted with points of light,

larger and smaller, brighter and fainter. "I don't much want to see the real tropics," I heard the gardener tell *Nyctanthes* only last night. But what *are* the real tropics, mister gardener? And where, if not at least partly rooted in Flinn? These exotic ladies of yours: where are they really from? Exactly. And knowing that, of course you don't want to follow the bird of paradise to its nest and find a heap of twigs and shit.

'Such metaphysical speculations are not to everybody's taste, of course, and evidently beyond the capacity of most things in this House. (One notices *altensteinii*'s head hanging a little lower this morning, does one not? Or is it pure illusion? So much is.) But tug on the wire, gardener! Hoist the poor old thing up! He can manage a little higher even though he'll never make sixty feet and stand on equal footing beside – what were his phrases? – "a mere cliché of the exotic" and "a symbol of longing". Thus spake *Encephalartos*!'

TEN

To his chagrin Leon was obliged to have the rest of his hair cut to match the missing chunks, which meant a style little different from that of a concentration camp survivor. He left the barber's shop as though wrenched out of civilian life and back into a wartime world when half male Europe had its head shaved for convenience, discipline, lice. The angry shock gave him a confidence close to insubordination. Going back to the Botanical Gardens' main gate office he said he must see Dr Anselmus at once. The secretary raised her eyes from a romance with a look of amazement as if she hardly recognised him, which further enraged him.

'Doesn't come in Thursdays, does he?'

Since the enforced shutting up of the Society's mansion, which until the war had furnished graceful offices for the Gardens' director as well as for senior research fellows and administrators, Dr Anselmus had been obliged to work from home.

'It can't wait.'

'It'll have to. You can see him first thing tomorrow.' The secretary, whose own hair had dulled over the years to a carefully supported heap of smouldering embers, gave his skull another look.

Normally Leon enjoyed sparring with the Dragon Lady, as she was now universally known, but today he was too pressed and savage to dally. 'I'll just have to find him at home, then, shan't I?'

'Gee, sure,' said the Dragon Lady, who was seeing American films and G.I.s with equal enthusiasm. 'Why not, sugar? And when you've seen him you can stop by the Palace and have a chat with the King about his begonias. You might get a royal warrant. "Consultant plant doctor to the crowned heads of." Gee.' She waved a glittering hand. 'Tomorrow.'

Leon went for a walk beside a canal. Though indifferent to clothes he had changed out of his military remnants into the suit he kept for whenever he left the Gardens. Not a fancy affair, it was lumpy at the seams, especially around the edge of collar and lapels: the sort of suit an upholsterer might have run up for himself in hard times. What with that and the haircut he looked fairly indistinguishable from the demobbed soldiers wandering the city trying to find a door which would let them back into normality. The only difference was that he was older than most and not wearing a military greatcoat hopefully dyed to look like an overcoat. The curator of one of Europe's most important surviving palm houses – genius, philosopher, communer with plants, visible companion of an invisible – wore against the cold a plaid ulster, a truly Sherlockian affair which a visitor in 1938 had shed in the heat and, bafflingly, never retrieved. Finders keepers, Leon had said proudly after a decent month's interval. He had inherited in one pocket some small change and in the other a pair of orange pigskin gloves and a brand new mousetrap. Now, his head roaring with thought, he stood on a quay and gazed down at a family of kittens investigating the snow on their barge's deck. With his cropped scalp, ulster and orange gloves – particularly the gloves – he was assumed by passers-by to be an NKVD officer engaged on an inscrutable Soviet surveillance mission.

This was a wealthy district known locally as Little Venice, in common with several other such canalside neighbourhoods scattered throughout northern Europe. Nothing about it was particularly Venetian. The mainly seventeenth-century houses which overlooked the waterways, often through wrinkled panes of very clear, thin old glass, were those of well-to-do bourgeois merchants. Counts, margraves, princes and other exotics tended to roost elsewhere, generally in plain, gloomy houses with too many rooms and too little garden for the height of the estate walls. It was exactly the district where one would expect to find the director of a Botanical Gardens living, and was indeed where the young Leon had once come as an apprentice, bearing a message for Dr Anselmus. His thoughts stilled to a purposeful hum, Leon the cropped and sinister turned and crossed to the remembered house, read the copperplate script beside the bell-pull and was in due course admitted reluctantly by an old factotum.

Once inside the door the visitor, surrounded by the panelled and carpeted vistas of gracious living, felt his scowl melt and fall away like slush off his boots. The factotum's 'Kindly wait here, sir' and the glance at the grey half-moon clots of ice on the polished floor reduced him further. What idiotic temerity could have brought him here? He looked at the prints on the wall, at the tall, moulded double doors on either side leading to salons and dining-rooms, closed and mute. He listened to a morning silence only intensified by the slow, hollow-chested tick of an immense grandfather clock in walnut across whose decorated face a golden schooner rocked the seconds away. Far off in the depths a pan clattered. From closer overhead a door shut and feet returned to the shrill squeaks and detonations of ancient parquet. Leon was shown straight down the hall, along a corridor and into a wooden cabinet of a room overlooking a long, thin garden. Curiously he stared down. Given its owner's profession it was

a surprisingly ordinary plot, as far as could be judged from the shapes beneath the snow. Bulgy bits would be flowerbeds, the flat bits strips of grass, with between them the straggle of rose stems on trellis work *à l'anglais*. Horticulturally, it suggested a perfunctory state of health bordering on neglect, like that of a successful doctor's own children. Presently Anselmus himself came in.

'Leon!' he greeted his curator affably, after a startled glance at the haircut. 'It must be important to bring you here. Nothing serious, I hope?'

The gardener thought that despite the friendliness of the tone the social lines had been quite adroitly drawn in a couple of short sentences.

'I'm sorry to trouble you at home, sir,' he said. 'It is a bit urgent, yes. The fact is, I'm afraid I have to report some damage to two of the plants. Wilful damage.'

'Damage? What kind of damage? Which plants? Who?'

Leon explained. 'I take full responsibility, of course,' he finished.

'No, no, my dear fellow. You can't be everywhere at once. You're a curator, an expert botanist, not a policeman. None of us will forget the immense debt the Society – indeed, the country – owes you for having brought our Palm House through the war practically singlehanded and looking better than ever. But tell me – and this is in complete confidence – whom do you suspect?'

'It's hard to imagine any of our visitors doing it, sir.'

'Quite impossible.'

'So really that only leaves the staff. Our assistants are . . . Well, you know how things are. These aren't easy times and we have to make do with what we can get.'

'I know, I know. We've all done our best to screen out the most unsuitable but really we've nothing much to go on except their own claims to have worked in greenhouses before.

There may be some poor, twisted fellow with a completely unfathomable grudge in our midst. I'm afraid the casualties of war are by no means all lying in sanatoria and cemeteries, Leon. Well, well. Never mind. Banana flower, eh? That's sad. Don't get many of them to set, do we? It has to be an assistant. Unless – ' the director tried for a joke to lighten the gloom given off by his curator's scowl and institutional haircut ' – unless of course *you're* doing it yourself and don't know it. Like Dr Jekyll and Mr Hyde, eh? You saw the film, presumably? By day the man of quiet scholarship and learning, by night a crazed fiend stalking the Palm House and committing unspeakable acts.'

The riposte took Leon as much by surprise as it did Dr Anselmus, so quickly it came and from an unguessed patch of his brain.

'Or you, sir. I mean, if that could happen to me without my knowing, so it might to you.'

'I . . . well, of course, I suppose you're right.' The director smiled wanly and in that moment Leon could almost believe it himself, could imagine the pink, pettish sobriety of Claud Anselmus's features melding and distorting at around midnight to remould themselves into those of the monster who slept within. 'Of course it was merely a jocular theory I was advancing. This isn't a film. No, it'll be one of your men all right. Only thing you can do is keep your eyes peeled, I'm afraid, and just hope it doesn't happen again. If it goes on we'll just have to bring the police in. Very well, then. Carry on. I'll drop in tomorrow as usual.'

'There was one other thing, sir.' Dr Anselmus's 'jocular theory' had tweaked Leon's anger, and hence his courage, back. 'There've been a lot of rumours recently about the Palm House's future, even of moving the entire Botanical Gardens into the country so our land can be redeveloped. If I'm not

197

being presumptuous the House's future is connected with my own and I'd like to know what's going on.'

'Ah, of course, of course. Perfectly reasonable.' Anselmus was all Jekyll now. A further glance at the shorn head of his most celebrated employee, the gaunt and smouldering features, increased the doctor's emollient urbanity. 'I was in any case intending to have a chat with you about that nonsense, knowing how these stupid rumours travel. Of course you've been worried, my dear fellow, but I hope not seriously? You surely can't have imagined we'd even contemplate taking any such step without consulting you? Why, you are – or you would be – the lynchpin of any such move. No, no.'

'No, no move? Is that what you're saying?'

'Yes,' said Anselmus testily. 'That's of course what I'm saying.'

'There is,' pursued his employee, 'no plan being proposed, no intention of selling our land and moving out?'

'Let me make myself absolutely clear,' umbrageously offered Anselmus, whose administrative duties had brought him into contact with politicians. 'This is simply a typical example of the sort of rumour which circulates at times like these. People look around and see all the damage and disruption – bombed-out areas and so forth – and they naturally wonder whether the old world can be restored or if instead it'll be supplanted still further by change and decay. But from all those trying years – the occupation and the anarchy, pure anarchy, really – we've got back not only our beloved King safe and well but our country's entire legal framework intact. In short, the *status quo ante*. The Botanical Gardens are not ours to sell, even if we wanted. They weren't before the war, and nor are they now. They belong to the nation, held in escrow by the University. This is our lawyers' professional verdict. There.'

Leon was staring out into the director's meagre garden even as

his words blossomed unconvincingly inside the boxlike room. 'I can see the attractions of a hundred acres in the country instead of fewer than ten in the city,' he said musingly. 'A far bigger collection laid out in a modern way. New, efficient houses devoted to specific regions or habitats. Impossible not to see the advantages. Better science so better funding. Room for a seed bank, especially of commercial varieties. Proper public subscriptions and membership. More visitors of the right sort, not just foreign diplomats trying to keep warm.' And, nerved by having accidentally introduced the chiefest topic of all, the real reason for his presence in this humidor of a room, his eyes wandering between the garden and its owner's fingers as they fiddled with a topaz fob (a large, faceted yellow lozenge which revolved around a golden spindle hanging from a golden chain) he added: 'That princess, by the way. I imagine you already know what she wants?'

'I'm afraid . . . ?'

'I know she's spoken to you, sir, because she told me. So you must know that only yesterday she offered me a job in her own country.'

Anselmus's fingers paused as if finding his words for him. 'Oh, that plan of hers. She did mention something of the kind. I can't imagine how you'd have replied. With your usual pungency, I expect.'

'It was left open.'

'A curious, even misconceived scheme, I first thought. But on further consideration I found it did have merit. It's really quite imaginative. As far as I know it would be the only thing of its kind anywhere. An international feather in your cap, certainly.'

'Are you plotting behind my back, Director?' Leon asked bitterly. 'Do you want to get rid of me? Would it make things easier?'

'Good gracious! How can you even think such a thing? My

dear man, you of all people! What, you mean conspiring to let you go? Our most distinguished employee? The very idea.'

'Perhaps not me, then. But the Palm House, yes, I think that's possible. Just now it's more of a liability than an asset, isn't it? Or at least, a majority of the trustees and board think so. Why throw good money away on installing new boilers if the entire place is due to be scrapped? By modern standards the place is a museum piece and when funds are low museums seem like useless luxuries. Oh, there's a lot of virtuous talk about national heritage and artistic patrimony and priceless educational and cultural value. But those are just phrases for public consumption, aren't they? We all know the talk that counts goes on in bank and government offices and the finance departments of places like City Hall.'

'I hadn't realised you'd been brooding to this extent. I – '

'What is hard,' went on Leon unhearingly, 'is convincing people that the Palm House has a future, especially when its own trustees don't really believe in it any longer. They're all rotted with this new egalitarian stuff the British are cooking up over there: free health, free education, free everything. Wonderful, this liberal democracy. You can do by money everything the communists have to do by force. But by God it's going to take a lot of money, and that means ever more centralised economic control, ever more centralised powers to tax and organise and regulate and restrict and exploit. That's not a scheme into which a palm house fits, according to their wisdom, is it?'

'I'd really no idea you were so well – ' began Anselmus with breezy admiration, but his gardener had not finished.

'Now *I* can see a future for our Palm House even if no-one else can. The board already know some of my ideas but they seem not to have paid them much attention. No,' he waved away an encroaching 'I assure you – ', 'they just see schemes. They don't understand the main idea behind them because

200

they know almost nothing of the history of such places. They might know enough to say, "Oh, nineteenth-century utopias, enchanted shelters from industrialisation and urban grimness" or something of the sort, though why that mightn't seem quite as valid today I can't think. What could be grimmer than parts of this city? Bombed, run down, no jobs, no homes, no money about. People ought to be flocking to the Gardens and the Palm House at times like these, reminding themselves of what beauty and richness and fecundity still are. But they're put off. It's all too surrounded by an aura of dry learning and crankiness.' Leon reached for an insult in his best *lèse*-majestic fashion. 'They take one look at Professor Seneschal and get one whiff of talk about black snowdrops or whatever abortion he's trying to breed, and they see a run-down Gardens full of what look like war criminals in gaiters not replanting the trees cut down for firewood, and not dredging and clearing the lake, and not restoring the Temperate House or the summer houses. And they stay away.'

'While denying the least validity to your personal remark I agree there's much in what you say. Do you think I'm not just as interested as you to bring the Gardens back to their former splendour? I might remind you', the fingers twiddled wildly, 'that I am currently the Director of the entire Gardens, whereas you are curator of the Palm House alone. It is, of course, the Gardens' main attraction, but nevertheless your area of responsibility is a good deal more limited than mine. The fact is, our funding is still in an equivocal state. We're awaiting a financial injection from the government.'

'Which is not likely to be forthcoming. Or rather', Leon tacked implacably on before his passion's stiff breeze, 'it'll be made dependent on our agreeing to move.'

'I really can't think what gives you the right to make these conjectures. Your job is to run the Palm House and not, I'd

201

suggest, to speculate about policy matters which are hardly within the terms of your employment.'

'And there we have it.' Leon turned from the window.

'More like a ruffian than a botanist,' thought Dr Anselmus. 'A peaky ruffian at that. And anyway, he's no more academically qualified than my dog' (a schnauzer puppy, which perhaps explained the condition of the garden). 'There we have *nothing*,' he said firmly, 'except maybe a good place to end this conversation.'

'You haven't yet heard why I think the Palm House must be preserved, Director.' Leon was determined that at least one person in the Society's hierarchy should be made to understand. 'It's more than just an old building with a useful but not unique collection of tropical plants. It represents a stage in people's understanding of the natural world, part of the evolution of knowledge. It's a dream, a private paradise, a poetic statement even. That remains true at any time. But it's not even just that. In the eighteenth century they were still naively pleased by exotica for their own sake. Strange, unimagined plants and creatures from places which often hadn't even been mapped yet – things with an almost mythic quality about them. But by the nineteenth, systems of classification were mastering more and more of the world. New plants might still be strange, but once they could be shown to belong to an already existing class or genus they became tamed. The relationship of man to nature was no longer one of simple awe and delight, it had changed to one of power. Power of knowledge, power of ordering, power of subjugating. The great palm houses symbolised this in the most public and open manner by putting a far-off ruled world under glass back home. A museum, what else? The public could wander around and see plants grouped according to their taxonomy and marvel at this reconciliation of themselves with nature. Thanks to man the wild variousness and generosity of

God's creation now made sense. What's more, it was seen to be perfectly compatible with industrialisation, colonial expansion and money. Perfect harmony, in fact. That's by day, of course. By night . . . Well, it's another matter.'

Dr Anselmus, who had been waiting for a crack in his curator's flow into which he might insert a deft verbal scalpel to the effect that he hardly thought he needed a prepared lecture on the history of botanical gardens, was thrown by this odd turn. 'By night? What do you mean, by night?' He gave his topaz an irritable tweak. It was a gesture which had not quite worked up the nerve to commit the forthright rudeness of hauling out his pocket watch.

'Oh, it's somewhere else at night,' Leon assured him. 'You must have felt it. All those classifications melt away. It just becomes up to the senses again, the perceptions. That's the time to stop looking at the plants and to smell and listen instead. The whole point about museums is that everything's on display, under glass, made visible. But what happens to museums at night? Ah, now that's a most interesting question.' He broke off to cough painfully. Something in the way he leaned against the shutter forestalled the director's retort.

'A most interesting question,' resumed the gardener, wiping the sleeve of his ulster across mouth and nose, eyes glistening. 'Now, what about this century? This is where my idea comes in. I think we've stopped being proud of our power and have begun to be afraid of it. Look at those atom bombs the Americans dropped on Japan last year. Power beyond our control, if you ask me. Look at the destruction caused by the war. Not just the people and the cities, but nature ravaged and battered. Entire jungles set on fire, according to the newspapers. Whole islands in the Pacific reduced to cinders. Millions of rubber trees and crops burnt to stop them falling into whoever's hands. And what can botanists and horticulturists do about it? Why, collect

plants as fast as they can, to protect as much as to display them. Our job will be to help nature survive the bullying of man.'

'I'd hardly expected our very own Palm House curator to be such a *futurist* at heart.'

Evidently surprised by a lack of patronage in the tone rather than the words Leon said mildly, 'How can one not think about the future if one knows any history? As a horticulturist I can see a clear pattern over the last hundred years: that of increasing destruction and despoliation and mechanisation. Now, what would you do with all those Flying Fortresses and Dorniers and Lancaster bombers if you were responsible for them?'

'What?' Again Anselmus was baffled by a change of tack. 'Melt them down as quickly as possible, I suppose.'

'For ploughshares? No, you'd sell them off to the air companies and travel firms like Thomas Cook. They'd get them very cheap and fill them with all those people who haven't been able to travel since 1939. Tourists. That'll be the way to make money in the future. The more people do it the cheaper it'll become. Not this year, not even perhaps for ten years. But one day everyone will be able to hop on a high-speed airship or aeroplane and go and see all the plants we've got here in the Gardens, but in their natural habitats. By then the habitats'll probably be huge nature reserves just as they have game reserves. But – and this is the point – they won't quite find what they're looking for. People will spend their time going ever further to ever more remote places in search of pure virgin nature, the realest, the most utterly authentic and unspoiled. But they'll never find it because *they're* there, and if they can be so can everyone else. They'll think they're looking for plants and animals, but it won't be that. They'll also be trying to discover what relationship they could possibly have with a natural world now completely in their power. Well, things like that retreat even as they're searched for, don't they? And that, among other

reasons, is why I shan't be taking up the princess's offer. Within my Palm House I'm authentic, and so is it. Far, far away there's a vast natural simulacrum of what I already live in. Part of our job as I see it is to train the public to understand that museum, memorial, research centre – whatever it is, the place is priceless. It's *because* it's so unnatural it can make people think and change their minds. We must preserve it at all costs. At any cost at all, really, since it'll never be rebuilt.'

And the two men, employee and employer, directed and director, found themselves staring at one another in astonishment until Anselmus's eyes slid away beneath the visionary gaze. Leon's surprise was by no means at his own eloquence, which as we know he had been practising day and night for years with an audience of gently transpiring green ears, but at the way Cou Min's phantom had unexpectedly shaken itself free of plaster dust somewhere up by the moulded ceiling which had received the main thrust of his speech, and floated down as a third presence in the room between himself and Anselmus. Had his pleading been on her behalf after all? Was the glass and iron structure which contained what felt like his lifework no more than her shrine, the truest expression (patched and unrepaired) of that far-off summer with Dr Koog, learning to look systematically at the natural world? How meagre was love, how flimsy its supports, how suspended its animation! he thought, coughing and coughing as the dust reached his lungs. Distantly he was aware of activity. A sleeve advanced into his aqueous vision.

'Here, take this. My dear fellow, you're in a bad way.' The door had closed behind the factotum and Anselmus was offering him a generous glass of brandy. When the spasm had eased and the brilliant display of retinal pyrotechnics was over Leon took the drink with a shaking hand and drank it off at a gulp. 'You're ill,' his employer advised him.

'No iller than usual. But it might be convenient, mightn't it?'

'Now, now, don't start all that again. You've said some hard things this morning and I won't deny they needed saying. Absolutely. Clears the air. But you really must agree you're not well. Might you please try to suspend your paranoia and take a much needed fortnight off? God knows you've earned it. I'd like you to see a doctor friend of mine – the question of money doesn't arise, of course. He's an excellent fellow: chief thoracic consultant at the Royal. We'll get you right, first, and then we'll have a proper joint effort with all the board and trustees and departmental heads to thrash this whole thing out. Actually, I'm most grateful to you for being so forceful. You've convinced me we urgently need an overall policy based on absolute agreement as to our role in the future.'

Leon was leaning heavily on a table, staring down at his large hands.

'I'll see your doctor,' he said hoarsely. 'Why not? But I must get back to the House now. There's work to be done.'

He was thinking of no single thing, perhaps, but a world hovered over by Felix's uneasy spectre. This morning the gypsy had appeared chastened and contrite, rather pettish over his pricked feet. But what was happening? Last night beneath the coconut, possessed by or else possessing some demon, there had been a hallucinatory instant when Leon had glimpsed his own tiny figure as if frozen by a camera's magnesium flash or the revolving beam of a lighthouse. White, contorted, hunched; staring at nothing with open eyes and mouth, incorporated in an even smaller manikin, as inscrutable as maggots caught in mid-maggotry at a stone's turning. In that instant he could not have named either creature, still less the act they were engaged in. He had felt his body thrust itself downwards as if through layers of other bodies to reach whatever or whomever it sought: through gypsies and students and store-owners' wives, through nameless dalliances to – (no, oh not to Cou Min: that was love, not lust) – to faceless imaginings and genderless pollutions in pursuit of the virgin real, the most utterly authentic, the ever-receding. And the harder he had thrust the more it had fled him: wan, enticing, repetitious, inexhaustible. But this morning the point had been, what must be done to avert scandal? Felix had to go; Leon couldn't bear him to go.

'If you're thinking of your new arrivals,' Anselmus began. 'What are they, by the way? Imagine, on order for nearly seven years. I think Seneschal told me one was a *Gnetum*.'

'It's already planted. I've still to unwrap the pandan and the *Pritchardia*.'

'And as for that nasty vandalism business, you must put it out of your head. It'll probably never happen again. Just one of those unexplained things.'

His mind still full of Felix, Leon was fascinated to hear his mouth produce an audacious inspiration. 'It wouldn't surprise me if this so-called vandal was actually part of a plot. If enough damage was done I reckon it could be pretty convenient for some people. Don't you see? While funds are withheld someone is hired to cut up the plants. Stealthy, strategic damage over many months. Sooner or later people will say "Just look at the place. Not worth saving. Needs complete overhaul and repair, new boilers etcetera, and there's not really enough botanical interest left to make it worthwhile." Why mightn't that be happening?'

Oh devious, devious, he thought as his mouth went about its business, implying that Anselmus himself had engineered the whole thing. He could almost believe it himself, it fitted so neatly. That was what happened in wartime, after all. Agents were planted in the subtlest manner . . . The brandy had gone to his head, despite having entered his body under medicinal pretext. Empty stomach doesn't help, of course, nor being half starved. Why have you led me here, Cou Min, my love? he wondered, looking curiously at the little room, the little man in suit and topaz, the little glass with its drop of topaz. 'I'm old,' he thought in amazement, since it was suddenly how he felt in respect to her. How had he got from then to this? Had it really taken all those years? Nothing aged one like loyalty. It was surely punishment. The gypsies, the men in suits, the dismantling of the beautiful – all were punishment for having loved remote things, for having abandoned the timeless austerities of Flinn.

'Go home at once and get some rest, Leon,' the director was saying. 'We'll find you a cab if we can but this damned petrol rationing's making perfectly ordinary things next to impossible,' he added irritably.

When eventually the front door closed on the back of the ulster Dr Anselmus walked slowly up the grand staircase and along the passage which led, with the sound of ancient kindling, to his study. The irritation persisted as he sank into his chair and gazed around at his booklined walls, at the brightly polished brass microscope he had used as a student, at the black hump of American cloth covering a modern German binocular microscope with Wetzlar optics. Why mightn't collaboration be a form of heroism, too? he wondered. For, indeed, it had taken considerable nerve and canniness first to have helped hide the Society's treasures from its headquarters and then, by deft dealings with the Gestapo, to have ensured the Botanical Gardens' immunity from sack and spoil. This was the part which would never be known, could never be acknowledged. A man like Leon took all the credit for having pulled the Palm House through, but all would have been in vain had it not been for the director's work behind the scenes. Anselmus thought how unfair it was that having supped with the devil for the best part of five years, often with spoons of terrifying shortness, on behalf of the Royal Botanic Society and a national treasure and science in general, he should forever be unable to speak about

He had failed, then. He had done his best but his oratory, his arguments had come to naught. Anselmus – crass, shifty Anselmus – hadn't heard a word, while pretending it had been a useful 'clearing of the air'. Pure bluster. Then finally Leon's lungs had betrayed his head and he'd been unable to go on. Cou Min, Cou Min, have you brought us to this? he wondered. Is it you? Despondent he walked his House whose very panes seemed to tremble about him, the ground to quiver underfoot. He found himself back at the Acacia farnesiana, *instrument of his guilty triumph the previous night. The shrub seemed not to have suffered much from the trampling. Quite the reverse, as it soon made clear in a soliloquy:*

'Well, of course I can bite! Ours is an adventurous and risk-taking species, boldly going where no man dares to tread – certainly not barefoot, that is. For this reason our shoots are well armed; and I may say it was a pleasure I'd hardly dared even dream about, sinking my full length into those tender tawny boy-feet. The meaty plush of it! The whine of muscle tone as it tenses in agony! The succulence of blood! It was, I can confirm, altogether worth being trodden on. Not since I dipped into the back of a gardener's hand in 1937 have I felt anything like it, and that was a mere sip of pleasure compared with this beatific gorging. The warm, cushiony embrace is the most satisfying thing this universe has to offer. What makes it even more piquant (*mot juste*) is that one can't experience it without first having been abused. Thus the boy took a liberty and straightway rewarded me with solace and revenge. How I adore him! He has the most exquisite sole. Even now, I daresay, he can feel where I was inside him. I may well have caused a little oozing and affected the way he walks for a day or two. I do hope so. Such thoughts fill me with a kind of afterglow, a happy hum of remembrance. Humans, of course, being slavishly egocentric, can't talk about us without resorting to the usual weary epithets, "cruel" thorns being the most over-employed, judging by several centuries of their rumty-tum poetry. "Cruel", indeed. By provoking that adjective we could hardly have presented a kinder gift to their sonneteers, whose constant need for padding or pruning is so easily satisfied by the word's metric ambiguity: a single long or a trochee according to necessity. More to the point (*juste* again) "cruel" is notoriously never the way the human foot is described as it unheedingly attempts to walk all over *us*. Oh, no. This is, for dimmer listeners, of religious significance. Why, you dolts? Because it's proof that we're the offshoots of a thoughtful, loving Creator. It was He who ensured that even as we were downtrodden we would be rewarded an hundredfold. You'll find that practically all the thorny species are pretty religious. It's only the ones who *should* have been thorny and – by some accident of heredity – aren't, that are cynical and atheistic. I'm told that thornless rose varieties are the worst. They might smell wonderful but underneath they're one black rant of blasphemy and frustration.

'But back to the boy, my divine and punished trampler! The gardener – whose new hairstyle so faithfully reflects the brutal chic of the times – is filled with nagging worries concerning this lad, as well he might be. Among them is the very pertinent question: did the princess mention him to Anselmus? Since she was standing right behind Leon while he was trying to cough his lungs inside out she had ample time to observe Felix in that cool, objective, Asian manner of hers which gives nothing away. She might have been saving the information to explode later like a bomb in a marriage bed, or to present on ice at a military tribunal. That's part of her power, which is why she causes such a stir. *Elle est arrivée*, forsooth! They yearn to be noticed by her, dazzled by her, raped by her.

'Very well, then: she must have seen Felix. And what did she think? That he was some new assistant Leon had been given? Some tatterdemalion apprentice who with the right training and influence might grow into a useful horticulturist? (Well, he might at that if he could curb the urge to vandalise the plants.) Of course, she might have thought that. But those Asian eyes with their mysterious canthic fold which lets everything sidle in and so little out, would have been trying to see patterns, make sense of peculiar Western *mores*, dress the fabled world of science and technology in the rotten flesh she knows is the common human denominator. And those eyes would have taken in the slippery, unmarried man in early middle age living in his crystal shell whose very air blurs the outside world, who refuses even to lodge out and simply go to and from work like everybody else. They would have taken him in, dispassionately, as he coughed on his knees in that abject way (is this, after all, the genius one has heard so much about? The man of vision and ambition who might abandon us and go off to create a Snow House for Kuala Lumpur or Jesselton or wherever?). Her eyes would also have taken in the way this supposed apprentice stood in the doorway watching him, neither tense with helplessness nor indifferently lounging but full of a wry domestic *déjà vu*. And she would have thought, "Good God, they're lovers. Of course."

'All right, play dumb. Fine, if you insist then: no, she wouldn't. She would hardly have noticed the boy at all. The great Leon was the centre of her picture, her plan. Anybody else in the vicinity was merely a labourer on the estate: a tangential figure such as painters daub into landscapes to fill up the gaps and add a vague sense of activity. Go on believing that version if you prefer.

'But if she *did* notice him and think him significant the remaining question is, would she have told Anselmus? If she'd seen Felix and Leon as a couple, wouldn't that affect her plan? Mightn't she now have to consider importing them both if Leon were to accept her job offer? And meanwhile mightn't Felix be a useful lever for Anselmus to ease out his curator before (oh, so regretfully, the traitorous hound!) pulling down the Palm House in exchange for a new site, more power, a bigger salary and a generous backhander from the dark fiscals? There are excellent prospects for a nasty scandal, are there not? Behaviour which might elicit amusement in Jesselton or Kuala Lumpur is a different matter in these cold, unforgiving latitudes. How badly, then, did Anselmus need to get rid of Leon? Would he be capable of doing a deal with this potentially useful and powerful lady? Had he already done it?

'I've watched him tonight, the gardener, stumbling and mumbling in the candlelight as usual, more than ever unable to read his fellow-humans and their motives. ("Stumbling" – what an erotic word that is, with its rich possibilities of the randomly-descending foot!) Nearer, gardener! You owe me a debt. It was I who caught your sportive faun for you, never forget. Had it not been for me and a few simple prickles you'd never have got your hands on him and rewarded his abuses as I just had. Oh, between us we could make a pincushion of that juicy gypsy!

'But you're not just worried, are you? You're lost and muddled, too, even as you patrol your domain, your private landscape of congealed time with the pipes sighing underfoot and the snowflakes sizzling on the panes overhead. She's no mere scheming bitch, this princess of yours, is she? You're in love with her, too, in your eccentric fashion. *Is* it because she reminds you of someone else, long ago? Somebody who was scarcely even real for a summer but to whose imaginary memory you've abandoned your one and only life? You've been taking this line quite a lot lately, we've noticed, in your nocturnal rambles both physical and verbal. You seem to think it has to do with something poetic bound up with your whole life and this place. I can't comment on that. We thorny species are beyond poetry except, as I said, when co-opted as metaphors. We assume it must be connected with the beauty of retribution . . . "Cruel"? Did I hear "cruel"? Ah, on the grounds that clichés generally reflect truisms and truisms some banal aspect of truthfulness? You really do have the strangest notions of cruelty. May I remind you of that night-flowering South American climber, *Araujia sericofera*, which you yourself have planted down at the far end of this House? Its popular nickname is "The Cruel", I believe, because the peculiarly tight arrangement of its flowers often traps moths by the proboscis overnight, releasing them at dawn. I think that's beautiful, both functional and mischievous. Nor are we thorns cruel, as I keep making clear. We merely raise points; others impale themselves on us. Proceed, unhappy man.

'Yes, I'd agree: she's obviously attracted to something in you, though thanks to her cultural difference it's not plain what it would be. You like to think it's a certain rough animality? That might have been more plausible ten years ago. In any case it sounds like dismal male vanity. But you're intriguing, I'd allow that. Both powerful and elusive. That's an unusual combination, and some people are excited by the unusual. You're right. Dull, dull, dull the courtship rituals we've witnessed in here. People who've seen nothing, done nothing, felt nothing, heard nothing, smelt nothing. Dull, dull, dull. The meanest periwinkle has more

ELEVEN

Winter had drawn itself out as if to hold in hibernation the infections bequeathed by war. Now and then it would seem over at last, that the sun could get to work and, in thawing out the corruption, brew compost for spring's flowers. On such days the sky above the Palm House was an intense windscrubbed blue against which the golden galleon scudded bravely along, her sails stiff. Then after a day or two fresh draughts arrived from the Steppes bringing with them first a dimming cirrus, then a pearlescent overcast and later the familiar rugs of dark cloud which miraculously frayed to earth as white feathers.

Leon had ventured out less and less, so painful was the raw air to his chest and so long the coughing fits it provoked. Once or twice he did find himself in the Gardens, viewing his domain from the outside, and could only be depressed by what he saw. Such stove houses needed repainting every four years, especially the putty which otherwise dried out and cracked. His Palm House hadn't had a lick of paint since 1938, almost exactly eight years ago. In that time it had become shabby. Much of the glass didn't even match. In an average year five hundred or so panes broke as a result of the structure's flexing and corroding. This tally had multiplied considerably during the war because of blast and shrapnel, to say nothing of a hailstorm in 1943 which alone had smashed nearly four thousand panes in twenty minutes. As the war had progressed new glass had been slower and slower in coming and was finally unavailable. No commandeered factory had been allowed to fill special orders for a palm house whose panes were long and narrow and precisely curved.

At the war's outbreak Leon had circumspectly over-ordered glass and the extensive store had at one time contained twenty-three thousand panes. Over the last year, though, he had been reduced to drawing on crated stocks discovered at the back of the gravel bins. This was antique, dating (according to an enclosed invoice hand-written in rusty ink) from 1907. He thought it was probably the last batch of tinted glass ever ordered. Up until then the Palm House, in common with that at Kew and elsewhere, had been painted green and glazed in green. The glass was coloured with copper oxide because it was thought necessary to protect the plants by shade of a natural tone. By the turn of the century the air pollution in many cities was fogging the glass enough to cut down light severely and tinting was abandoned. When they had unpacked the ancient stocks Leon and his assistants found that over the years much of it had changed colour to a variety of hues ranging from a nearly opaque bottle to malignant pink. Several dozen panes were quite colourless while almost as many were as black as thin sheets of jet, except at the edges where they were the dark grey of X-rays. The wartime maintenance crews had used the least discoloured glass but the place had still emerged looking patched and piebald. He could hardly decide which were worse: brilliant cold days which picked out his building cruelly against the snow's whiteness, showing every rust streak, every peeling gutter, every bizarre tint mottling its surface; or the leaden days whose sombre light made of it a sad mineral lump, its skin dull as slate, blinded from within by steam and from without by soot. After such confrontations with appearances he would return bitter and morose. It all confirmed his glummest suspicions. The moving finger had written, on glass and in condensation. His vision, that jewelled airship which had hovered in its bright new livery among the trees in 1938 as if tugging at its moorings, impatient to be gone, was long grounded. He could scarcely believe it was ever intended to soar again. On the contrary, it lay as if partially embedded after a disaster. One expected at any moment to see its envelope sag and collapse, its iron ribs poke through.

Increasingly in these pessimistic moods he wanted to be rid of it, hankered after the killing air outside, nearly yearned for the pitiless expanses of Flinn and its estuarine consolations. Long ago (it seemed) in his intense, driven, 'prentice years when by the glow of lamp and candle he had read himself an education in a potting shed, he had come across a story about Mendelssohn, for in those days his omnivorous reading included much that had no connection with Linnaeus and the *Genera Plantarum* or Wendland and the *Index Palmarum*. The story described how the composer, on a visit to Denmark Hill in London with his wife in the spring of 1842, had eagerly planned a picnic outing to Windsor Great Park. One balmy morning the hampers were packed, the carriage arrived, the ladies were handed up. Then at the last moment Mendelssohn had hung back, returned to the house, and eventually his wife emerged alone. 'We shall drive on without him,' she told the disappointed party. 'He has something in his mind and begs to be excused.' When in the early evening after a glorious day the picnickers arrived back in Denmark Hill they were greeted by a musician eager to play them his latest composition, 'Spring Song', which he did to cries of admiration. 'That's what I've been doing while you've been at Windsor,' he said.

What was it about this story which had impressed the young Leon enough for him to recall it in 1946 while brooding on his

Palm House's ruin? Not, at any rate, the urgency of genius, that cliché of cinematic proportions. Rather, it had to do with versions of truthfulness. Ordinary people went and sat out in nature and steeped themselves in views, marvelled at the painterly effects of sunlight on leaf and grass blade, were enchanted by Her Majesty's deer, filled themselves with cold hock and jellied fowl. Extraordinary people knew all that by heart, stayed at home in South London in dark rooms crammed with pictures and ferns and furniture and created something faithful to all sunlight that ever was, all blue skies and shifting grasses, and which would outlast every tree they saw. Artifice again. The deft dream always would supplant the conventional vista . . . And in *this* film, at any rate, the earnest young autodidact with the yellow hair would have got up from his peat bale and gone outside to gaze at the Palm House shivering in moonlight like a tinfoil mirage. One day . . . Ah, one day.

And the day had come, and the day had gone, and all was leprous and obscured.

Inside, the House appeared remarkably normal – at least to the casual visitor. The occluded light of dud glass went scarcely noticed, was merely a reminder that times were hard, that this was a period of make-do-and-mend. Whose shirt cuffs were not turned? Whose sheets not resewn sides-to-middle? Why should a building be any different? It had even acquired a heroic, rakish look in certain lights, like one of those ex-soldiers glaring on the pavement outside cinemas and restaurants through one clear lens and one smoked. What couldn't be denied was that botanically it had never looked better. New plants burgeoned, the mature grew in stature. It was this the visitors came for and for this they praised the gardener. Hitherto, praise had evidently cheered the man but just lately seemed to have no effect on him, might even have deepened the creases which had appeared on either side of his stubborn mouth.

Tonight, suspicions of his growing strangeness were at last confirmed by unequivocal symptoms. The cropped skull was amazing, though none dared give it such a knowing look as the Italian chargé. They also noticed he was walking with a slight limp and at once began to imagine a set of circumstances in which he might have had a brutal haircut and gone lame, trying to connect them with that same compulsion which makes people look for a narrative thread between a stranger's tattoo and his heavy cold. It was an intriguing game since it prompted them to invent a hidden life for him, one not spent beneath glass and open to public scrutiny.

'*Est-ce qu'elle est arrivée, peut-être?*' The usual enquiry could be heard as the sound of the double doors tweaked pairs of eyes out around fronds and stems.

'My dears . . .' The cold, which was extreme, maybe provoked the chargé to more than his usual waspish languor. 'My dears, *elle ne va pas arriver, tout court.* I'm not at all sure I care for this – ' he had sunk his beak gingerly towards the sparse greenish flowers buried unassumingly at the heart of some fleshy blades. 'Now you must tell me, do you have these in Brazil?' This was addressed to a tall, handsome young man whose sideboards still trailed into silky wicks like a boy's rather than being shaved square. 'Never mind what they look like, you couldn't possibly forget the smell. Like a tom-cat sitting in a jasmine bush. Fairly hateful, I'd say, but authentically exotic.'

'We have flowers which smell of decaying cheese,' offered the young man. 'They attract flies and insects which pollinate them.'

'And are they beautiful?'

'Exquisite.'

'One might have guessed.' The chargé lit a cigarette. 'I only did that to attract you,' he said as Leon surged darkly forward, 'though not, I confess, with pollination in mind. What are these spear things called?' He stubbed out the cigarette and courteously handed it to the gardener.

'Down there to the left there's a label.'

'Good gracious, so there is.' The diplomat bent forward from the waist like melting toffee. 'It flowers day and night but is only scented after dark,' he announced at large. 'Very frugal, I'd say. Now then, sir, I have a message for you.' He took from an inside pocket a small creamy envelope embossed with a crest and sealed with green wax. 'It's from the lady whose absence you'll have noticed tonight. She begs to be forgiven but is unable to see you in person. As a matter of fact,' he consulted his slim watch, 'I imagine she's at present somewhere over the Middle East. You're surprised? My dear sir, I'm sorry to be the bearer of sad news. Evidently you've not read tonight's papers? There's been a coup in her country.'

From the way his listeners moved a little closer to him the chargé was not after all relaying common knowledge but imparting genuine diplomatic intelligence. He basked as Leon turned the envelope over and over between stained paws. 'It's confused, to say the least. It seems to be a coup led by the princess's own uncle, a military man. He claims to have placed the entire royal family under arrest. Yes indeed, you're asking the same question as all of us. Since the uncle must himself be of royal blood, how has he managed this trick? *Chissà?* What we do know is that he has loudly denounced her father for the usual evil misrule, despotism and tra-la-la but also for having collaborated in a most unpatriotic and abject manner with the recent Japanese occupation. It's even rumoured that the princess herself is implicated, but I'm sure everyone here who remembers a young, sophisticated and dazzlingly beautiful lady – a true diplomat – will find the charge wholly incredible. Our embassy was told that her uncle's agents, among them the sinister fellow who used to accompany her here, escorted her to the aeroplane. The

223

poor girl had no choice but to go. It's conceivable that when it stops to refuel in one of those dreadful hot places like Karachi she might find a moment to slip away if the British feel it's in their interest to be sympathetic. I couldn't bear to think of anything happening to that exquisite creature.'

The chargé fitted another Egyptian cigarette into his oval holder and lit it. For once Leon seemed not to notice. His mind was seeing an aircraft standing, engines ticking over, its propellers flicking off their silver rays as a small figure jumped from the open door into Asia's immensity.

'She adored this place, of course, but you know that already. She adored you, too, mister gardener, Don Juan, Lothario. Whence this strange charm, I wonder? It's proof even against your hairdresser, though in future I beg you to consider Giorgio's in Palace Square. He understands hair just as you understand plants. I once had some slight – '

'What will happen to her?' interrupted Leon fiercely.

The chargé waved a hand and left the gesture's signature on the air in fragrant smoke.

'Who can tell? Asian politics are a closed book to me, as they are to everyone else. She may escape, she may not. She may be in jail, shot or on the throne by the end of the week. Her family is immensely powerful and immensely rich. One waits breathlessly for the outcome. There's even been talk of their all being tried by military tribunal on charges of war crimes; there's quite a vogue for such things just at present.'

'She? A war criminal?' This time Leon heard his own belligerence and remembered himself. Never before had he been part of his visitors' conversation. He had always answered their questions more or less politely, more or less brusquely according to mood, but he had never taken the liberty of hanging on the edge of a circle of talk until sucked into its centre to offer opinions of his own. Oddly, the chargé seemed almost to be addressing his remarks directly to him as part of a private conversation the others might overhear if they chose.

'You must endeavour to be a little worldly,' he said kindly. 'In these circumstances to be accused of war crimes may mean no more than that one has been eclipsed, whether temporarily or not. It doesn't mean that the princess herself committed atrocities with those beautiful hands. Did you ever notice the half-moons of her nails? The most delicate pearly mauve. You must remember that her family were on the throne during both the Japanese occupation and the American liberation. They need to have done nothing. Merely to have survived both régimes confirms guilt in their opponents' eyes.'

'But she was interested in city planning.'

The lame absurdity of his protest apparently didn't strike the chargé whose tone, on the contrary, suggested complete sympathy. 'And she liked Lancôme. I never could respect a woman who hasn't learned how to wear Guerlain and Lancôme. Both houses produce scents of the utmost sophistication and complexity. The princess had perfect taste in scent, which is very unusual in one so young. She was – ' a razory note here ' – naturally interested in city planning, too. The recent efforts of the Americans to dislodge the Japanese from her country have left the capital in some disrepair. "Partially destroyed" would be a better description, according to diplomatic friends of mine. She and her family own large tracts of land in the capital including, one gathers, a royal game park. Doesn't that sound exotic? A private game park in the middle of a city with a gilded hunting pavilion at its centre. That's the East for you, that's power. Now along comes the West with another kind of power: oil. The Americans have discovered large deposits along the coast somewhere. Well, my dear, it would hardly amaze one to hear that deals of a Byzantine intricacy were being hatched, would it? Let me see: the uncle takes over with American backing in return for the promise of exclusive drilling rights. The ex-royal family are allowed by the skin of their teeth to take a suitcase and a servant apiece and fly into exile in somewhere ruinously déclassé like Vientiane or even, God help us, Hawaii. It will emerge that they were secretly planning to sell off the nation's patrimony, the royal game park and hunting lodge, to the highest bidder in order to build offices for the expected postwar boom. The greedy fiends! Was nothing sacred to them? And so on and so forth. Then after a discreet interval the royal game park is ploughed up and put down to office buildings as part of the government's democratic and enlightened plan to abolish the last traces of feudalism and restore the nation's assets to the people. Tra-la-la. My dear, American *diplomacy*. It's like watching somebody trying to do joinery with a chainsaw. Whatever that is.'

The chargé raised an amused eyebrow at the dead stub of his cigarette which, lost in the throes of his oratory, he had smoked down to the holder.

'But she wasn't like that at all,' said Leon. 'She would never have sold off a city park for development. She had this extraordinary plan – ' He couldn't complete the sentence. He suddenly had no desire to throw titbits into the gossip pool, to give away anything of his princess. The diplomat's account was shocking, delivered with that worldly nonchalance which always made hearsay sound like fact, conjecture like truth, knowingness like knowledge. What did these people know? How? And why did they always make it appear as if they knew yet more? The chargé was still watching him with his odd kindness. He detached the cigarette stub and offered it gracefully.

'This really ought to be framed or mounted,' he said. 'It's the very first I've been allowed to finish in this enchanting place. I believe you're slipping. And this extraordinary plan of hers?'

Leon only shook his head, candlelight glinting on his hacked fur. The story he had just heard had done something savage to her presence. In any case mentioning a job offer by someone who no longer had the power to appoint would perversely suggest a failure of his own.

'Nobody', said the chargé obscurely, 'is proof against the past. Not her, not you. Nor even I,' he added with a quick smile at his young companion.

That night Leon's wretchedness wrapped him in a sheet of flame. He burned on the mattress beside Felix in the spilled light of the half-open fireboxes. Everywhere he looked he encountered the same falling away. Several times he reached out and laid a hand on the gypsy's shoulder, left it there until it grew to feel as heavy as a toad. Only when he tried to turn him over was there any response. Then the unyielding rigidity of the boy's body, as if bolted through the mattress and into the brick floor, was so eloquent he lost heart.

'I'm ill,' he remarked, but more to himself. He had lived on his own for too long to have acquired habits of demand. His chest scalded him. He got up and drank feverishly from the tap, selected an infusion from the cupboard, drew off a cupful of hot water from a spigot on the boiler, sipped it. 'I've failed,' he said. Then, remembering, 'I'll read to you.' He got up again and searched the pockets of his trousers draped over a chairback. He found the envelope, slumped on to the mattress with it and ran a nail beneath its flap. Absently he inspected the thumb as if for scale insects, then took out a single cream sheet.

' "Cher Maître," ' he read aloud, ' "for that is how I think of you. In my country we have holy men, some of whose qualities I see in you. I had not expected to find any such thing so far from home and perhaps I allowed my pleasure and relief to show too obviously. For this I apologise.

' "The snow is coming down and I have heard terrible

news. His Serene Highness my father has been taken ill and I must fly to his bedside at once, even before saying goodbye to you. As I believe I hinted, our country did not have an easy passage through the recent war and in the present circumstances it becomes impossible to predict what will happen. Our plan together – or at any rate my own dream – will have to wait a little before going ahead. I believe I may have been guilty of rushing you the other day. This was improper and I am sorry if it seemed I was applying pressure. It was nothing more than my own eagerness. You are a great man, I am sure of it, and will find your own way.

' "And so I must bid you adieu for now, with the greatest sadness and sincerest thanks for all you have taught me, only part of which you will know about. Your beautiful exotic poem in which you live and work will remain the happiest memory of my first diplomatic posting and an inspiration in whatever upset the immediate future holds for me. Once I, too, had hopes of being a poet. Maybe one day I shall be after all. Whenever it happens, and wherever we both are, it will have been as much your doing as mine. Plant something for me. Tahassa, HRH The Princess Imluk." '

When he had finished Leon fell silent. Fuel collapsed in a boiler with a cindery rush and the glow intensified for a moment, lighting up the letter he held. Beside him Felix lay like a stone bolster. He seemed not even to be breathing and, leaning aslant, Leon saw his eyeballs' staring gleam. His own fever was affecting him like alcohol: not enough to blur but, on the contrary, enough to sharpen the emotions. Under its influence her words were not those of someone announcing an unforeseen journey and the separation of two people whose relationship appeared to be based more on the admiration of one party than on the shared allusions of friends. Instead her letter had left him with the distillate of farewell, of valediction, speaking for his whole existence with the fatuous punctuality which pretends to significance. He could not for the moment have uttered a word without at once falling into tears. Why had she described the Palm House as a poem? Or had she meant his life, his vision? It was unfair of her to write on a page, with easy strokes of her cultured hand, something he himself had surely never thought, could never have thought, but which now stood as a humiliatingly truthful proposition. Unfevered, sober, he knew how gruffly he would dismiss such pretentious nonsense, in public at least. 'I'm a gardener. I dig the ground and plant things and hate wireworm and spider mite. I worry constantly about the shitty boilers and the shitty assistants and the shitty coal they send me whose smuts drift down and stick to the shitty glass I'm given to work with. Otherwise, of course, it's a right little sonnet we've got here. Seen the paintwork? The putty on the south side of the lantern? It'd break the heart of the fellow who built this place.' Now, with the fever on him and the scent of loss disguised as 'Cuir' drifting up from the writing paper, a capitulation occurred and he was forced to admit there might be something else beyond the bare profession thus crudely sketched. Was it this which had gone wrong? His expertise betrayed by a dreamy flaw? And what did she mean by 'exotic', anyway? Hardly the plants, since palms were as workaday in southeast Asia as plane trees in the municipal park across the way. Didn't exoticism simply depend on being outside or somewhere else? Maybe she meant he always was somewhere else, always would be; that even the place which most reeked of him and his labour was no structure of putty and glass and iron ribs but rooted entirely in his mind where it glowed and brooded and festered and hung its unsettling fruit. Living out a dream rather than in one? No, that was far too explanatory. There was a vulgarity about the whole idea. He wished she hadn't mentioned poetry at all. He quite wished she had returned the lotus, too. It had been blighted by events, having progressively fallen from the category of outright gift through that of 'indefinite temporary loan' and was now unrecovered property.

'Oh Felix,' he murmured, swaying as he sat, 'what are we going to do? How did all this happen? It was the war, wasn't it? The damned, bloody war.'

The thought gave him some comfort but not enough. He was still ambitious. To grow plants was not the same as watching plants grow. He could almost see how he wanted things to be: almost, but not quite. The princess's departure had unaccountably muddied the view.

'Who was she, this princess of ours? Perhaps after all what the newspapers call a raven-haired temptress? Enticing us with opportunity – "name your own salary", that's what she said. Can you believe that? Enticing me to selfishness, to abandon you and rush off to a country which for all I know may be completely imaginary. Do you feel as I do sometimes?' he laid a hand on the immobile figure's hip. 'As if everything takes place in a far country? We're a little ill, I think. That's all it is. Hungry, too. Tomorrow I'll go down to the market for a bag of snouts and we'll rig up a fine stew. Strange things we're expected to eat nowadays. Butcher's shops selling whalemeat! I know, and what's more they still snip coupons out of your ration book for it. A few years ago we wouldn't have touched the stuff. Reindeer, too. What are we, bloody Eskimos? And that horrible fish from Africa somewhere, what do they call it? *Snoek.* No, tomorrow we'll have a good old stew, I promise. Potatoes, carrots, and a proper set of teeth grinning up at you from the bottom of the pot as if to say "Oh yes, we're the real thing."'

At this point he broke into coughs which were finally eased with a draught of tarry substance from a bottle.

'Let me tell you about my plants, my Felix,' he resumed when able. 'It may be a discovery of my own or it may not, but I've never read it in any book. It's about their juxtaposition, which means which plant is placed next to which. They used to say that shrubs in tropical houses ought to be placed according to region. So you'd get New World shrubs all up one side and Madagascan in a little group over there and those from Malaya and Sumatra and other southeast Asian countries up the other side. Then they said no, they should be arranged according to the order assigned them by botanists. So you'd have the cycads in one place, no matter where they were from, and near them all the Gnetales – only three surviving genera of those, though. Like that. Then still other people thought the arrangement should be entirely aesthetic. How will this look with that? Will this area balance the damned palms which really have to be stuck under the lantern, most of them? Will these leaf colours go well together? Will that tree's aerial roots obscure this bush? I still think aesthetics are important and I admit I'm not yet happy about how we've arranged all our night-scented varieties, are you?

'But my discovery's something else. I now see that certain plants actually dislike one another and never do well if they're put side by side. I know what you're going to say with that sharp little mind of yours – that it'll have something to do with parasites or fungal infection or a plant changing the chemistry of the soil around it. Sound good sense and not only possible but likely in many cases. You'll have heard of the mythical upas-tree of Java which poisoned everything for miles? The principle's well established. But my idea is still that certain plants simply dislike each other and should never be put together. If you were a prison governor and wanted to run a quiet prison you'd make an effort not to put two men in a cell together who were bound to fall out, wouldn't you?

'You think all this is barmy, just your old gardener rabbiting on with his usual highfalutin ideas. Mystical harmony or something. No, you're quite wrong. I've watched, I've seen, I've learned. Did you know there are certain rare people who can blight plants? You can't explain it and nor can you predict it. If a person like that touches a plant something goes wrong with it. It starts to wilt, or it sheds all its leaves, or it's suddenly covered in thrips. Remember that piece in *Picture News* a few weeks back? That one about the girl who wrecks anything electrical just by going into a room? Lights swing about and bulbs explode and perfectly good wireless sets blow all their valves. They say she's bewitched, which is a pretty funny diagnosis for the middle of the twentieth century. Once she made an electric milk van crash. There'll be a reason but it won't be witchcraft, just as there'll be a reason why some people can blight plants and some plants blight each other. Just opposite harmonics. I read somewhere that you can make light- and soundwaves cancel themselves out if the peaks coincide exactly with the troughs. All you get is darkness and silence. That's very interesting.'

He talked and swayed and talked to the glacial figure beside him, perhaps hoping to calm the gypsy by irrefutable accuracy, via sooth to soothing. He became drowsy, then briefly agitated by an incoherent desire to extract any sort of recognition from the boy. He tried again to turn him over but this time felt his hands angrily thrust away.

'Damn you, boy!' he coughed. 'Do I bore you? Do I stink? Do I stink worse than you did, matted with slum-juice? I took you in my arms then but you won't have it now. You run amok in my House with a pruning knife and when I tell you I still love you you become stone. I even turn down jobs so I needn't leave you. Of course I wanted to go! What future is there here? They'd pull down my House about my ears if they didn't know I had connections . . . town councillors, diplomats, royalty, famous and powerful people in every country . . . And now all because of you I've lost my chance.'

In this way feverish invention became raving lies, which

in time blew themselves out. At this point there was a lull. Then he got unsteadily to his feet and disappeared next door. A cupboard door squeaked, there were sounds of rummaging. He returned with a much creased manila envelope from which he shook a small cardboard box little bigger than a cigarette packet. Opening this he took out a piece of white fabric like a folded butterfly.

'There,' he said, laying it tenderly on the boy's uncommunicative shoulder. 'That's just to prove she was real all along. You thought I'd made the whole thing up, didn't you? But it really happened. This is her handkerchief. This is Cou Min. It wasn't her fault she went away but oh how I wish she hadn't. I know it's silly, but not a day goes by that I don't think of her. Sometimes I even pretend I might find her in the House, that suddenly an ordinary visitor will turn round and it'll be her. "Just thought I'd drop by and collect my handkerchief," she'll say, sort of casually and mischievously. "I do hope you've been keeping it nicely. Since you stole it I'd think that's the least you could have done. Did you really imagine I hadn't noticed? Did you really think I hadn't dropped it on purpose?" And then . . . But of course it's all make-believe. I don't seriously suppose it could ever happen; I just pretend for a bit. I don't think about her being over thirty with an elderly Chinese husband and several children . . . Have I told you this? I never know . . .'

Gradually, his cheeks wet and his eyes closed, Leon toppled forward into a rasping sleep. Far overhead on the House's lantern the golden galleon still headed briskly east into the prevailing chill, its rigging thick with ice.

This time the lotus spoke to the gardener in his sleep:

'They all left, carrying her suitcases. The front door closed and I could hear it being locked. Soon the radiators began to clink because they'd turned off all the heating. My water's growing cold and I shan't last long. I know I shall never see her again.

'Here she is, writing a poem for you about distances. She looks down at things as she passes: at Arabia, that happy land, at the wrinkled sleeve of the sea. At the end of her journey are the forests whose canopies sag beneath the weight of butterflies. It's a short poem because I'm dying, but I promise it will be strong enough to carry your heart to the princess's land and thence to the person she knows all about. Too good to be true? But no. It was a fable, wasn't it? A fairytale that turns out happily in the end.

'But what a strange leavetaking, all the same. Dear gardener, dry your eyes or you'll miss the final scene. Do you see it now? You're watching a tiny aeroplane high in the sky, droning and receding. It seems to have snagged your sweater, for an end of wool is caught in its tailwheel and as it recedes so you unravel. High across the cirrus sky it goes and its propellers sparkle their spokes of light, *sprrixx*, *sprrixx*, as you grow cold.'

TWELVE

Next morning Leon awoke frozen and alone. Felix's side of the mattress was empty. He wondered where the boy was and why it was so cold. He thought the boilers might be low but almost at once he began to sweat and blaze so that he dragged himself off the floor and put his head under the cold tap, turning his face sideways and drinking as it ran.

He shook the drops from his furry scalp and made a decision. It hurt him to breathe. His left lung jabbed him as though he had broken a rib in his sleep. Very well, then, this time he would see a doctor. He blundered about until he had found a slip of paper with the name and address of Dr Anselmus's friend, the famous thoracic whatsit at the Royal Infirmary for Palm House Curators with Collapsed Lungs. Give the man a bit of practice, he thought. What else? Stew. He'd promised to make some stew for Felix. Build the boy up. A fine bag of snouts, that was what Dr Leon prescribed. So, then: market first, then doctor.

On the way out he passed a habitual, affectionate hand over the leaves of the tamarind just inside the main door and threw a fond glance at its unofficial neighbour. This was a *Conium*, a common hemlock about two feet tall to which he had taken a sentimental fancy since it had no business in a stove house and ought long since to have been weeded out. He had first noticed it some weeks before but had left it because of its determination to establish itself in an alien clime. It grew perfectly well all over Europe and he supposed a stray seed must have blown in from outside and casually taken root. It was odd it had survived at all in this tropical heat and in recognition of its tenacity he had left it and now couldn't bring himself to grub it up.

'Did you just see our famous Palm House curator tottering out?' enquired the Dragon Lady of her fingernails in the office by the main gate. 'Looked more like one of those poor people from the camps in the pictures, specially with that new hairstyle of his. Must be he's caught a dose of this flu.'

'Half the staff off today,' agreed the gateman, who had already been on duty an hour. 'None of his have come in yet. Reckon he's on his own.'

'I thought he looked worse than just flu. But then, our resident genius's always acting peculiar, one way or another.'

'Never really know what's going on in the head of a man like that.'

'A good deal more than goes on in yours, Albert, I dare say.'

'How'd you know? 'Tisn't heads you girls are interested in. Not in my experience.'

'Saucy.' This was the sort of repartee the Dragon Lady liked. It considerably leavened the drudgery of typing out the day's quota of envelopes and the membership secretary's dreary letters to go inside them. 'It's not even as if he'd got a nice wife to look after him.'

'Who has?' said Albert, whose own wife was something of a slut just as her husband was most of a cad. 'You ought to ask Willesz about Leon. He and his gang are always in the boiler house for tea and that. Says it's unbelievable how the man lives. Not dirty, mind, just basic. Nothing soft anywhere, no comfort at all. You're always thinking you've overheard a bit of conversation, too. Willesz says it's downright uncanny, exactly

236

as if he'd got someone hidden there who's for ever vanishing a couple of seconds before you go into the room. Says it doesn't matter how suddenly you go in, it's like somebody's just gone out in a hurry as if they were scared of being seen. They've all kept their eyes peeled but Willesz's positive there isn't anyone, it's just the way the man behaves. Spooky, though.'

'You're not kidding,' said the Dragon Lady in her best Hollywood. She had forgotten her nails and was staring at Albert. 'But he's quite normal to talk to, isn't he? I mean, certainly no odder than anyone else. Even quite witty sometimes. Lonely, that's his trouble. If you ask me men like him live in their own world. He's got no idea what ordinary people are thinking. It's sad, really. Remember when he first came here? Scrawny kid. Not what you'd call conventionally handsome, but he had a real something about him. He always did.' She shivered. 'God, it's cold in here, Albert. Can't you scrounge us something to burn in this piddling little grate? Otherwise we're going to freeze to death before lunchtime. There's more important things to worry about than gardeners with flu, like us catching it. Plus ration books and petrol coupons and not even being able to get a bit of coal. I met this swell guy from Ohio last night. Great big blond. No shortages *there*, I can tell you.'

'You're a scarlet woman, that's your problem.'

'I can't think what you mean,' said the Dragon Lady with a filmic pout and shaking out her erstwhile flames. 'I'm talking about Luckies, Camels, Hershey Bars, nylons . . . You name it, this boy can get it. It's like there's never been a war. The States,' she said dreamily. 'I think I might go to the States. They don't know what gasoline rationing is. Bill – he's Bill – says even the kids in his family have cars. His is a Hudson Terraplane.'

'I'd be jealous of the Yanks if it wasn't that they take slags like you off our hands and leave us with the nice girls,' Albert told her as he went out, jingling his keys.

'Still won't do you any good,' she shouted after him. 'Nice girls like gentlemen, not spivs.'

It was settling down to being a good day.

Meanwhile with reckless abandon Leon blew two months' meat ration on half a pig's head wrapped in newspaper. He walked with it cleft side uppermost so the brains wouldn't fall out. The wind cut achingly from the northeast straight into his face as he made his way coughing through the side streets skirting Palace Square and the Opera House to the Third of August Boulevard. There, behind leafless planes and sycamores, the Royal Hospital stretched its grey façade. The chill pierced his plaid ulster and cooled him pleasantly although it froze his chin. The pavements, which in this area of town were regularly cleared of snow and salted, nevertheless felt spongy beneath his feet and a long way off. 'Didn't I tell you, Felix?' he muttered. 'It's all in a far country.'

It took a while for his identity to be checked for at first the great doctor's receptionist was reluctant to believe he was who he said he was. Actually he looked like a murderer, what with the haircut and the newspaper-wrapped lump seeping blotches of watery blood. Once admitted he sat peaceably, leaning against a green-painted radiator reading creased back numbers of *Picture News*. He even came across the feature about the girl whose disruptive powers had led her to be accused of witchcraft. There was a detail he'd forgotten: she had gone into the sitting room where her prospective brother-in-law was learning to play Mendelssohn's 'Wedding March' on his Hammond organ. At once the tune had broken off and the keys had begun to skitter of their own accord beneath the terrified young man's fingers. So frightened had he been that he couldn't even take his hands from the keyboard and had to watch, paralysed, as some crazed automaton within the machine had given a groaning, vindictive rendition of the 'Danse Macabre' by Saint-Säens, complete with

rattling skeleton effects. At the end of this involuntary performance the poor fellow had collapsed and was even now (at the time of writing) under doctor's orders while a priest had tried to exorcise both girl and Hammond organ. At this point in his reading Leon's immoderate laughter set off an agonising coughing fit from which he recovered to find the consultant watching with concern. He was helped to his feet, ushered into a technical-looking room and examined for a long time. Then he was handed an appointment card for the X-ray department downstairs and told to report there at noon. By now there were only fifty minutes to go so he was brought a cup of tea and a bun and re-installed by the radiator. In due course the X-rays were taken and he was sent back upstairs to wait for them to be developed and for the consultant to return from lunch and read them. This time he was brought a plate of spaghetti and parsnips in gravy by an apologetic nurse who said it was all the kitchens would send up.

At two-thirty the doctor returned and delicately retired behind a screen to view the films presumably, Leon thought, to prevent his patient seeing the sad half-shake of the head and the pursed professional lips. The idea amused him and he was grinning horribly when the man emerged and told him (while fondling the coils of his stethoscope) that he was really rather ill and had to be hospitalised at once.

'Oh no, I can't. I mean, it's quite impossible.'

'I've already spoken to Dr Anselmus, if that's your worry. As a matter of fact we've just had lunch together. I'm afraid I suspected what we'd find. Nothing to worry about, of course. But chest infections, especially in this beastly weather, are all potentially dangerous. You're a valuable man, sir, a valuable man. Claud – that is, Dr Anselmus, stressed that we mustn't take any risks with you. He says you're unique, and I shouldn't wonder. I've been to your Palm House many times, you know.

239

One of my favourite haunts. You may not know me but I recognised you at once this morning.' The doctor glanced at Leon's scalp. 'Though I notice you've left your syringe behind today in our honour.'

This note of medical humour signalled the start of some hard bargaining in which the patient pleaded for his liberty like a man condemned, eventually striking a deal which allowed him to be driven in the consultant's own car back to the Botanical Gardens in order to collect some things and (though of course he didn't mention it) warn Felix he would have to fend for himself. He was escorted downstairs, by now a little giddy with fever, while alarmed glances were shot at the bloody parcel tucked beneath his arm. Then the doctor's chauffeur drove him sedately through the freezing streets as strengthening gusts whirled eddies of snowflakes beyond the car windows. He sank back in the aromatic leather, one paw upstretched and clutching on to the handhold's silk-netted bobble like a very frail old invalid.

Most of the day had evaporated, he thought as he climbed stiffly out at the gate leaving the chauffeur to talk to Albert. That was the worst of hospitals or, indeed, of anything to do with doctors. Once you were in their clutches normal clock time disappeared and was replaced by a hallucinatory sort of calendrical time so that when you finally escaped you were surprised to find it was still the same day outside as it had been that morning. Such musings brought him to the Palm House door. It was locked. The Closed to Visitors sign was propped inside the pane. That was strange. He let himself in with his own key and at once felt the drop in temperature. Compared to the weather it was warm, but still far cooler than it should have been. The nearest thermometer read 11°C. He lurched through No Admittance into the boiler room. The fires were out, damped right down so they had choked on the

inferior fuel. This was incompetence amounting to sabotage. It was all the fault of Anselmus, sending him assistants too stupid even to be navvies. Where, though, was the boy? Only Felix was strong enough to get the fires going again.

He went back and stood helplessly. The House was silent. No drops of condensation pattered down on leaf and gravel. The air seemed brighter and bleaker as more of the insidious snowlight was admitted by the clearing glass.

'Felix!' he shouted. The sound vanished. He swayed as he stood, certain the air was cooling by the moment. He sensed the freezing northeasterly wind outside as if over his own naked body, scrubbing the heat from the glass as it rushed past. He could see it banging puffs of snow out of the leafless trees and bushes becoming visible over towards the Orangery. If only he weren't so weak. It was perfectly simple to light the boilers and reverse things but it took strength. Help. He would go for help. That was it. 'Felix!' he called again. 'I need you.'

A movement up in the clerestory distracted him and in that instant he knew something was about to repeat itself. He knew it as though it were not external to him but, on the contrary, a flaw of self at the edge of vision which ensured repetition, like the dumb stump of a tree to which a man lost in a fog involuntarily keeps returning. There would be the same ghostly figure flitting always off at an angle, mocking, seducing, destructive, leaving him to stumble through darkness back to the same beginning, beseeching, fond, ashamed. That sudden crash of glass! Had he not just broken something without raising a finger? He was surely responsible even though he couldn't tell how.

So the hateful smashing began. High along the clerestory ran the figure, wielding what must be the long-handled coal hammer like a club, shivering the curved glass into glittering shards which blew away outside among the snowflakes. Within seconds there were great rents in the roof through which Europe,

so long excluded, greedily poured. Down below, as he vainly tried to coax his body into movement, Leon could feel it cold on his neck and hear the taller plants rattle their topmost leaves in alarm. And among the din of smashing and the whispering rush of wind and naked feet on iron catwalk he heard words being gasped out.

'Enough! Finish and get out! It's not natural! Just because (*crash*) it doesn't mean I'm not a man, you bastard.' A long series of crystalline explosions progressed along the clerestory, paused, resumed on the opposite side. 'Your reward for being a hero, right? Yours to do what you like with? (*Crash*) and (*crash*) and (*crash*) night after bloody night? Eh, mister spraygun?'

The left side of his chest was transfixed with a bright spear of pain, pinning Leon to the gravel where he had fallen.

'But I thought you couldn't speak,' he said, his eyes wide. 'I thought you couldn't speak, Felix.'

(*Crash*) 'law says I have to speak if I don't want to? To you or anyone?' (Running footsteps. Falling glass. Icy gusts.) 'Gives you the right to treat me as dumb, then? No cock, (*crash*) no balls, (*crash*) no voice? That it, master-gardener? Just do what you like with the poor riff-raff gypsy?'

'Felix, Felix. You're wrong, boy. You were dying. And we were lonely, weren't we? You can't deny that.'

The wraith with the hammer had descended and now flickered across Leon's vision. The smashing began again all around him, louder. The gasped words resumed.

'Fine, you rescued me. (*Crash*) would love their rescuer. Of course. I was (*crash*) wasn't I? But repayment? Stoke boilers and shut up? Lie doggo by day and lie still at night, that it? (*Crash*) Saviour, nurse, lover? Can't tell me that's natural. (A loud gonging as the hammer, wielded by tiring muscles, flew off and struck a girder.) Who'd want that? Forced on me. Whoever wanted to *have* to be saved? (Still the feet whisked

over the gratings and winter billowed behind.) All that (*smash*) about your Chinese bit of stuff, Keemun or whatever her name was. On and on about her (*crash*) bloody months on end. Stupid cow. I still think you made her up. (*Crash*) thought a lot more of her than you ever did of me. What does a handkerchief prove? Nothing! (*Crash*) Nothing! (*Crash*) Nothing!'

Now the voice was becoming fainter as it ran off down the far end of the aisle, shivering panes as it passed. Leon had to strain to hear above the wind the tatters of words as they twirled fiercely like the eddies of straws and dead leaves in an empty street. Alone on the gravel with a mortally ill companion, dreamed girl, imagined boy, he could only repeat 'I thought you couldn't speak,' helplessly. 'Oh Felix, my poor Felix, I thought you couldn't speak. If only you'd said.' The wind was terrible. All at once the brightness in his chest grew, filling the House with remarkable light. All his plants wore fragments of multicoloured glass and were jewelled. Blazing gems fell slowly through the air. In this radiance only his own voice grew dusky. 'Look, oh look,' he murmured wonderingly. Then, 'Felix, my love,' his mouth spoke directly into gravel which tasted of foreign lands. 'If only you'd said. I thought you couldn't speak.'

And at these words his heart, carneous fig, burst to pieces, each fibrillating with wings awhirr. They fluttered inside their bonework cage and yearned to be gone. One by one, as the snowflakes drifted through the ribs of his shattered House and settled on his back, they began finding their way out.

How, then, could the tamarind which grew beside the Conium *near the door have broken in, half drowning Leon's 'I thought you couldn't speak'? What commentary is possible from a man near death? Who could believe in a mind, embarked on its last short wandering, finding refuge in the branches of a favourite tree? Yet on the edge of nothing a voice spoke to itself, neither plant nor man:*

'With what mixed feelings we watch our gardener fail! This man whose hands we loved, whose scent we knew, who spoke to us in a tongue we nearly understood: did he not give his health for us in desolate times? This atrocious cold from which he sheltered us, the wind puffing through shattered panes speaks, *shuuuff*, of treason. For, as we feel the sap thicken and grow sluggish, as our leaves turn numb and roots shrivel at the seep of this mortal chill, we recognise the scale of the deceit.

'Some time ago the coconut palm voiced one of his tedious theories. Apparently his idea is that the wall around the Gardens must support another, vaster, transparent dome which contains this House. And beyond that there's probably another, and another: an infinite regress of ever-larger structures enclosing one another, each with its own atmosphere and temperature and pressure. There's no single house which can claim to be definitive, he said. I imagine he's too ill to speak now.

'The rest of us did our best to ignore the way mere loftiness of stature was presumed to license banal philosophising. Frankly – and this is the deathbed frankness which has neither time nor will to dissemble – I've always tackled these Great Questions with a device of my own invention which I call "Bunkum's pruner". Wielded with the right dexterity I find it lops away at proliferating theories much as a vine, shorn of its pretentious intercoils, can be satisfactorily reduced to an essential and quite humble expression of its vineness. Chilled to the marrow as we now are, I can see my pruner's value is going to be proved right to the last. Never mind concentric universes, the one outside's killing us so to hell with the others. There *is* nothing beyond it and it's pouring in so fast the House echoes to tickings and crunkings as the pipes cool. Pipes, you see? It's all artificial. It was always artificial. For as long as it lasted – and we were practically all of us raised here, knowing nowhere else – this place was everything and everywhere. But there again, what could any of us have done about it had we known? It was never anything but lethal outside.

'So what are we to make of this poor man lying at our feet, the breath leaving him like moths from a bottle? Do we hold him to blame, who until so recently was the god with the brass wand, the great prestidigitator who magicked us through our lives so that we thrived and grew, heading only for the siren sun and cursing the glass which kept us from bursting through? He, of course, knew that the sun is nothing but a great thermal deception. It is in fact as stone cold as the moon, and had we really managed to grow through the roof and walls we should have perished as surely as we're perishing now. So what was it all for? My patented pruning hook whispers as it slices: *it was for his benefit alone.* What else? A falsehood he wished to sustain for obscure private reasons, hiding behind glass, showing off his menagerie to his own kind, people who blew smoke in our faces and smudged our blossoms with lipstick and sebum. To his greater glory, then, since they evidently thought he was no end of a fine fellow.

'It's growing very dim and I can no longer feel most of my body at all. My darling neighbour, my hemlock, overheard that and says tartly that she was numb from birth so why don't I stop moaning? Her words pierce me utterly because they show – oh, too late! – that not only does she have wit but is, after all, quite capable of hearing the truth without going into ecstasies of childish confusion. Very well, then. Dearest *Conium*, little hemlock: I love you. I always have, and will for however many more minutes. My last formulated thought will be of you; it's your fading image I shall carry with me. How could it be otherwise? I don't for one moment believe you can magically cancel the dark but your presence will be what it has always been – something to hold as I'm released for ever from the messiness of love and the absence of redemption. Don't cry, little hemlock, you shan't die just yet. You were designed for cold climates and I rejoice in whatever chance or error brought you here. That *Annona*, who's more soppy than he's sour, used to say you weren't made for this world. Were any of us, I should like to know?

'But ... ah, I can just see people gathering around our gardener, vainly trying to catch the moths. They turn him over and there is a coal hammer under him which would not have helped their artificial respiration. Others are hurrying in with hand trolleys, spades and sacking. We – that is, those of us still alive – gather the intention is to move us at once to the Temperate House. No thanks. I've never known where I came from and now I never shall, but let's say I feel in my roots (as would still have been possible until quite recently) that I, too, was meant for a different place, a different land, even a different universe. They can shunt my remains from one phony house to another but I shall put forth not one green shoot for them. Never. We were always dupes and I wish I'd paid more attention to what my roots were telling me. I must admit, though, that the great duper could even now coax some green out of me were he not himself beyond it. He did have the most wonderful hands. Not one of us failed to respond to those remarkable fingers. Since my frankness now knows no bounds I'm obliged to add that I actually thought it was a disgusting thing to do, drenching us in festering tobacco juice every so often. When it dried on one it gave off a stench of tawny spittle which will be with me to my dy—. Ah. Well, they do say laughter's the first and last sign of intelligence.

'No time for that now. We're pinched, frozen and blackening. We're being dismantled. It's ending after all. I'm sorry, for I used to love the way the light stole in at dawn when we were all together, bedded down in our humous thoughts. It was like a slow scent rising into the air and the flittering birds beyond the panes sang it up. Everyone began stretching at the same moment and the sound was a soft hum. I imagined it spreading out on all sides in a space a million times vaster than this House such as I know couldn't exist. I seemed to hear this illimitable hum as if there were nothing under the sky between one horizon and another but growing things all tensing themselves at the light's silky command. Hard to believe I heard it this morning for the very last time.

'I used also to love the sun's decline, how the galleon's shadow sailed a curving course across the roof. In summer months its keel would cut overhead, skid off into evening and vanish into the darkening sky. Often I would wake in the night and see it up there, tacking in the moon's cold mauve. I felt such affinity for it I wonder if my ancestors may not have arrived thus, borne in a golden ship from wherever it is the wind begins. Never again, then. Nothing can possibly follow cold like this. (Oh, this dark!) And all right, to be fair to the man, he did speak like the wind itself and he loved and loved us as best he knew. But love's a worthless disease; there's nothing to learn from it. He wore himself to the selfish bone and beyond. He heard our hum. In a minor way he was our sun.

'I believe they're taking him away now with a mask over his nose. I can tell them it's in vain, since I am he. And as for the rest of us . . . "Transplant". What a vile smell that has! It's one of their words, and carries. They're coming this way, I think, although I can no longer see. I sense mutilation and sacking. I'm frightened, Cou Min, my hemlock. I've tried to be brave but I'm terrified now it's happening. No redemption, none. Remember me? Promise me that, my dear? That I truly loved you, for all the good it did us. You alone will survive. Remember me . . . Are you still there? You are? Oh, then, farewell my House! Precious hemlock, little *Conium*, farewell!'

THIRTEEN

Nowadays the Royal Botanic Society's elegant old mansion is, most likely, the Museum of Historic Instruments, beautifully restored and smelling of beeswax polish. Here the more culturally-minded tourists may stop for an hour on the way to the Zoo (trams 8, 9, 17 and 26a pass the door) and wander through rooms of zithers, cimbaloms and portable organs, passing an immense gilded piano made for Liszt by Pleyel. They can pause before a harpsichord whose ebony keys were once depressed by the fingers of Mozart (*aet.* 10) while touring with his father who was claiming his wizard son was not yet nine. On all sides the building is jostled by shops. The plane trees are still there but the great wall went quite recently. In its place is a half-mile frontage of stores, including the apotheosis of the music shop whose wartime window felled a lion. This now sells jazz in the basement, classical CDs on the ground floor and Japanese electronic pianos under its post-modern eaves.

Of the original Gardens themselves not a stick remains. Their site has become a chic residential precinct. The tropics are represented in a well-patronised corner delicatessen which sells blowsy mangoes and cans of a fizzy drink claiming to be made of 18 per cent pure maracujá juice. The nearest jungle is one depicted in a poster in the local travel agent's window. Very occasionally, as when spring thaw coincides with heavy rain, a particular quarter of this enclave has the tendency to flood. None of the residents there know they are living on a lake; that at any moment the concrete of their apartments might turn to glass and, peering down past other people's cut-price Iranian rugs, they might spy a ghostly yellow-haired gardener far below hauling in a fowling net in whose meshes are snared the brilliant webs of an oystercatcher. But like everybody else they suspect nothing of what preceded them. Solidly rooted (as they would assert) in the present, they turn out to be helplessly caught up in a directionless future.